SCOUT'S HONOR

2-19-15

To Steve,
coaching is the next
best thing to playing —
& makes you fully
understand that life
is a metaphor
for hoops.
Good luck.

Jerry Rosen

SCOUT'S HONOR

A NOVEL

by Charley Rosen

Foreword by Phil Jackson

 Codhill Press

New Paltz, New York

Codhill Press books
are published for David Appelbaum

First Edition
Printed in the United States of America
Copyright © 2013 by Charley Rosen

ISBN 1-930337-68-X

Cover and interior text design by Alicia Fox.

This is a work of fiction. The characters and events depicted are products of the author's imagination. All institutions and locations are used fictitiously. Any resemblance to actual persons living or dead is coincidental.

Library of Congress Cataloging-in-Publication Data

Rosen, Charles.
Scout's honor / by Charley Rosen.
p. cm.
ISBN 978-1-930337-68-8 (alk. paper)
1. Basketball stories. 2. Sports stories. I. Title.
PS3568.O7647S36 2012
813'.54--dc23
2012030836

To the memory of Al Dufty,

A remarkable basketball player—skilled, courageous, savvy, unselfish—who inspired his teammates and earned the universal respect of his opponents. Even more importantly, he was an extraordinary friend, husband, parent, brother, teacher, and diligent truth seeker.

So long, Big Al. Thanks for the run.

FOREWORD

■

by Phil Jackson

One night, some forty years ago, while I was playing with the Knicks, I hosted a postgame get-together at a loft I owned on the Lower West Side of New York City. I extended an invitation to Stan Love, a player for the Baltimore Bullets, a team we were currently competing against in the play-offs. And Stan brought along a guest, who turned out to be the most interesting person at the party: Charley Rosen.

Since that meeting Charley and I have been fast friends and have collaborated on two books and several magazine articles. I'm also one of the lucky people who can claim to have a copy of each of his nineteen books in my library.

In addition to this long-term friendship of ours, Charley was my assistant coach for three years when I was the head coach of the Albany Patroons in the minor-league Continental Basketball Association. From there I went on to coach in the NBA, while Charley began a six-year stint as head coach with various teams in the CBA.

One of the toughest decisions I had to make when I became the Bulls' head coach was not to hire Charley as an assistant. My rationale was that his career as a writer would be more important to him than wasting his time on an NBA bench. This book justifies that difficult decision.

This latest novel by Charley Rosen is his best basketball book to date! He uses his expertise as a basketball maven to give the reader an inside look at what makes a player NBA-skilled. At the same time, he accurately depicts the trials of an NBA scout's life-on-the-run. Of course it wouldn't be a Rosen book without his trademark curmudgeonly humor and graphic details of food, sex, and music. I couldn't help but laugh out loud several times.

Best of all, Charley's narrative refutes the misguided ethos that currently dominates the media and also the management of virtually every NBA team. The fact is that the league is currently going through a period in which numbers-oriented *Moneyball*–type general managers are completely running the show, because owners have let themselves be convinced that the much more knowledgeable "Old Guard" are passé. These new "experts" believe that computer-driven technology and irrelevant statistics should be the sole determinant of all personnel decisions. The outcome of such narrow vision is a conviction that team chemistry, team systems, and coaches in general are merely minor factors in a given ball club's success or failure.

Charley's book, *Scout's Honor*, challenges this all-too prevalent idea via the sensibility of his protagonist, who states his case, lives his principles, and thereby puts his very job in jeopardy. Nobody can make this case more dramatically and entertainingly than Rosen, who fervently believes that in order for a team to earn the right to be a champion, they must first appease the basketball gods.

Both basketball fans and pundits alike will benefit from this novel's critique of the idea that talent alone wins NBA championships. In truth, this game, more than any other professional sport, requires team play.

Scout's Honor is the champion of the how, why, and who of this sport, which requires the sacrifice of personal glory for the greater goals of the team. It's required reading for anyone who loves the game of basketball.

AUTHOR'S NOTE

This is a work of fiction, so the time frame of several actual players has been altered for dramatic purposes. Similarly, while there is a summer league in Las Vegas, the official NBA Pre-Draft Combine is routinely held in Chicago.

FIRST HALF

CHAPTER ONE

The harsh ring tone startles the fragile images of my dream and chases them into oblivion. Although I am used to getting late-night phone calls from a long list of fellow hoop-o-maniacs, before I reach out and lift the receiver, even before I open my eyes, I know who the caller is.

"Earl, what time is it, and what do you want?"

"Almost two thirty, Rob, and what I want is to switch jobs with you. I'll be the scout and you'll be the general manager."

"No fucking way. But how about we switch paychecks instead?"

"Yeah. Yeah. Whatever . . . So how was he? What do you think? I saw that he scored forty-nine points."

"Mostly lay-ups against what looked like a team of ninth-grade nerds. I mean, they won by forty points, and Johnson played the whole game. The coach wanted to sit him after the third quarter, but the kid told the guy to go fuck himself. Tell Weiss the kid's a total asshole. Maybe that'll change his mind."

"Are you kidding, Rob? We just got an advance copy of next week's *Sports Illustrated* and the kid's on the cover. Listen to this: 'DeLeon "The Lion" Johnson Is Primed to Be King of the NBA Beasts.' Weiss is creaming in his pants. The idiot told me he'd be happy if we lost all the rest of our games just so's we'd have the best shot at the number-one pick. Just to make sure we screw up, he told me to fire Greg and replace him with that shit-for-brains Joe Brownley. But, hey, if that does happen, I'm sure I can convince Weiss to replace Brownley on the bench with you."

"Forget it, Earl. Haven't I told you a million times that I'm done with coaching?"

"Yeah. Yeah. Anyhow, I can't sleep and I can't wait for you to file your report. Tell me . . ."

"Well, there's no question that Johnson is a legit six-eight, two-fifty. He's also an amazing combination of speed, quickness, size, and strength. He reminds me of Magic except the kid's a better athlete. More like LeBron, only he doesn't see the court like either of them. But who does? I must say, though, that the kid goes to the hoop like a locomotive. Plus he's got a terrific left hand and he's a great finisher."

"What else? What else? He's only eighteen, so there's got to be some serious holes in his game."

"I don't like his stroke. His release point is so low that he has to lean back when he shoots to keep from falling on his ass. Also, when he pulls up left, he has to bring the ball across his body and it never winds up in the same place, so his release point is always slightly different. Which means he's just as likely to shoot an air ball as a bull's-eye."

"That's what I want to hear. Give me some more good news."

"He does look to pass, but only if he can deliver a home run, so he tends to force the ball through heavy traffic."

"What else?"

"Let's see . . . His right-to-left crossover needs work because the ball gets too far away from his body before he can corral it. And his defense is awful. His weight is too far forward, and he makes a few half-assed stabs at ripping his man, then he starts to fade downcourt looking for a long pass and a breakaway dunk. But I'm gonna see him again in a couple of weeks when they play Chicago's top-rated high school team. That should be more of a test. But tell me this, Earl. Why did you send me to Fuckbutt, Mississippi, to see him play against these little boys."

"It was strictly Weiss's idea. He insisted that—"

"Oh, there's something else. I hung around after the game just to see what I could see. Right? So it turns out that while the rest of the team boarded the bus, the kid hooked up with a pimpy-looking black guy in a fur coat and went off with him in a chauffeured Rolls-Royce."

"Big deal. There's a million guys sucking around the kid. I'll bet it was an agent. . . . Anyway, did you speak to his coach?"

"Sure did. The guy's a pussy and the kid does whatever he wants. If we do wind up drafting him, we're gonna need a stronger coach than Greg to control him. Somebody like PJ or Pop or Sloan."

"Fat chance of Weiss spending large for anybody who'll get more publicity than the kid."

"That'll be *your* problem Earl."

"Fuck you, Rob."

"Can I go back to sleep now? I've got an early flight to Philly."

"Yeah. Yeah. But you know something, Rob? It was much more fun playing for you in the Crazy Basketball League. Not much money, but a lot more fun. Now it's the other way around."

"Don't complain. When you were playing in Peoria, you would've given your left nut to get called back up to the NBA. Enjoy it, Earl, you're a big-leaguer again."

"Yeah, and wading in the same old big-league bullshit. How the fuck did all this happen, Rob?"

"Say good night, Earl."

"'Good night, Earl.'"

CHAPTER TWO

Here's how the fuck all this happened to Earl:

He started out as a leansome six-foot-seven, 210-pound, high-scoring small forward at Nevada State, drafted early in the second round by the Utah Jazz. Earl played about six minutes per game during his rookie season in the NBA, backing up the primary backups at point guard, shooting guard, and small forward. Strong hands and a high basketball IQ made him an above-average defender. Heavy sneakers and an erratic jumper destined him to be a perpetual tenth man in an eight-man rotation. Still, his biggest contributions came off the court where his upbeat, gregarious presence did much to foster team harmony.

"I could have played in Utah forever," Earl swears. "The Mormons loved my white ass, and the general manager, Jerry Hart, appreciated the way I saw the game and the way I related to everybody."

But Earl was canned, and most likely blackballed, early in his second season. The villain was Utah's Bible-thumping coach, Toady McGraw, who had actually fined the Jazz's sixth man, Damone Bradley, thirty dimes for griping to the press about his limited playing time. *Thirty pieces of silver!* When Earl publicly sided with Bradley, McGraw petitioned the owner to override Hart's strenuous objections, and he was cut. Since no other NBA team contacted Earl, a complicated system of rules and procedures assigned his rights to the Peoria Stars of a minor-league outfit called the Commercial Basketball League—where he became my star player. After one season in Peoria, Earl went on to play in France for five years.

Back then, the competition in Europe wasn't nearly as rigorous as it is now. There were very few international tournaments, and except for a rare exhibition contest, teams only played one or two games per week. Earl is also quick to disparage the coaches he had over there. "For fifteen minutes every practice, one guy made us run up and down the court bouncing balloons off our fingertips. He said it would help our shooting touch. I made about three hundred grand a season and it was like stealing money."

Then, during a summer back home, he got the magic phone call.

Hart left the Jazz when Utah's owner wouldn't let him fire McGraw after one particularly disastrous season when the team failed to make the playoffs for the first time in over a decade—and Hart was quickly hired by the New Jersey Nets. After one dismal season in the Swamplands, Hart fired the incumbent coach and all of his staff, put Greg Dodge (who had been the lead assistant in Utah) in the command seat, and brought Earl in as an advance scout. Earl then spent two seasons charting the plays and the personnel of the Nets' upcoming opponents, before being promoted to assistant coach.

During the six years Earl spent on the bench, he was celebrated throughout the league for his thorough knowledge of X's and O's, his player evaluations, and his continuing ability to enhance the togetherness of the entire organization. Along the way, Hart also tutored Earl on the intricacies of the salary cap and contractual negotiations, going so far as to let him have preliminary discussions with various agents—clearly grooming Earl to replace him. Which is precisely what happened three seasons ago when Hart retired.

As for me . . . I was born, bred, and buttered in the Bronx.

My father was thin, bespectacled, bald, and crippled by heart disease as well as what he called "sugar diabetes." His lifelong ambition had been to teach mathematics at one of New York's prestigious high schools, either Hunter College High School, Stuyvesant, or Bronx Science. But a heart attack terminated his college career late in his junior year at CCNY. Until his death thirty years later, Daddy was a prisoner in our low-rent, cockroach-infested two-bedroom apartment on Fulton Avenue in the East Bronx, where he earned a meager wage as a part-time bookkeeper for a local settlement house. He was unable to walk ten steps without stopping to gasp and cough. "What did I ever do to deserve this?" was his perpetual lament. "My life is shit."

To him, I was the doltish son who wasted my time playing "stupid" ball games (anything to escape from that crypt of an apartment) and who was only good for ferrying books to and from every public library within easy reach of public transportation.

Every so often, he vented his understandable angst by unbuckling his belt and whipping me across my back and shoulders. My immediate crime might be a dirty shirt I'd thrown on the bathroom floor instead of stuffing into the laundry basket, or a cup that I broke while washing the dishes, or perhaps a too-loud sneeze that woke him from a pain-free nap. Given his slow, tortuous limp, I could easily have dodged the blows. "Don't you dare try to run away," he'd say, "or I'll get you while you're sleeping."

Daddy's only joys were to read advanced mathematical texts and biographies of famous scientists, as well as to argue the shape of things to come with his cronies over rye bread and steaming bowls of my mother's borscht.

Momma labored mightily in the laundry at the nearby Bronx Hospital, collecting, cleaning, drying, and sorting shitty sheets and pissy pajamas. She was a sweet woman, long-faced, sad-eyed, and stubbornly incapable of abstract thinking. They had daily arguments—perhaps the flanken was too well done or the bathroom floor puddled with piss because he used to read while he stood to relieve himself.

What with working at the hospital, shopping, cooking, washing *our* laundry, and keeping the apartment reasonably clean, she was routinely too physically and emotionally exhausted to attend to my little-boy's needs. The best she could offer was to give me an occasional hug (which always made her weep), and to get hysterical whenever Daddy beat me.

And nearly as much as I hated my home court, I detested school. Being so much taller than my classmates, I was expected me to be more physically coordinated and emotionally developed than I had any hope of being. Moreover, my size made my every clumsiness painfully obvious while also subjecting me to constant bullying from my erstwhile peers. So I had several reasons to constantly misbehave in class, talking back to teachers, shooting spitballs at pretty girls, and worse—always trying to be a hero to my classmates.

During a pre-Thanksgiving third-grade art class, we were required to outline the spread fingers of one hand on a small square of drawing paper, then transform the resulting scribble into the representation of a turkey. I hated the fatuous blabbing of Miss Eichelbaum, the art teacher: "Now, children, let's fold our little hands on the desk, sit as still as tiny statues, and listen to every single word I have to say as much as you would listen to your mommies." So instead of following her orders, I cut an arc in the middle of the paper, wrote "Bullshit Protector" on one side, and hooked the paper over my right ear. My classmates roared with laughter, but the teacher was not amused, and my mother was forthwith summoned to the principal's office (thereby causing her to miss a half day's work and earning me another belt-whipping). My official punishment was to spend three school days squeezed into a tiny chair in a kindergarten class. Unfortunately, when I returned to my rightful class, the bullying continued unabated. But the good news was that my mischievous school-time antics subsequently led to my initial contact with a backboard and a rim.

At the tender age of nine (while appearing to be at least three years older), and facilitated by Daddy's contacts at the settlement house, my failure to protect myself from bullshit caused my banishment to a summer camp for troubled youths in Pittsfield, New Hampshire—where I discovered a crude plywood backboard nailed to one of the telephone poles lining a dirt road that bisected the campgrounds. In the absence of any kind of balls, I tried to throw stones through and at the hoop: pebbles and baseball-sized missiles from long range, as well as large rocks that I had to shot-put toward the rim in approximations of lay-ups.

Nobody seemed to notice, or perhaps it was believed that my rock shots had some beneficial effect in overcoming what was described as my "antisocial behavior."

By the end of the summer, my shooting percentage was about 20 percent, the backboard was reduced to splinters, the rim was scarred and bent, and the pole was seriously gouged.

Maybe that explains the occasional brick I subsequently launched over the course of the next forty years.

During the remainder of my tenure in elementary school, I was a regular in the lunchtime games played in the cold, windy schoolyard. Getting humiliated for being so big and so clumsy. Getting "the strap" from Daddy for periodically tearing my pants.

In junior high, I played organized ball in a local community center with the Apaches. Our coach had played varsity ball at CCNY and was forever scolding me for being such a "stiff."

After long, lonesome sessions in a nearby playground, I ultimately developed an awkward, but adequate corkscrew jumper to compliment an awkward, but adequate hook shot. At sixteen I was a senior at Theodore Roosevelt High School, and having grown to six foot six and 212 pounds, I tried out for, and made, the varsity team as a third-string center.

It was early in the season and we had just finished routing the High School of Art and Design in an afternoon home game—and I was absolutely ecstatic because I had come off the bench to score my first varsity points. Five of them—on a put-back lay-up, an elbow jumper, and a free throw.

Five points!

I was so happy that instead of taking the Third Avenue Elevated for the four stops from Fordham Road to the 174th Street station, I decided to undertake the two-mile journey by foot. Merrily I skipped through Little Italy and across Tremont Avenue. *Five points!* I aimed to cut about fifteen minutes off my travel time by taking a shortcut through the wide construction site that obliterated 177th through 175th Streets in preparation for the Cross-Bronx Expressway.

It was already dark, and the dug-up landscape was beyond the reach of the bordering streetlights, but my neighborhood buddies and I had easily scampered across the same route during the daylight hours on our way to the movie theaters on Tremont. And besides, I was floating in my own delirious reverie.

Five fucking points! I literally came down to earth when I tumbled into a freshly dug ditch. Fortunately, the ditch was only four feet deep, and I escaped with only a deep cut just over my left eyebrow. With blood gushing all over my face, I managed to traverse the remainder of the construction site with no further injury, whereupon I ran the ensuing ten blocks to the emergency room at Bronx Hospital.

Turned out I needed five stitches to close the wound.

In my dazed adolescent mind, the five stitches somehow equated with the five points. And I would gladly have suffered twenty stitches to someday score twenty points!

Alas, those were the only stitches and the only points I amassed for the rest of the season.

Next stop was the freshman team at Hunter College. The coach was Tony Russo, who stressed guts and grit and ridiculed me whenever I played "soft." His philosophy was that a big man's ruthlessness would always trump a smaller player's skills.

By now I was bigger (six foot eight) and stronger (230 pounds) than most of my opponents, so I overcompensated for my basic shyness and confusion by being mindlessly aggressive. Too bad Coach Russo employed some kind of high-post offense that I was spectacularly unsuited for. I was constantly in foul trouble, averaged only eight points per game—and went scoreless the night before my father died.

Daddy was forty-six going on a hundred when he finally succumbed to the massive heart attack we had all been fearing and expecting for so long. I accompanied my mother in the ambulance ride, and just before we reached the hospital, Daddy roused himself. I remember that his blue eyes were tightly clenched and staring at a place just above my head. The last words he ever said to me were, "Hi, kid."

He died that evening.

After flunking out and spending two semesters in night school, I was older, a tiny bit wiser, and ready to play varsity ball.

There was one game during my sophomore season that was much more significant than any of the others. We were being soundly trounced at Brooklyn College when our coach, Arnie Goldman, officially surrendered by emptying the bench. The Brooklyn College coach quickly followed suit, and everybody settled back to watch the scrubs try to make garbage time last forever. The only trouble was that one of the home team's scrubs (Number 46) was out of control, throwing indiscriminate elbows, undercutting the legs of airborne jump shooters, and even throwing a punch in a close-quarters rebounding melee. The referees, eager for the lopsided game to end, sucked on their whistles and let the clock run down. Coach Goldman was furious as he stood up and shouted downcourt to his opposite number, "Hey! Why don't you get that jackass out of there before he hurts somebody?"

The other coach's rude reply was, "Screw you, Goldman! You coach your team and I'll coach mine."

With that, Goldman walked over to where I was sitting comfortably on the pines and said this: "Go back into the game, Rob, and take that jerk out."

"What do you mean?"

"Elbows are like Christmas presents," he said. "They're better to give than to receive."

Moments later I found myself side by side with Number 46 along the foul lane while one of my teammates prepared to shoot a free throw. As the shot was released, Number 46 leaned into me and assumed the proper "box out" position, thereby hindering me from rebounding a possible miss. Standard operating procedure would have been to muscle him closer to the basket, but instead I cocked my right arm and aimed my elbow at the middle of his face. *Wham!* I connected so solidly that several of his teeth were broken and a small fountain of blood splashed in the lane. In their haste to keep the clock in motion, neither ref noticed anything amiss. While the Brooklyn College coach screamed bloody murder, Goldman just shrugged.

In the locker room I received Goldman's congratulations. "Good job, Rob. The guy got exactly what he deserved."

I was flushed with the elation of my first kill. So that's how it felt! The power. The reckoning. Now I was a man. Mess with me or my teammates at your own peril. Tony Russo would have been proud.

Over the course of my three-year varsity career, I mastered the sternum smash and broke virtually every school scoring (24.2 points per game my junior year) and rebounding (16.0 as a senior) record as we barely managed to play .500 ball (a combined 31–28).

Since I majored in English while most of my teammates were physical education majors, we didn't spend much time together off the court, with one meaningful exception. Isaac Giambalvo played point guard and was affectionately known as "Ike the Half Kike." His parents were divorced, with his father a successful banker in Columbus, Ohio, and his mom (having retired from teaching junior high school) overseeing Ike and his two younger sisters from a luxurious apartment in the ritzy Riverdale section of the Bronx. Although his mom was Jewish, she cooked incredible Italian delicacies. Ike was also the only guy on the team who had a car and, after Saturday morning practices, he'd drive me to his home to pig out on one of his mom's luscious feasts.

He had a higher basketball IQ than Goldman, and Ike's per-game assist average of 6.7 (mostly on cookies fed to me in the low post) exceeded the combined total of all the rest of us. We also sat next to each other on bus rides to away games, had adjacent lockers, and talked about our fathers (he loved his, and I was jealous), our futures (he wanted to be a coach, and theoretically I aimed to be a high school English teacher), and getting laid (or not, as was the case with me until my senior year after I'd scored 43 points against Bridgeport and the homeliest of the cheerleaders literally waylaid me in the nurse's office during a postgame dance).

Upon graduation, I discovered that the Scranton Miners of the Eastern League (the forerunner of the CBL) had somehow obtained my rights. The players were one skill and/or a few inches short of being bona fide NBA players, nevertheless they were still outstanding performers. With a per-game pay scale that ranged from $150 to the $50 that I received, games were played only on weekends in high school gyms in front of at best seven hundred fans. With nary a practice session with my new teammates, I made my debut on the road against the Allentown Jets.

I entered the fray late in the first quarter, and my initial task was play defense against Allentown's center—a six-five, 270-pound strong man named Tarzan Penman. He was averaging about 32 points and 27 rebounds per game, and had once tallied 68 points in EL competition. But, hey, I was a rough-tough guy, so I wasn't at all intimidated. In fact, as Penman settled into the pivot and caught the entry pass, I commenced to jab an elbow into the small of his back while simultaneously furiously banging him with my right shoulder and hip. But he didn't seem to notice.

Then, with the ball palmed in his right hand, he used his free hand to grab my left arm just below the armpit. Showing no strain whatsoever, he proceeded to lift me to my tippy-toes and then fling me across the baseline as though I was made of straw. As I slammed into the padded wall and sank to the floor, Penman laughed, wheeled, and executed a monstrous dunk.

But the play wasn't finished yet.

The nearest referee tooted his tooter, pointed to where I was still sprawled on the floor, and called the foul on me. Which was exactly why teams rarely lost at home in the Eastern League.

Okay. The next macho move was mine, so a few plays later I hauled off and belted Penman with a 'bow that was aimed at his face, but he either expected the assault or saw it coming. In any case, he grabbed my elbow before it could make contact, and flipped it upward with such force that once again I was sent crashing to the floorboards. Once again, the laugh and the foul were on me.

His coup de grace was a massive elbow that crunched into the cartilage that extended just below my sternum. Gasping in pain, I asked out of the game—and out of the league. The EL's bequest to me was a painful lump on my chest that lasted for about three months.

From then on, during runs at the local YMCA and at various playgrounds and school yards, I played a strictly finesse game.

Meanwhile in the real world, I moved into a one-bedroom apartment on upscale Claremont Parkway only ten blocks away from where my widowed mother lived. Except for Sunday afternoon dinners at her place, I ate only takeout Chinese, pizzas, or greasy fare from a neighborhood kosher deli. My "breakfasts of champions" were instant coffee and a large bowl of Wheaties. Teaching jobs were scarce in New York, but Ike's mother made a few phone calls and I was fortunate to get hired teaching English at a junior high school in a squalid neighborhood that was only a short bus ride away. (I wouldn't risk taking my car there—a ten-year-old Oldsmobile with flying fins—and leaving it parked in the mean streets for seven hours.)

The student population was about half black, half Hispanic, and at least seventy-five percent functionally illiterate. Whereas I could comfortably have instructed them in the Christian exegesis of "The General Prologue" to *The Canterbury Tales,* or Billy Budd as Jesus, I was totally incapable of teaching them how to read. The official curriculum called for them to spend entire classes busying themselves in workbooks. During alternating class sessions, I would go over each exercise. "Their" as opposed to "there" and "they're," and so on.

In fact, my main task was to keep the kids under control. This was primarily accomplished by lulling them to sleep.

Oh, and I also got married.

Ike's mother was also responsible for my meeting Rachael (the daughter of a woman in her knitting group), who was a first-grade teacher in the upscale Inwood section of Manhattan. My standard site for a first date was Chinatown so I'd at least be guaranteed of having some good eats, and Rachael turned out to be cute, just a mite overweight (I didn't find out until our first petting session a few weeks later that she wore a girdle!), quiet, and agreeable enough to eat my favorite dish, snails in black bean sauce. Since I believed we had the possibility of a meaningful connection, for our next date I proposed an excursion to the Palisades Amusement Park, located in New Jersey just over the George Washington Bridge. I was anxious to make a good impression, so the day before escorting her there, I made a solitary scouting trip.

Naturally, I zeroed in on the basketball-toss booth—three shots for a dollar. But the game was rigged. The rim was slightly smaller than normal and much tighter, and the front lip was higher than the back. Also, the backboard was slanted backward, and the ball was oversized and overinflated. If the ball so much as touched the rim, it would bounce away.

It cost me two bucks to make adjustments and find the range.

The first time I nailed three for three, I won a four-foot-high teddy bear. In quick succession, I also won a huge stuffed penguin and a somewhat-scary-looking stuffed owl—all of which I presented to whatever kiddies happened to be in the vicinity.

All right! I had it down! There was no way that Rachael wouldn't be totally impressed.

The next night, I confidently steered her over to the basketball toss, saying, "Watch this"—and proceeded to miss shot after shot. After spending twenty dollars, I had won two tiny plastic dinosaurs!

How could I have missed the message: *The ball never lies.*

We had a Jewish wedding and a reception with all the trimmings: Waiters sashaying around the room bearing trays of Cherries Flambé. A buffet table featuring rows of Stars of David fashioned from chopped liver and nestled in beds of endive. Igloos made of deviled eggs.

Her parents never approved of me, which showed at least a modicum of good judgment. Her mother repeatedly nagged me about my habit of not wearing socks in the summer. "You look like a Bowery bum. Besides, you'll get an athlete's foot."

My father-in-law's distaste for me was solidified one fine April day just a few weeks after the wedding, and just before the Red Sox were scheduled for a three-game weekend visit to Yankee Stadium. "I've got tickets for Friday night," he announced.

"Really!"

"Yes, and they're good seats, too. For the whole weekend!"

"Wow! How'd you get them?"

"The rabbi is my cousin's brother-in-law."

"Great! Thanks for thinking of me."

"No problem," he said. "But you will have to wear a suit, and socks with dress shoes."

"Sure. Whatever."

Later that same evening, Rachael told me that the tickets were actually for the upcoming Yom Kippur services at the synagogue down the street. Since my parents were strictly gastronomical Jews—potato latkes on this particular holiday, gefilte fish on that one—I was more familiar with Arbor Day and Flag Day than with the Jewish holidays.

When I called with some patently absurd excuse for changing my mind (I had papers to mark; I'd sprained my ankle playing a pickup game at the Y; my only suit was at the cleaners—perhaps I offered all three of these), he hung up the phone in a fury.

He was barely civil to me from then on. Indeed, the only way to soften his anger was to present him with a grandchild—something that neither Rachael nor I was ready for.

Trouble was that Rachael and I seldom agreed on anything. I liked Chinese food; she insisted on Indian fare. I squeezed the toothpaste tube from the bottom; she pinched it from the top. She required separate knives for the peanut butter and the jelly jars, while I made due with one. I liked life rare; she liked it well done. I hid *Playboy* magazines under the mattress so I could choke my chicken in peace when she wasn't home. She hid candy bars in the night table on her side of the bed. She rightfully complained about my bad breath, my belches, and my farts. I rightfully complained about her talking to me like I was one of her students: "Robert, even though the glass you just washed may look clean, germs are invisible, so you must do a better job. That means more soap, hotter water, and more elbow grease. Understand?"

"Yeah. Whatever."

Except for an occasional trashy novel, she never read a book, a magazine, or a newspaper, and had no interest in politics. The eleven-o'clock news telecasts were her only source of current events.

My part of this dismal equation was my being sullen whenever I didn't get my way, and occasionally lashing out at her as though she were a referee who had negated a successful jumper and called me for charging.

"You're intellectually retarded!" I would shout at her.

Her retort was "You're emotionally retarded!"

And we were both correct.

After only three months I felt as though we'd been married for fifty years.

In the meantime, Ike had become an assistant coach at Illinois State University. My marriage was temporarily saved when, largely through Ike's connections and recommendations, I became the head coach of the expansionist Peoria Stars and spent six months of each of the next four years all by my lonesome on the road.

The highlights and lowlights of my tenure in the CBL were these:

A player was traded from Savannah to Albuquerque for a blow job performed on the former team's general manager by the latter team's incredibly beautiful public relations directress.

A player, unhappy with being pulled from the starting lineup, attempted to drown his coach in a toilet bowl.

A coach, unhappy with a referee's call, raced onto the court, grabbed the ref's whistle lanyard, and began twisting it. When neither his fellow ref, the coaches, nor the players came to the rescue, a security cop finally intervened, even as the ref's face was turning a bright blue.

Alfrederick Smith was a former number-one draft pick with an afflicted jumper who had just been released from the Cleveland Cavaliers and wound up in Peoria. Upon his arrival, he instructed the Stars' general manager to call him "Al," the owner of the team to call him "Fred," and me to call him "Rick." He proved to be a terrific player, but only for every third game.

Bench players (on other teams!) often munched on peanuts or popcorn during games.

Players would often miss practice sessions and then come up with fantastic excuses: "The dog ate my sneakers." "I had an argument with my wife and she hid the car keys." "Today's Tuesday?" But a guy named Sammy Franklin came up with the most creative one.

"I was out all night with a babe I met at a club," he told me. "There's no question that my wife is freaked out, because I didn't come home, and I knew she'd be sure to come looking for me at practice. Man, the screaming and the cursing would've been incredible. And I would've been totally embarrassed in front of all the guys. The only way I could've maintained the respect of my teammates would've been to slap her around, and she definitely would've called the police. So I missed practice to stay out of jail."

And the guy was right! His wife had stormed into our practice session, searching for him in the locker room, the bathroom, and even under the stands.

So I fined him fifty bucks, and the team put him up in a cheap hotel for a few days.

But the drama continued.

"Me and the bitch had it out," he told me, "but we were okay when I promised to give her all of my next paycheck. But when she saw it was fifty bucks short, she accused me of going out clubbing without her. She doesn't believe that you fined me. You could save my marriage, Coach, if you wrote out a note saying that I was fined for practicing without getting my ankles taped, or for losing my practice jersey, or something like that."

No problem.

Except that after our next home game, his wife got into my face about stealing their money over stupid rules. "That's what the white man always does to black people!" she raged. Leaving me no choice but to trade the guy (and his wife) ASAP.

I arranged a trade for another player when I discovered that he was the CBL's unofficial drug dealer, but he was averaging 14 points and 10 rebounds (broken down to about 25 and 15 when he was straight and 5 and 5 when he was high), so the general manager squelched the proposed deal.

Earl carried the team during my rookie season on the bench. He was primarily responsible for the team finishing with the best regular-season record and earning the top seed in the playoffs. Unfortunately (even tragically!), he broke a bone in his shooting hand in the very first minute of the very first post-season game and we were swept by an inferior ball club. Over the course of the subsequent three seasons, Earl was in France, while Peoria won some games, lost a few more, and never again qualified for the playoffs.

During my second year, the team desperately needed a backup center, and I had just the player in mind—a rawhide-tough Texan who had been fired from a team in Spain for fucking the owner's daughter. But the Stars' general manager refused to pay the airfare from San Antonio to Peoria, claiming that the budget was limited and the most pressing need was to buy new bras for the cheerleaders.

The owner of the franchise—a red-faced and red-necked playboy who owned and operated the largest accounting firm in the city—

was increasingly unhappy with my performance. As a result, my bench-side manner became more and more manic, and every loss became a personal tragedy.

However, as frustrating as all of the off-court absurdities were, even worse were the on-court agonies inflicted on the good guys by the league's referees. The NBA had total jurisdiction over the officiating corps, and many of the tooters periodically worked games in the League. After they'd just adjudicated a confrontation between the Celtics and the Lakers in Los Angeles, their discontent at having to work the next night in La Crosse, Wisconsin, or Wichita Falls, Texas, was understandable. Still, what nettled me most was their arrogance, as well as their bias toward those of my fellow coaches who had bona fide NBA experience. And since I expected truth and justice to abound, I yapped at their every miscall, and was routinely nailed with costly technical fouls—$25 for the first 5 per season, then $10 more for each additional 5. My total annual fines amounted to about $750. Not that I didn't have good reason to complain.

When our chartered bus broke down en route from Peoria to Fort Wayne, we arrived at the arena fifteen minutes before game time. Claiming that the hometown fans were "restless," the refs allotted us only a single minute to warm up. Subsequently, we trailed by 20 after the first quarter, and lost the game by a mere 4 points. To add insult to absurdity, I was nailed with a T when one of the refs mistook a fan's loud, drawling complaints for mine. I responded by calling the ref an "asshole," but once he'd perceived his error, he refrained from banishing me with another T.

At a home game two weeks later, the asshole ref got his revenge when he was the prime tooter that resulted in the visitors shooting 18 free throws in the fourth quarter while we shot none.

After my team yielded 6 consecutive offensive rebounds in a game at Omaha, I said this to the ref of the moment: "This is like a hockey game. We can't clear the puck across the blue line." Even if he'd misheard "fuck" for "puck," I was still an innocent victim.

Similarly proving that refs are deaf as well as blind, I was booted from a game in Rockford, Illinois, when I questioned the ref's focus by saying, "You're missing a good game." Later I was informed that the ref thought that I had called him "gay."

I started my coaching career believing that refs were a necessary evil, until I came to understand that they were cops with whistles instead of guns, hanging judges, insane dictators, and just plain crazy motherfuckers. Also, because they focused only on penalizing mistakes and illegalities, they missed the beauty of the game.

Here's how the problem could be resolved: Equip every referee at every level of competition with a wire vest and a small battery. Each coach would be given an apparatus containing a small button that, when pressed, would create a short but powerful electric charge in the vests. By rule, however, each coach would be limited to instigating only one zap per half.

I got a call during one off-season asking me to participate in a charity doubleheader somewhere in northern New Jersey. "Sure." I was then asked to bring another player, and Ike Giambalvo was eager to come along for the run.

The first game pitted an all-star pickup team (that included me and Ike) against a squad that had won the city's recreation-league championship. In the second game, the winner would be matched against a team composed of players from a high-ranked semipro football team from the area. The gate receipts were earmarked to benefit local children afflicted with cerebral palsy.

The stands were filled with dozens of young CP victims, their friends, and their relatives. They were all somewhat downhearted when their townie team was easily defeated by the all-star ringers, but they clearly enjoyed the competition and were eagerly looking forward to the finale.

Against the rec-leaguers I had played with reticence, but I was eagerly anticipating the banging and roughhouse tactics that competing with football players would entail. Here was a chance to reassert my macho game plan.

However, between games, the two referees—crew-cut bozos with slight paunches and bleary eyes—demanded a bonus for officiating the second game. The promoters were outraged, but they were also stumped. Perhaps a pair of the defeated rec squad could do the job?

But half of them were already gone, and the rest were either still in the shower or had declined. No refs ostensibly meant no game and an early and disappointing end to the children's good time. The promoters pleaded, but the refs were adamant.

That's when, seemingly out of nowhere, I came up with a great idea. What if we played the game without the greedy refs? If all the players were agreeable, we'd just call our own fouls.

Everybody seconded the motion. And the subsequent contest turned out to be the most enjoyable basketball game I've ever played in.

The football players were powerful, athletic, and eager for chest-to-chest combat, but the big men (defensive and offensive linemen) lacked the instinctive footwork necessary to work effectively beyond the line of scrimmage. We respected their professional status, and although we were only civilians, they respected our superiority in performing the requisite dance steps.

As the game unfolded, a wonderful camaraderie developed. Even though we all played hard, we played clean. And we talked to one another constantly, complimenting good plays on both sides and apologizing for any undue contact that fell short of being foul-worthy. There were no arguments and not a trace of ill will.

On one drive hoopward I was bumped off stride and missed the ensuing lay-up. When my defender (a six-foot-six, 270-pound tackle) offered to penalize himself for the illegal contact, I said, "Naw, that's all right. I should have made the shot anyway."

During the brief half-time intermission, the players mingled near the scorer's table, identifying ourselves and exchanging personal information, even though we knew we'd never see each other again once the game was over.

"I'm Harley Richardson," said my opposite number. "Originally from Maryland and working hereabouts as a bouncer in a nightclub."

"Rob Lassner from the Bronx. I'm a basketball coach in a minor league, the Commercial Basketball League."

"Can't say's I ever heard of it. But you sure do have the moves down right."

"And you set the best pick I ever ran into."

Meanwhile, the kids lined up for autographs—and we remembered where we were, why we were there, and how fortunate we were to still be able to run up and down the court. So we turned our full attention to the kids. The beautiful, tragic, cheerful children.

"Hey, buddy," we'd gently inquire, trying in vain to match the innocence of their joy and their forgetfulness. "What's your favorite team? Who's your favorite player?"

Too soon, the game resumed.

As before, the body collisions were aggressive and intense, yet within acceptable limits. The fouls were seldom called, particularly among the bigs. Each play, each move and countermove, was executed with a sense of joy that transcended any consideration of shots made or missed, of botched passes and faulty dribbles. We were all riding the crest of the same unexpected, yet delightful experience.

"Nice shot, man."

"How'd you get that pass through all that traffic?"

"All right!"

The final buzzer came as a rude shock. Only then did we bother to look up at the scoreboard—and it didn't matter who had won and who had lost.

Instead of Us versus Them, instead of five against five, we were ten players playing one ball game.

Ah, hoops were paradise enow.

Alas, within a matter of weeks, I was back to reality.

One night in my last season in the CBL, I returned to my hotel room in Tampa Bay after we had lost a ballbuster of a ball game. We were up by 19 to start the fourth quarter, only to lose by one on an offensive rebound at the buzzer. Naturally, I had just finished crashing a chair against a wall when the phone rang.

"We can't go on like this," was Rachael's opening gambit. "We're more like roommates than a married couple. It's not my fault that we can't have children. You're selfish and lost in your own world. You love basketball more than you love me."

"But, Rachael. I love you more than I love baseball."

"I don't give a shit anymore, Robert. I want a divorce."

Nineteen points! And we lose because that big stiff of a center doesn't box out. Nineteen fucking points! "Yeah? Well, fuck you, Rachael! Fuck the horse you rode in on, and fuck everybody in the world who looks like you!"

Two days later, after I'd been nailed with a technical foul (for calling still another ref an asshole) in my seventh consecutive game, one of my players—Bill Woodman from Lehigh University—asked me this: "Rob, are you having fun right now?"

I scowled, pointed up at the scoreboard, and quickly said, "If we win, I'll have had fun. But not if we lose."

After my fourth season, the owner was brought to trial by the federal government for his responsibility for the illegal deductions on clients' tax returns. He was quickly convicted of fraud, fined 100K, and locked up for two years. I was more relieved than disappointed when the new ownership group gave me the boot.

I did not contest the divorce proceedings, and spent the next two years subbing in the local schools and coaching the women's varsity at Rhinegold University, a small Divison III school in Queens.

Coaching the women was a challenge, compelling me to watch my language and to utilize about one-tenth of my available basketball expertise. Yet they were responsive, diligent, didn't define themselves as basketball players, and even the occasional lesbians were friendly. Since I refused to actively recruit, we only won about every third game. And since the athletic director, James Looney, only paid attention to the doings of the men's team, he virtually ignored us. All of which was okay by me.

But there was one particular game that effectively ended my coaching career. Guess who the terminators were. . . .

Late in my second season we traveled into Manhattan to play against Hunter College. Since I'd been admitted to Hunter's athletic Hall of Fame several years back, I was looking forward to the game as a kind of homecoming.

Hunter had a top-notch team, but it was obvious from the get-go that one particular ref was a blatant homer and, unfortunately for us, he was making virtually every call. Every time he tooted his tooter, we got a raw deal.

Okay. That's what happens on the road. So my protestations were rather mild, even as Hunter built a double-digit lead.

But what eventually pushed me over the edge was when this knucklehead started laughing at every miscue that my players made. Misdribbles. Botched passes. Bricked lay-ups.

"Hey," I finally shouted. "What're you laughing at? They're working harder than you are."

That triggered my first technical foul.

Okay. In the CBL (and NBA) coaches sometimes deliberately got themselves T'd in hopes of "buying" more favorable calls. But this jerk started making calls that were even more biased than before, while his partner continued to suck on his whistle.

"Yo," I said to the silent ref. "Doesn't your whistle work?"

Tech number 2.

We were behind by 17 at the half, but I made a rousing locker-room exhortation, and we began the second half playing like gang-busters. Our flex offense was working like a clock. Our shots began to fall. We played terrific position defense and controlled the boards. In a matter of minutes we trimmed the lead to 7 and had possession—when the lead ref made an atrocious charging call that was quickly compounded by an imaginary hacked-in-the-act call at the other end.

In rapid succession, another bogus charge and still another invisible foul went against us. Suddenly we were down by 14, our enthusiasm was depleted, and it was clear to me that the offending ref simply would not let us win.

"You should be arrested for stealing the game, you jackass!"

Tech numbers 3 and 4. And automatic ejection.

We lost by about 20, and I happened to be waiting in the corridor when the refs exited their dressing room.

"You guys are an embarrassment to the game and to yourselves!"

It was when I started cursing them that they flinched and ran out of the building.

The next day, Looney called me into his office. Complaints had been filed. My behavior was unacceptable. But if I wrote a letter of apology, all would be forgiven.

And I did write the letter—a craven, humiliating mea culpa. Why? Because, despite the aggravations, I truly loved coaching my wonderful hoopettes.

Anyway, after the season concluded, the AD presented me with a choice: Regardless of the letter of infamy, I could either resign or be fired. Clinging to what I deemed to be my last and only vestige of self-respect, I told him that he'd have to fire me.

After the ax did indeed fall, I discovered that in his spare time Looney refereed local high school games!

Of all the games I've lost because I didn't play well, missed critical shots, or made faulty decisions on the bench, the most painful I-wish-I-could-do-it-all-over-again basketball memory that still haunts me is my writing that letter.

But I've really got no complaints. Sometimes all's well that doesn't end well.

A month later, Earl hired me as a scout for the Nets.

CHAPTER THREE

My mother stubbornly believed that my separation from Rachael was only temporary and that a reconciliation was inevitable. I waited until the off-season and until I'd signed a contract with New Jersey before telling my mother that the divorce was official. "No!" she wailed. "You're my only child! My only hope to have grandbabies! How could you do this to me!"

"It's not about you, Mom."

After blubbering for a few moments, she said that I had only two acceptable choices: "You can still make up with Rachael, she's a lovely girl. Or get married again in a hurry while I'm still alive. A son, especially an only one, owes his mother *nakhes*."

She was even more distraught when told of my plan to move out of the city. "What? Where? Who else should I make a fancy Sunday dinner for? With the flanken and the mashed potatoes. For who else?"

"Ma, I'm not moving to Outer Mongolia. Just within a hundred miles of New York."

"A hundred miles, a hundred light-years. I'll never see you again!"

I promised to visit as often as I could, but she was sobbing when she hung up the phone.

Anyway, I bought a map, and with my mother's apartment as the epicenter, I drew a circle of a hundred miles. Then I took off on a week's journey to explore the possibilities.

Despite Bruce Springsteen's advocacy, New Jersey was out, especially since the Nets were destined to relocate to Brooklyn. Besides, a state full of slums, miasmic pollution, broken cities, and plastic suburbs, and ruled by the Sopranos held no attraction for me. Most of all, it would be too embarrassing to live in Noo Joizee.

The sections of Pennsylvania within the bounds of acceptability were appealingly rural and unsophisticated, but too far from a major airport.

In Connecticut, what I saw of Stamford, Norwalk, Bridgeport, New Haven, and Fairfield were either too depressingly industrial or too pocked with low-income ghettos—and the outskirts were too ritzy.

That left New York.

The locations closest to the city—White Plains, Haverstraw, Croton-on-the-Hudson, and the like—contained either the worst aspects of the city or were outrageously expensive. I bypassed Peekskill because of the violent redneck riot there that greeted a 1940s concert by Paul Robeson. Newburgh and Poughkeepsie were classic examples of metropolitan blight. Indeed, the Newburgh Motel had scurrying cockroaches in the bathroom, a space between the front door and the threshold that let in frigid drafts, and a heating system that clanged on and off every fifteen minutes.

My last stop—and designed as such—was Woodstock. For sure, the main drag was flanked by hipper-than-thou boutiques, art galleries, tie-dyed T-shirt emporiums, and the kind of upscale knick-knackeries that appealed to wealthy tourists. But there were also two interesting hardware stores, a fantastic bookstore (The Golden Bough), and a superb library.

It was fate that my car—Zippy, a ten-year-old Subaru, so-named because no matter how late my departure, he always gets me to my destination on time—broke down a few feet from a service station. To be at the total mercy of a merciless out-of-town mechanic: a traveler's worst nightmare. However, the problem was quickly diagnosed as a broken fan belt, got fixed in just a few minutes, and the bill was a mere ten dollars.

This was the place for me.

After being chaperoned around the environs by a chatty real estate agent, I found a two-room cabin-in-the-woods approached only via a half-mile driveway, and furnished with pleasantly shabby essentials. The electric heat would be costly, but it meant that I wouldn't be disturbed by deliveries—and was augmented by a wood stove that could be fed, I was assured, throughout the winter by an already well-stocked woodshed.

The landlord was a dentist who lived in Saugerties, fifteen miles away. Plus there were international airports in Newburgh (forty-five miles south) and Albany (sixty miles north). And the Nets played their home games in East Rutherford, New Jersey, an easy eighty-five-minute cruise away.

Privacy, isolation, convenience, cable TV, all for a mere $750 per month. As long as I put up the first month's rent plus two more in advance, I wouldn't even need to sign a lease.

When I got back to my apartment, a voice mail from a distant cousin had distressing news: My mother had died of a stroke three days ago and the funeral had taken place yesterday.

My poor mother. Her life full of travail, caring for an invalid husband, raising a goonish son, working in a citadel of filth, disease, and infection. No, she never had pleasure from me or anybody.

How could I not blame myself?

Even as I packed my things, I wept.

By now, though, I've forgiven myself, that dumbo whose failure to box out cost us (me!) that agonizing loss at the buzzer, and I've also forgiven God.

In any case, let me count the ways in which my NBA job kicks the snot out of my CBL gig:

My former 40K salary is now doubled. In Peoria, the per diem was $36; here it's $120. Instead of the mandated tie and jacket (under threat of a $250 fine), I can now go to work wearing jeans, sneakers, and any kind of shirt that has a collar and buttons. Also freebie first-class plane tickets, top-of-the-line rental cars, and spacious rooms in fancy hotels. In the CBL, all of the non-playoff coaches were surreptitiously vying for each other's job; here (because having a player drafted is a boon to their program) I can enjoy a cooperative, non-competitive connection with the coaches on my circuit.

My favorite coach is Michael McCue, who's been at Villanova since, as he puts it, "Jesus was a pup." During his tenure, Michael's teams have qualified for the "Big Dance" a dozen times, made three appearances in the Final Four, and won what he calls the "whole enchilada" back in 1992. McCue only answers to "Michael," never "Mike." Nor will he permit anybody to call him "Coach," because, he says, "Then I'd have to call you 'Scout,' or call my guys 'Player,' or call certain sportswriters 'Bullshitter.'"

At sixty-something, McCue is no longer the slender, bright-eyed playmaker for the Villanova Wildcats as depicted in a forty-something-year-old team photo on the wall. His paunch is round but solid, his face is a topography of hard wrinkles and sagging pouches, his blue eyes sad and watery, his nose squashed like a prizefighter's, his mouth full of small yellow teeth. He wears a frayed, blue Villanova sweatsuit with the last white "A" dangling crookedly by a single thread.

I first encountered Michael during my time in Peoria, after I'd earned a modest reputation as a big man's coach. Indeed, by dint of personal postpractice drills I helped turn a shy, mistake-prone seven-footer named Andre Gaddy into an NBA-ready player. Unfortunately, Gaddy chose to quit basketball in favor of guaranteed full-time employment with the U.S. Post Office. David Wood was another big man who greatly benefited from my one-on-one tutelage, eventually moving on from the CBL to a seven-year NBA career. There were two other triple-X-sized students who likewise made terrific improvement, but both failed drug tests and instantly vanished from the hoops scene.

Anyway, that's why Michael recruited me to work at his all-star summer basketball camp. During the morning sessions, I'd conduct big-men classes. In the afternoons, I'd coach games. After dinner, the counselors scrimmaged, then we gathered to discuss the relative merits of the participants over beer and pizza—with our evaluations spiced with Michael's at-large ruminations: He hates the NBA because the passing is so bad, and because the influx of schoolboys and undergraduates have dumbed down the game. "Pick-and-roll, effen pick-and-roll. That's all that anybody runs anymore."

Michael also believes that drinking huge quantities of beer keeps a player's joints well lubricated and improves his jump shots. Also that eating pizza (but without extra cheese) provides "a solid base" that makes bigs better rebounders.

Since he's also infamous for the crushing power of his routine handshakes, I present mostly limp fingers as Michael greets me in his office. As ever, his opening gambit deals with his determination to retire: "I don't know how much longer I can take all this effen crap. But it's always good to see you anyways. Rest your keister, why don't ya?"

His office is situated directly beneath the gym, and is cramped with dented file cabinets, old newspapers, and game programs scattered on most available surfaces, and with wall racks containing hundreds of game tapes. Dozens of team photos are squeezed into the other available wall spaces, showing players hardly remembered by anybody except Michael. There's also a personally autographed head shot of JFK, one of LBJ, another of John Wooden. The only place for a visitor to sit is a sagging leather couch placed opposite his scarred, littered desk.

No need to inquire further about what the "crap" is, since Michael is always quick to complain without any prompting: "These effen kids these days, they think their doo-doo smells like Old Spice. Even when they're nothing but wet-behind-the-ears freshmen, they've already had high school coach coaches and AAU coaches kissing their keisters, and some of them are even getting under-the-table money from them effen leeches."

He means agents.

"Plus they don't give a rat's rump about seniority. These freshies come in here and want to play forty minutes a game and touch the ball on every possession. Eighteen-year-old crap-for-brains and they're already as arrogant as NBA all-stars. I'm telling ya, Rob, they're uncoachable. They say, 'Yes, Coach. I got ya, Coach.' Then they go out there and do whatever the eff they want. And get this: If they mess up, it's always somebody else's fault. Usually mine. I mean, it was knuckleheads like Rasheed Wallace what drove Norm Sloan into early retirement."

"I hear you, Michael, but the both of us know that you'll die on the bench."

"Yeah. What the eff? If I left this racket, my wife would have me hopping all day long. Fixing the effen kitchen sink, cleaning the gutters, spreading that powdered pig crap on her effen geraniums. Whatever.

Actually, the biggest thing that bothers me? All of them balls bouncing during practice. Too much effen noise for an old codger like me. Then I got to shout over all the racket to make myself heard."

"Speaking of practice. You've got a shootaround scheduled at noon, right? You gonna push them?"

"Yeah. It's a Sunday, so they got no classes. Why the eff not? But not too much 'cause they're liable to fall asleep in their classes tomorrow. If they go to them, that is."

He deftly pulls a tissue from a box atop his desk, noisily blows his nose, inspects the outcome, then rolls the tissue into a ball and tosses it toward a brown-stained garbage can squatting on the floor beside his desk—and grunts when he misses. "I'm losing my touch," he says with a small smile. "Okay, so let me guess who you're here to look at. . . . Marcus Ross, right?"

"You got it."

"Let me tell you this. . . . The kid can fill it. Put him on an outdoor court in the middle of a hurricane and he'll still shoot your eyes out."

I knew that already after seeing a few televised games, but I had several other questions: Is he coachable? Unselfish? Emotionally stable? Liked by his teammates? Does he always work hard? Does he take personal responsibility when he messes up? Is he a good student? What's his major? What are his parents like? Does he have a girlfriend? How much does he party?

Turns out the kid has a 3.1 grade average. His girlfriend is white and they're both prospective political science majors. Both of his parents are teachers, his mom in elementary school, his dad a sociology professor at Penn. No, he doesn't party much. And Michael had overwhelmingly positive responses to all my other queries.

"If I had a daughter," he said, "I wouldn't mind for her to marry him, so long as his side paid for the wedding."

A loud thud from overhead causes him to point at the flaking, grimy ceiling. "Whoops. Time to get the show on the road. I can hear those effen balls bouncing already."

The ancient gym is poorly lit, the floor is composed of some dark wood, and in lieu of bleacher seats, one sideline contains a single row of gray institutional folding chairs. Michael has two young, spry assistants (one black, one white, neither of whom I recognize) and they are charged with conducting the warm-up joggings and stretchings, as well as the usual three-quarter-speed ball handling and the three-on-two, two-on-one continuity drills. Then the players split up, with the bigs working at the near basket with one of the assistants and the smalls at the opposite end with the other assistant.

Unlike the Dean Smith routine that's followed by so many college coaches, during practice sessions Michael uses his assistants as teachers instead of loose-ball retrievers. Again unlike Smith and his disciples, Michael's voice is seldom heard as he sidles up to various players and whispers instructions and/or encouragement.

All of the players diligently work their way through the oft-repeated exercises. I only wish that more NBA coaches routinely devoted significant practice time to fundamental drills.

Here's what I discover about Ross:

He's a legit six-five, 210 pounds—a good size for a shooting guard. He has quick hands and feet, long arms and muscles on his muscles. His crossovers need work, and since Michael is strictly a zone guy, the kid's defensive stance, footwork, and ball-responsive instincts rely more on his considerable natural athleticism than on technique. Yes, his jumper is deadly, but his shot release is a mite too slow, so he'll require various combo screens to create the space and time he'll need to get clean looks in the pros.

In short, he does have the requisite tools, but he's a project—maybe two seasons before he can be a useful rotation player in the league. Too bad the Nets are such a sad-sack team and in need of immediate help. On the basis of what I see, I'd rate Ross as a low-second-round draft pick. Since we'll certainly be picking high in the second round, the kid is not for us.

Oh well, maybe the kid will step up and show me more when the lights are turned on tonight.

Back at the hotel, I adhere to the same pregame routine common to virtually all pro players—one that I'd also practiced as a coach: a small early-afternoon meal of pasta and salad in the hotel dining room while studying the NBA and college box scores in *USA Today* (NJ lost by 21 to the less-than-mediocre Timberwolves), followed by a short nap and a shower. Then it's game time.

The stands are jam-packed with postadolescent guys and gals with their faces painted in various designs and combinations of blue and white (Villanova's colors) or the crimson and gray of St. Joseph's. All of them screaming hysterically as soon as the players take the floor for their pregame lay-up lines, and not shutting up until the final buzzer. Adding to the overwhelming racket is the competition between each school's band—heavy on large. thunderous drums; blaring trumpets; and blatting trombones. Sometimes it's hard to hear the officials blowing a play dead.

I've even considered wearing earplugs, but from my primo seat at the scorer's table, I'm interested in trying to hear the play calls by the coaches. So I just grimace and bear it.

In truth, I'm not very fond of college ball, and here's why:

- There are normally only one or two players in any given game who could conceivably play in the NBA, and perhaps another one who might qualify for the CBL.

- The comparatively low talent level leads to sloppy play, ill-advised shots, incredibly poor decisions, and routine confusion.

- About 95 percent of the big men have identical post-up moves— one or two dribbles in place before undertaking a drop step, then unleashing a jump hook.

- The vast majority of college coaches specialize more in recruiting than in X'ss and O's. Accordingly, the set offenses I'm obliged to witness seldom generate open shots.

- The coaches make sure to stand, jump, and scream instructions all game long—demonstrating how hard they are working.

- The 3-point line is much too close.

- The unbridled zone defenses make for boring (and useless) offenses.

- The referees are the most pathetic I've ever seen.

- On the plus side, the undergraduates usually play hard. *Boola Boola.*

In any case, I always try to keep a low profile. Literally every other NBA scout is armed with a basketball-colored, basketball-pebbled Spalding folder that proudly sports the league's official logo—a white silhouette of Jerry West dribbling the ball with his left hand (something West rarely did) set against a red background on the ball side and a blue background on West's right side. At the bottom, "NBA" in prominent white blocked letters. The folder being typically carried and flashed about to insure that its bearer is seen and admired by every passerby. The scouts' notes and diagrams are usually scribbled on pads of yellow, tear-away foolscap. As for me, I use a five-subject spiral notebook.

Anyway, Ross shows me no surprises. He bags a shitload of uncontested treys against St. Joe's ragged zone, dives for loose balls, avoids putting the ball on the floor in traffic, forces a couple of shots, shows quick hands and slow feet at the point of Villanova's zone, and never misses a free throw. I'm delighted to see that he's also eager to take the win-or-lose shot, burying a buzzer beating, one-on-none 3-ball that gives Villanova a 75–74 win.

However, there's a six-eleven, 250-pound center on St. Joe's who attracts my attention. Isaiah Jones is a senior and a four-year starter. According to the pregame notes, most of his highlighted numbers aren't very impressive—6.2 points, 5.9 rebounds, and 1.1 assists per game. But he averages one rebound for every four minutes of playing time, blocks 2.3 shots, shoots 51 percent from the field (mostly on put-backs) and 78 percent from the stripe.

And the kid plays killer defense; has terrific lateral movement; sets rock-steady picks; has quick, adhesive hands, a smooth turn-around jumper over his left shoulder (he only took two of these); and he rebounds like the ball is a lamb chop and he's a hungry wolf. Also, he's a sky walker and is incredibly quick off his feet. His T-square shoulders are another plus. Guys with sloping, muscular shoulders are a quarter count too slow in raising their arms to challenge shots and are therefore vulnerable to foul trouble. Moreover,

Jones knows how to play without the ball (which is seldom passed to him), is never out of position, has uncanny anticipation, hustles on every play, and has an NBA body.

I'm impressed. I project him as a solid role-playing backup. A defensive stopper like Oklahoma City's Nick Collison. Or, in tandem with a point-making power forward and a pair of creative, high-scoring wings, Jones could eventually become a starter and the anchor of a playoff team's defense.

After the game, I try to catch up with St. Joe's coach, but after they've lost in such an aggravating fashion, the locker room remains closed for forty-five minutes. Subsequently, after dealing with the local media, the coach makes a quick exit stage left. By then it's too late to connect with Michael.

But I absolutely, positively must see this kid again.

Meanwhile, I'll write and send Earl my report in the morning. Then it's time for a time-out. . . .

I've been on the road for twelve straight days, eyeballing ten games in ten cities, and my itinerary calls for a three-day minivacation.

CHAPTER FOUR

The train station at Rhinecliff is just a thirty-five-minute drive from my new home, and Zippy is patiently waiting there for me.

I take advantage of the slightly-better-than-mediocre Chinese restaurant in town, to pick up three days' worth of takeout as well as the latest edition of the *Woodstock Times*. Then, after loading and lighting the wood stove, and filing my backlogged scouting reports, I settle in to do some serious reading.

The library and bookstore hereabouts are critical to my well-being, simply because of the long flights and the otherwise boring downtime in hotels. That said, I pride myself on discovering (and devouring) novels of generally obscure writers. Writers like J. R. Salamanca, whose *Wild in the Country* is a rich, stylistic master-piece—and which was bought by Hollywood and turned into a nonsensical Elvis Presley film. Also, Paul Horgan and his Richard Trilogy, the last of which—*Clean Mountain Air*—literally made me sob. Plus a pair of Englishmen—Malcolm Bradbury and David Lodge. Most of these are out of print, but are available through the interlibrary loan system.

Even so, I can't resist closing my book of the moment to watch the Miami Heat play the Chicago Bulls—a busman's holiday. Except when Marv Albert is doing the play-by-play, my practice is to mute the sound and avoid the temptation to take notes.

In truth, the only reason I'm watching the game is because I find LeBron James to be the most culturally relevant player in the NBA. And here's why:

Ever since he was a schoolboy, LeBron was hailed as a future Hall-of-Famer. And he devoutly embraced the media hype refer-ring to himself as "King James," having "The Chosen One" tattooed on his back, ad nauseum. This self-absorption was further ignited when the citizens of Sports Amerika rushed to love him and make him the focus of their vicarious lives.

But then LBJ's arrogance got the better of him. Witness "The

Decision" and his several premature announcements and celebrations of multiple championships in the near future. Even worse, his most recent playoff performances have revealed him to be a fraud and a loser. As a result, many sports fans of most persuasions are currently rushing to hate James. The point being that we (they!) need villains as much as we need heroes. And for much the same reasons: both mindless hero worship and mindless vilification boost our own deflated egos and become significant, and artificial, components of our internal identities.

It's also quite possible that, deep in his heart of hearts and despite his incredible talent, LeBron is basically insecure. That's why his boasting is so hollow, and why he is routinely AWOL in so many playoff games. Nor is it farfetched to say that LeBron acts as a mirror for the subliminal fears and insecurities of so many of us—all of which go a long way toward explaining our culture's pervasive racism, sexism, and homophobia. That's also why so many of us are so blindly devoted to absurd political and religious philosophies, denial of scientific proofs, and so on.

The twofold moral of the story being that (1) hero or bum, we need LeBron as much as he needs us; and (2) life is a metaphor for basketball.

Therefore, for my own reasons, I'm not happy that LBJ torches the Bulls for 38 points in the game I'm watching, and Miami wins in a wall-to-wall blowout. It's inevitable that James will win an NBA championship, or two or three. Also that he'll learn to nurture a more humble public persona. At that time, Sports Amerika will instantly forget his insufferable ego bleating and his on-court failures, and once again regard him as one of the finest human beings in the history of Western civilization. But no matter how many rings James may win, he'll still be an asshole.

And I am struck by the certainty that young DeLeon Johnson is another media monster in the making.

Ugh! Enough hoops for the nonce.

A brief perusal of the current edition of the *Woodstock Times* informs me that an open-house poetry reading is in session in town at the Colony Arts Center.

I've taken pains to be invisible hereabouts, hunching my shoulders and bowing my head in public places to minimize my extra-large presence. Thus far, in the supermarket, the Laundromat, the bookstore, and the library, I talk to nobody, and nobody talks to me.

But hey, why not get a taste of the local literati scene? I'll come and go like a ghost.

CHAPTER FIVE

The Colony is a large, dimly lit, low-ceilinged space. Two swinging doors at the far end lead to the kitchen, and much of the available wall space is covered with outsized framed posters celebrating the participants of the original Woodstock festival—Jimi Hendrix, Ten Years After, Sly and the Family Stone, Joe Cocker, and The Who (a quartet of first-basemen?)—each one featuring the familiar logo of a silhouetted white bird perched on the neck of a guitar. The floor space is crowded with round, brown Formica-topped tables and wrought-iron chairs with wafer-thin beige cushions.

A slightly elevated platform is wedged into a corner, upon which stands a middle-aged bearded man who holds his hand over an upright microphone while engaging in a rather spirited discussion with a younger man whose lips, eyebrows, nose, and ears are pierced with a dully gleaming assortment of metallic rings and studs. There was a tattooed eye in the middle of his forehead. The pin-cushioned youth grasps a ragged folder in one hand and repeatedly points at it with his other hand, while his opponent keeps shaking his head.

The only unoccupied seat is at a table perilously close to the kitchen doors, where an almost-young man slouches in an adjacent chair. He has a lean face and his brown eyes are squeezed tightly around his long nose even as he restlessly scans the room, perhaps searching for the return of a companion who's visiting the rest room. He's resplendent in a purple, ersatz-satin sweat suit that's adorned with gold piping. The colors of the Los Angeles Lakers. But his baseball cap bears the logo of the Knicks.

"Excuse me. Is this chair taken?"

"No, not at all." With an upturned palm he urges me to sit. Then he offers the same hand for me to shake. "Hi. I'm Jack, aka Jacques the Ripper."

Hmmm. "I'm . . . Robert."

"You're a newbie, right? I can tell at a glance."

"Um, yeah. Moved here just a few weeks ago."

"So, what do you do, Robert?"

"Um, I'm an insurance adjuster. Why are you also known as Jacques the Ripper?"

"It's a long story that I won't bore you with."

The tabletop contains a saucer, an empty cup, a spoon and a fork, a crumpled napkin, and a small plate littered with brownish crumbs.

"By the way, what's going on up there on the stage?"

"Dmitri wants to read his epic, and Carlo will only give him fifteen minutes. They'll spend at least that arguing. This happens every week. Dmitri always winds up reciting it on weekends on the Village Green with an open cigar box to collect change from the tourists. It takes about three hours to get though the whole shebang and it's awful. Some Buddhist nonsense about our lives and everything in the world being a dream."

"Are you a poet, then?"

"My entire life is a poem," he says, then proceeds to relate much more than I want to know about his "life experience."

After a woman named Gloria left him five years ago, Jack/Jacques spent a "riotous summer" in California. Then, following the advice of an "itinerant hippie," he hitchhiked to Woodstock.

"Nah," he responds to an unasked question, "I never made it to the festival. I wanted to go, but one of my sister's kids had a fancy bar mitzvah in Port Washington that I had to go to."

He lived with Rosie for a few months and was beginning to think he had finally found his one true love. "I'm an incurable romantic," he glints. But after Rosie developed a yeast infection and was prescribed two weeks of vaginal suppositories, he "was gone."

He says that he moves around a lot, but in an emergency can sleep in his battered 1964 Ford van that's replete with curtains Rosie made, two lumpy mattresses, and quadraphonic sound. "The only good head," he insists, "is a Dead Head."

Do I know anybody with a cabin to spare for the rest of the winter? Are any of my friends on vacation? Do I have a spare bedroom? "I don't have a lot of stuff, so I won't take up hardly any space."

His "stuff" includes two pairs of jeans, a shopping bag full of shirts, a backpack stuffed with socks, underwear, and toiletries. He's still "pissed" that somebody stole his down-filled sleeping bag from the summit of Slide Mountain last fall. His most valued possessions are one carton of CDs and three cartons of books. "Ess-eff, man. I used to go to conventions on Alpha-Ralpha Boulevard."

He considers himself a part-time carpenter. "But somebody stole my hammer, and I haven't worked since I split with Rosie." He's also suffered employment as a dishwasher, a cheese slicer, a summer-camp counselor at Levy's-by-the-Lake, and a night watchman at a car dealership.

"What I need right now," he says, his eyes still restlessly reconnoitering the room, "is to get a shit job and hold it long enough to get fired and collect checks." In the meantime, he shovels driveways and makes dump runs for $7.50 an hour, and sells a few ounces of pot. "I ain't ashamed. Someday I'm gonna write a novel."

Just last night he met someone new in the Grand Union, and was hoping she'd show up tonight. "She's got a build, and a kid." He readily admits to being sexist. "Let's face it. Chicks are sex objects. So are guys. So are the Grand Canyon and the Eiffel Tower. And if she does walk in the door, then you got to vamoose, right?"

"Right."

But why am I listening to this guy? And why are the other spectators glued to their seats while Dmitri and Carlo continue to argue?

Jack/Jacques is thirty-six and passes for twenty-eight. During the summer, he plays mixed doubles at the Rec Field, and when the weather turns cold, coed volleyball on Wednesday nights at the Woodstock Elementary School. But he never plays basketball. "You can't get laid playing hoops."

On the stage, Dmitri and Carlo have reached an agreement. The ostensible poet grabs the mic and says this: "This fucking asshole says I can only read one of my short poems, and if I try to do more, he says he'll pull out the plug."

The audience's laughter annoys him. "Yeah?" he says. "Well, fuck all of you, too. I know who you are. A bunch of dumb shits that think you're all undiscovered geniuses. You'd do anything to be more in with the in-crowd. Or else you're Trustafarians who live on the checks mommy and daddy send."

The crowd responds with laughter and a few hoots, but Dmitri is undeterred. "So here's my fucking poem." He shrugs, straightens his shoulders, stretches his neck, and then adds, "I'm gonna make artistic pauses so you can imagine the unique spacing of the lines. It's called 'Happy Birthday to Tzu,' as if any of you has an idea who the fuck that is. . . ."

Clearing his throat with a fluid gasp, he begins:

Thousands of years ago, an old man went to the mountains to die.

   Some of you may be old men

   Some may live on mountains

     But today

       this evening

       right now

       what do you know about death?

         the old man's

         yours

The old man was a teacher

    even when he slept

    or pissed

    or chopped wood

Just before he reached the mountain pass, the old man was over-taken by one of his students. "Master," the student said. "We fear your wisdom will be lost when you die. I am younger than you and much stronger. I will not let you pass until you have transcribed your wisdom."

Words

words

   for rent

   help wanted

   special this week

   attempted assassination

why did the chicken cross the road?

The old man breathed an ancient sigh and surrendered.

What to say about life

> love
>
> death
>
> renewal
>
> about a finger pointing to the moon
>
> about silence
>
> about a river falling from the mountain
>
> > into the sea

So the old man wrote, "The truth cannot be spoken." But the student was not satisfied and bade the old man write more. So the old man wrote, "That which is spoken cannot be the truth." But the student was still not satisfied and bade the old man write more.

After three days, the old man stopped writing. "Words will never satisfy you," said the old man. "And it is time for me to go."

Thousands of years ago an old man went to the mountains to die."

A few people applaud (including me), a few laugh (including Jack/Jacques), and one wise guy shouts out, "Dmitri! By your own admission, your poem is a lie!"

As Dmitri stomps off the stage and heads for the exit, he says over his shoulder, "Pearls before swine!"

A tall, slim waitress with long black hair approaches the table. "Can I get anything for you?" she asks me.

I'm stumped because I don't know what's on the nonexistent menu.

Jacques points to the remnants of his own repast and says, "He'll have chamomile tea and a slice of carrot cake."

Okay," I say, and the waitress nods and heads toward the kitchen.

"As I was saying, all I need to get my life on track is the right chick. You know what I mean?" Then he points to a woman who's delicately approaching the stage accompanied by a slight smattering of applause. "Like her."

"Who's she?"

"Nancy Sanger, the unofficial poet laureate of the Woodstock Nation. She comes here every week and only reads one poem. Watch, the place will empty out when she's done."

Although she's probably only in her early forties, her hair is already gray and twisted into a pair of long braids that frame her face. Cold stone-colored eyes under untrimmed black brows, high shiny cheekbones, a small *goyish* nose, thin unpainted lips. Black leggings cling tightly to her slender legs and she's apparently busty under a loose thick-yarned brown-and-white-flecked sweater.

Her frosty sensuality suddenly reminds me that I'm as horny as a unicorn.

By dint of my willpower and stubborn sense of morality I never cheated on Rachael. Until that dramatic and climactic phone call after we (they!) lost at the buzzer. What a way to lose a fucking game and a fucking marriage!

From then to the end of my stay in Peoria, I occasionally convened in my apartment with the married choreographer of the Stars' cheerleading squad for hurried sessions of beddy-hi and beddy-bye. She was a ruthless, athletic lover, who, like me, was only interested in discharging certain thrilling energies. We never discussed our spouses or anything of a personal nature.

After I moved to Woodstock, I was propositioned by a second-string powerless forward on the women's team that I coached. Her lean, flexible body was certainly appealing—too bad she had such bad hands!—but after some ridiculously adolescent flirtations, I turned her down. Not because of any ethical considerations, but because I figured out that what she was really seeking was more playing time.

Since then, Mandrake the Magician stands at attention only in my dreams. Until now. . . .

I can't prevent myself from saying to Jacques, "She's absolutely gorgeous!"

"That's why every guy in town is in love with her. But you ain't seen nothing yet. Her poems will always blow your mind. Hmmm . . . I've got something else she can blow."

His crude lechery is rendered forgivable and even meaningless by her sheer presence, even as she settles comfortably behind the mic, expertly lowering it to suit her slightly hunched posture. There's a glow about her suggesting innocence lost and innocent wisdom found. A palpable feeling is silently communicated that she's a wise, middle-aged angel bereft of her gossamer wings, returned here among us mortals to demonstrate that grace, beauty, and hope are not exclusive to the young.

She doesn't deign to glance at her audience, smiles to herself, places her hands on her hips in gentle defiance, then closes her eyes and recites from memory in a ringing yet mellifluous voice. Ah, but I also get a feeling that despite her on-stage persona, she's more than a little scared. Conflicted, too. Of voluntarily making herself so vulnerable. Indeed, the sheet of paper she holds trembles ever so slightly.

"This one is called 'A Resurrection' . . .

So silently has another equinox slowly turned the world—
    Gray leaves twirling flying already dead
Only a few blazing flowers to survive the frosty curtain
    Of nightfall
Runny noses
    winter cough
The fearsome nocturnal sigh of an oil furnace coming alive
The hawkwind whipping your face
Wild ducks arrowing southward and blackly under sere
    clouds of doom
Vitamin C and thermal undies
Snow tires and tired batteries

So silently does death come upon us
>dancing our imaginary lives macabre upon the crumbling
>edge of despair
Turning the earth to stone

Spring seems so far from here
>escaping like a warm tailfeather of dream from a cold
>and rheumy morning
Even so
>some joyful someday
>shall the barren heart-stones of winter
>suddenly burst forth into luminous blossoms."

As she steps down from the stage, shouts of "Bravo!" and "You go, girl!" shrill above the enthusiastic applause. But she ignores the fuss, and the audience respectfully makes way as she strides, head turned downward, out the front door. After waiting another few respectful minutes, the crowd likewise makes a swift departure.

I turn to Jack/Jacques to say, "Hey, that was great!" But he's gone.

As I pull on my jacket, the waitress approaches, hands me the bill, and waits for me to pay up. It seems that before I got there, Jack/Jacques had feasted on a large portion of nachos, some chicken wings, and two glasses of wine. The bill I'm stuck with amounts to $43, but when I hand her two twenties and a ten and tell her to keep the change, she sneers at me before huffing through the kitchen doors.

Before I take off my coat and change into my floppy slippers, I listen to my voice mail. The only message is from Earl:

"Rob, there's a change of plans. Weiss wants to meet with the entire coaching and scouting staff before Wednesday night's game. Who the fuck knows what he wants? Anyway, I'm sorry to cut a day off your free time."

Here's my altered itinerary: New Jersey for the meeting, next is Duke vs. St. John's in Madison Square Garden; Georgetown at Syracuse; the CBL's all-star game in Rockford, Illinois; then on to Salt Lake City; Los Angeles; Oklahoma City; and back home again. I'm responsible for scheduling my own rental cars, hotel reservations, and flights—the one part of the job I detest.

Other than having to deal personally with Weiss.

CHAPTER SIX

The entire scouting staff, plus the video coordinator, has been imperiously summoned to one of the several smallish meeting rooms in the upper reaches of the Prudential Center. In the middle of the windowless room, four plumply cushioned leather chairs line each long side of an impressive oak table. There's also a chair at either end, but these two are larger than the others and have swiveled bases. Both the low-slung cabinets and the sidewalls they hug are faced with matching small-grained oak panels.

The only defining decoration hangs on the far wall. A long, silky white banner with gold tassels at the bottom, and in the center a large blue-black shield. Half of a basketball seems to protrude from the downwardly pointed end of the shield, and what can be seen of the ball is encircled by a small dark-blue ring. Across the top end of the shield, "Nets" is emblazoned in large white letters.

This official logo of the team looks like it's been fashioned for the Big Game by a team of high school cheerleaders and their moms.

One of the cabinets supports the fixings of a help-yourself buffet. But the stacked paper plates, the basket of plastic forks and knives, the dual steam-trays of greasy hamburgers and withered French fries, the wilted salad stuff lying listlessly in a large plastic bin, the mushy buns, and the packets of salad dressing, mustard, and ketchup suggest a cheapo meal for starving, homeless sinners at a low-rent church.

The meager menu rudely and crudely obliterates whatever sense of self-importance and independence any of us might have brought into the room. We are reminded that we are mere wage earners, bottom-feeders in this multi-million-dollar organization, who have come with our tails wagging hopefully when summoned by the Power That Is. And since none of our contracts are guaranteed, we can't help fearing that the Nets' miserable performance so far this season will cost some, if not all, of us our jobs.

I've added a black herringbone sports jacket to my normal working attire, but everybody else is spiffed up in suits and ties. Including the senior-most scout in the organization, John Ballard, who used to be a ferocious, elbow-wielding six-ten center for several NBA teams back in the day. It is said that before playing against Ballard, opposing players would have nightmares. These days, he's a hunched old man who wouldn't measure six-six if he could straighten up. But he's been with the Nets since the franchise was in the American Basketball Association, so he knows everything about everybody, and it's inconceivable that Weiss would can him. Ballard covers the West Coast region, and is the only one among us who helps himself to the food.

"How's the boy?" Ballard asks me as he looks up from a serving of two burgers and a pile of fries.

"Plugging along. Trying hard to remember what city I'm in."

A grin contracts his crinkled face and hides his eyes. "I know what you mean, but shit, at my age it doesn't matter where I am as long as I'm someplace."

"Any clue about what's going down here?"

"Fuck, no. And I don't really give a shit either. All I know for certain is that the older I get, the faster I get older."

The Midwest scout is Alfonzo Wallace, only five years past his NBA active career. His cleanly shaved head emphasizes the furrowing of his brow, yet he's cautiously friendly as we exchange waves from opposite sides of the room.

Evander Plochman is a weasly little twerp with pale white skin and a large shit-colored nose, who covers the South and the Southwest. He never played hoops at any organized level, and started out in the business by coaching at an obscure community college in Kansas before somehow getting a gig as an at-large gofer during a long-ago session of the old Los Angeles Summer League. The story goes that, a few years later, when Plochman was working on a part-time basis for the Chicago Bulls, a veteran scout (and onetime NBA player) on the team's payroll chanced to mention a Division III player named Hayes Wright, whom he had been studiously tracking. "He plays all five positions for a nowhere school called Montana Central,"

Plochman was informed. "I've seen Wright play seven times and I swear this kid's got the goods to be an NBA all-star."

Plochman then took the next plane to Kalispell, rented a car, saw Wright play once, and was equally enthusiastic. From his hotel room immediately after the game, Plochman then called Chicago's general manager and praised the kid up, down, and sideways. Subsequently, Wright was drafted by the Bulls late in the first round, indeed became a repeat all-star, and Plochman's claim to have discovered him was vouched for by the GM. When the original scout objected, he was summarily fired, and Plochman was promoted to take his place. When a new GM took over in Chicago, Plochman was canned and was subsequently hired by Weiss as a favor to a party or parties unknown.

No wonder Plochman trusts nobody. He sits by himself near the far end of the table, clutching his official Spalding-NBA folder close to his chest, responding to my casual nod by looking down and studying his fingernails.

In truth, Plochman and Wallace have legitimate grounds to both dislike me and pity me. The former because Earl has designated me—a mere rookie scout—as the "checker," that is, the guy who provides a second opinion on blue-chip players to either substantiate or repudiate the reports of the others. To them, I'm Earl's pet and spy. As for Ballard, he's happy to be employed and couldn't care less what happens to his reports after they get filed.

I'm pitied because of the routine transcontinental flights I have to suffer.

There's something else that sets me apart from my coworkers: They all have agents while I have always negotiated my own (mostly boilerplate) contracts. To keep us both on edge, and theoretically working 24/7, Weiss has guaranteed both Earl's my jobs until June 30. This despite Earl's having an agent who eats 15 percent of his salary.

In any event, I believe that the all-too-common circumstance of an agent representing a member of the coaching staff and one or more of the players on the same team inevitably leads to the kind of favoritism (unduly increased playing time, skewed play calling, tolerating mistakes and laziness) that can destroy team harmony. Plochman, for example, is represented by Harry Mayerson, a super agent who speaks for dozens of NBA players and who will undoubtedly lock up many of the draft-eligible blue-chip players.

The video nerd has bloodshot eyes that are magnified by his thick spectacles. I have no idea what his name is. Conspicuous by their respective absences are Weiss, Earl, and the coaching staff.

Suddenly the door swings open and Weiss is here. He's a thirty-something six-footer trimly built. His perpetual tan sets off his blond wavy hair, and his blue eyes seem to flash even brighter than his perfect teeth. He wears a light blue denim work shirt with the sleeves rolled halfway up his thin forearms, also crisp chino pants, black socks, and black loafers. His roundish chin is thrust confidently into the future, yet there's an awkward roll to his walk and a tight dangling of his arms that indicate a lack of natural athleticism.

As his official bio states, Fred Weiss, Jr., once started at middle linebacker for Forsyth University in Biloxi, Mississippi. But the school gave up its football program over twenty years ago, and no records have survived. The bio pointedly fails to include any mention of Fred Weiss, Sr., a second-generation German American who made untold millions in the real estate business, bought the Nets fifteen years ago and made a gift of the franchise last June to his ne'er-do-well son and heir upon the fifth anniversary of Junior's climbing on the wagon.

Weiss the Younger is the classic example of a rich man's offspring who was born on third base but thinks he has hit a triple. And just the fact of his assuming control of the Nets has convinced Weiss that he knows everything there is to know about the game.

Following Weiss's commanding entrance into the room, his taller and heavier general manager seems obliterated by his boss's shadow.

All of us stand to greet Weiss, who humbly waves us to our seats, but remains erect as he delivers his message. Meanwhile Earl walks around the table and lightly taps my shoulder in passing as he heads for the seat at the other end.

"Perhaps you're wondering why I've called you here," Weiss says, quickly glancing at us from right to left but then addressing the banner on the far wall. "That's actually a line from an old Charlie Chan movie that I've always wanted to say."

His tight, expectant grin prompts general laughter from my workmates, including a few insincere chuckles from me.

"Actually, I wanted to discuss, and also get your opinions about, the future of the ball club. Specifically about the upcoming draft." He pauses to extract a sheet of paper from one of his back pockets, then reads some numbers. "'Thirty-six points per game. Seventeen rebounds. Eleven assists. Fifty-nine percent from the field and eighty-four from the foul line. And his team is undefeated.'"

He flashes another smile at the banner, this time with an all-knowing showing of his teeth. "Actually, those are the stats so far this season of DeLeon 'The Lion' Johnson, who's on the cover of the current issue of *Schwartz Illustrated. . . .*"

Like a veteran stand-up comic, he waits for the laugh before continuing. "I know he's only a schoolboy playing against other schoolboys. But numbers don't lie. And actually, in the accompanying story, the number-one sports magazine in the country declares that Johnson can't miss being an NBA all-star. That's a given. That case is closed. And that's exactly why we must draft the young man."

He clumsily shifts his weight and has to put a hand on the table to maintain his balance.

"Now, there is of course, one formidable problem. We'll surely wind up in the lottery. That's actually another given. But as you all know, whichever team winds up with the first pick is strictly unpredictable. After all, you can never tell which way the Ping-Pong ball bounces."

Earl glances at me in quick conspiracy and actually says, "Ha-ha." The best I can muster is "Hish-sh-sh," a watery ghost of a laugh. Everybody else is nearly convulsed with hilarity.

"So, then . . . In the event that we are denied that precious first pick, I'm determined to offer the team that does luck into it a trade that they can't refuse. Not that we want to cripple our team completely. So here's my own personal assessment of the players on our current roster: who are the keepers and who are the losers. Now,

I'm aware that you guys are the professionals and know much more about talent evaluation that I do. . . ."

He beacons another knowing smile around the table, clearly demonstrating that he's lying only to be polite. Then he goes down the list:

"I'd say that we have two untouchables. Rodney Betts scores over twenty points per game and shoots forty-nine percent from the field. Even I know that you never trade a starting center for a wing-man. But everybody else is on the table, with the exception of our point guard, Darrell Harman, who's a bona fide all-star."

Weiss doesn't like Ralph Layne, the starting power forward. "Look it," he says, again consulting his gyp sheet. "Nine points a game, more turnovers than assists, and, get this, only fifty-two percent from the foul line."

Also deemed expendable is Tyrone Howard, our shooting guard, who "can't do anything but shoot." Also Kevin Brownbill, who "can't guard his own shadow" and "never hit a clutch shot in his life."

To buttress his opinions, Weiss quotes more numbers: 12.2, 7.7, 41 percent, 2.5:1.5 A:TO ratio, plus 12 points, minus 7. In addition, this guy "makes too much money." That guy is "always hurt." The other guy "still makes rookie mistakes."

Through it all, Plochman diligently takes notes.

Of course, in addition to whichever disposable players the lucky top-drafting team may want, Weiss is agreeable to including whatever future draft picks are necessary plus "a ton of money."

His imperial pronouncements completed, Weiss sits down and, starting with Ballard on his right, indicates that he will now suffer to hear our opinions.

"Well," says the old scout, "seeing as how I'm almost always on the road, I hardly ever get to watch the team play. So it doesn't seem fair for me to judge the players. I guess I have no choice except to defer to your opinions."

"Thanks," says Weiss.

"You bet."

With a broad, toothy grin, Wallace seconds everything Weiss has presented "only because the hotel chain I stay in has the NBA channel." And the video guy thirds the motion.

Plochman stands and says this: "You're right on, sir, on every count. You can't fool me, sir. You must have studied hours of game tapes."

In lieu of an answer, Weiss accepts the praise with another gleaming grin.

By virtue of my sitting at Weiss's left hand, I'm last.

This motherfucker doesn't know an X from an O. It's influential dickheads like him who twist the game into something unbeautiful and mechanical.

Before I can say anything, Earl glares at me and shakes his head with a slight but unmistakable warning. Then Weiss turns to me and says with an almost sneering condescension, "And last, but probably not least, the newcomer to our staff . . ."

Fuck him!

"First off," I say, "Betts is a stiff. Yes, he can shoot some, but his moves are mechanical, he gets confused when he's doubled, he can't rebound worth a shit, and his feet are too slow to play defense. What he is, is a white hope."

Now it's my turn to look at Weiss, daring him to respond. He shifts in his cushy chair but says nothing.

"Harman is an erratic shooter who habitually overpenetrates. Yes, he's a wonderful finisher and he's excellent at the stripe, which is why he scores so much. Trouble is, he can't run an offense. He also thinks he's a leader, but he's so selfish that nobody wants to follow him. If you want Johnson that bad, I'd trade both of these guys for him—although I'm not completely sold on the kid."

Weiss responds by sadly shaking his head and giving Earl a subdued yet furious glance. After all, it was Earl who begged the Nets to sign me.

"I also disagree about Layne. Yes, he can't shoot himself in the foot, but he can defend and he can inhale rebounds. With Betts pussyfooting around the boards, we absolutely, positively need somebody who can rebound. Otherwise, sir, I'm in total agreement."

Earl is holding his head in his hands as though he has a massive migraine.

"Thanks to you all for actually being so honest," Weiss says sourly as he stands and quickly exits stage right.

He's hastily followed by everybody else, who all avoid coming near me as though I were glowing with radioactivity. Not even Earl dares to look my way. Except for old man Ballard, who not only stops to look me in the eye but shakes my hand, and says, "It's been nice knowing you, kid."

CHAPTER SEVEN

Earl and Weiss habitually watch the game from the owner's box. Ballard, Wallace, and Plochman are probably en route to their next assignments or else to parts unknown since the spaces reserved for them in the upper press box are vacant. And by "upper" I mean just below the nosebleed section.

So here I am, situating myself so that there's an empty chair on either side of me, to fend off the uninformed opinions of writers employed by low-level web sites and foreign-language newspapers, the wire-service stringers, as well as the kids bent on doing "in-depth" pieces for their high school or college weeklies.

The ID card taped to the long table in front of me says only "NETS STAFF." For all my neighbors know, I could be a public relations intern, so I'm grateful to be ignored by the surrounding hubbub.

From way up here, the players are even smaller than they appear to be on my forty-six-inch TV back home. Since I'm always seated courtside at the scorer's table when I'm working, I can't keep my attention focused on the game below. Besides, there's a buxom blonde sitting on the aisle about ten rows down from where I'm perched. From this angle, I can see her right shoulder, her fulsome right breast, and a partial profile of her apparently bright, youthful face. But for the time being, my dinner actually interests me more than either the blonde or the actual game.

Having disdained the grub that Weiss had ordered for the meeting, I was hungry. There had been decent food available for free downstairs in the media complex, but the New York–based news-hounds are aggressively obnoxious. They habitually come at me one by one, initially greeting me as a long-absent best friend—where-upon the questioning commences. Who will we be drafting? Is DeLeon as good as the hype? Will Dodge get fired? If he is, who might replace him? Who should be chosen for the upcoming NBA all-star game?

Instead, I've bought a "foot-long" hot dog and a "Jumbo" cup of fizzy, pisswater beer (for which I was charged the outrageous sum of twenty-four dollars!), then climbed up to the press box.

Who the hell are the Nets playing anyway?

Ah, the San Antonio Spurs. So a loss is still another given.

Indeed, near the end of the first quarter, the visitors have assumed a 15-point lead, and the hometown heroes have shifted into cruise control.

The hot dog makes me belch and the beer makes me light-headed and playful.

Okay. Should I stay put until the bitter end, and hopefully hook up with Earl for a late meal at our favorite Italian joint in the East Village? Or should I call the hotel in Manhattan and see if I can expand tomorrow's reservation to tonight? If so, I could cancel my reservation at the nearby New Jersey Ramada Inn and then vacate the premises ASAP.

I guess I'll wait to hear from Earl.

Meanwhile, as the game progresses, shots are made or missed, whistles are blown or are silent, the fans roar or moan, and I couldn't care less. As a coach, I lived or died with the result of each game. As a scout, it blissfully matters not who wins or who loses.

Just as the second quarter is under way, an underling scurries along press row handing each of its inhabitants an official copy of the first-quarter stats. This consists mostly of a running timeline of points scored, fouls called, substitutions, and time-outs.

More fucking numbers!

Feeling sillier with every gulp of beer, I carefully fold the stat sheet to form a paper airplane, then launch it at the blonde. If I could get her to turn around, then I'd know if I was in love or not. Geez! As usual I must be drunker than I think I am. The flight pattern seems to be true, but the swirling air currents in the arena cause the missile to nose-dive and bounce point-first off the bald head of a man sitting five rows away. He grabs the paper and turns furiously around to locate the perpetrator. My smile and the happy wave of my right hand only stoke his ire.

However, a small boy sitting beside him—probably his son—unfolds the missive, reads the numbers, and excitedly pokes his dad. Ah, now the guy's thrilled to possess the inside info. His anger instantly turns into delight, and he waves a hearty thank-you up to me. Both of them neglect the game action and instead pour over the numbers.

Why am I not surprised?

Only because the most basic of the several cultural factors that are destroying the beauty of basketball-as-we-should-know-it is America's general obsession with numbers: The stock market and its fluctuations. The GNP and the unemployment rate. Ubiquitous rankings and poll results. Test scores. Gross and net worth. Digits wrought in red or black ink. What's your APR? Your IQ? Your credit rating? Who's number one?

In virtually every aspect of our society, value is expressed in linear, numerical terms. This allows the individual (and the collective) mind to reduce the ongoing, ever-changing stream of life to a static format that is presumably more easily quantifiable.

How I'd love to be locked in a room with Weiss as my prisoner and elucidate the inherent fallacies of his belief system. This is what I'd say to him: "Weiss, you fucking moron, numbers cannot evaluate the worth of a player, or the human spirit, or predict the future. In truth, most of your holy numbers are either partially or totally misleading. If you really want to know how good or how bad a player is, just watch him play."

Then I'd convince him with my incontrovertible proofs:

"Take minutes played. I'll bet you think that this particular measurement is carved in stone. That's only because you're a shit-for-brains and don't know that actual playing time is rounded off to the nearest whole number. So a player who's on the court for a single tick of the clock and a player who's on the court for eighty-nine seconds are both credited with one game played and one minute of action. Do the math, schmucko. This eighty-eight-second difference could conceivably include at least four possessions, and could therefore be the difference between a totally insignificant appearance and a critical one.

"Shooting percentages can also be unreliable, since they fail to differentiate between good shots and ill-advised ones, or between meaningless sixty-foot heaves launched before the buzzer ends a blowout, and botched lay-ups in the clutch. And while field-goal percentage is apparently an objective number, it's not necessarily an acceptable measure of a player's shooting prowess. For example, take Shaquille O'Neal, assuming you have sufficient medium-term memory to remember him. The Big Aristotle? The Big Diesel? Okay? Then I'll use him as an example.

"When Shaq was still able to lug his fat ass up and down the court, he'd routinely lead the NBA with accuracy rates that approached fifty-eight percent. In fact, Shaq had the worst "touch" in the league, and given the nature of the point-blank shots he took, the Big Load should have made about eighty percent of his shots.

"I must admit, though, that makes, misses, and accuracy of three-point shots are generally reliable reflections of a player's ability to dial from long distance. . . . Hey, wipe that shit-eating smile off your face. I'm not done here.

"As with field-goal percentages, Shaq's shooting form raises some questions as to the efficacy of free-throw percentages. Because there was such a pronounced hitch in his stroke, potential defensive rebounders were frequently faked out and drawn into the lane too early, resulting in the negation of the subsequent free throw (usually a miss) and Shaq's being awarded another try. If all of his true misses at the stripe were included in his total (as they once were), Shaq's career percentage would be considerably lower than the fifty-three percent that it was. Although this is admittedly a minor cavil, other current players who similarly benefit from their own awkward shot releases include Carlos Boozer, Samuel Dalembert, Brendan Haywood, Dwight Howard, and Pau Gasol. Do-over misses are not recorded in box scores. Got it?

"What? You want me to loosen the ropes? . . . Nah!

"Moving on to rebounds . . . Since poor-shooting teams miss more shots, their big men have more opportunities to snatch offensive rebounds. Conversely, the bigs on teams loaded with sharp-shooters are rarely among the league leaders in this category.

"Also, not all defensive rebounds are equal. Some players (such as Shaq) are so slow off their feet that they seldom come up with defensive rebounds in heavy traffic. And rebounding the opponents' missed free throws is easily done, since the defending team has both inside positions along the foul lane.

"Comprendo? No, no, I'm not going to take the tape off your mouth. Just nod your head.

"Of all the numbers that are bouncing around in your otherwise empty skull, assists are one of the most fraudulent. The operative definition is a pass that directly leads to a basket, with the scorer being allowed a dribble and two steps after receiving said pass. But there are several glitches here. One being that no assist is recorded when the recipient of such a pass is fouled in the act of shooting—even should he make both free throws and thereby tally the same number of points as he would have had he not been fouled. Also, proof that the awarding of assists can be highly subjective is the fact that most of the NBA's assist leaders garner more assists per game at home than they do on the road.

"The most outrageous abuse of home cooking occurred during the 1973–74 season when a point guard that you never heard of named Ernie DiGregorio was a rookie with the Buffalo Braves, a team you also never heard of. They were a mediocre ball club that finished with a record of 42–40, so the Braves' primary gate attraction was DiGregorio's attempt to lead the NBA in assists. He eventually succeeded—averaging 8.2 per game—even though it was later discovered that, during several games in Buffalo, DiGregorio had been credited with assists while he was sitting on the bench.

"Now, you can't be so dumb as not to have at least heard of Wilt Chamberlain. Wilt the Stilt? The Big Dipper? . . . Okay.

"For the 1967–68 season, Chamberlain was certified as the NBA's leading playmaker on the basis of his 8.6 assists per game. Until then Chamberlain had been renowned as a scorer of gargantuan proportions, peaking with a never-to-be-shattered record of 50.4 points per game in 1961–62—another news bulletin, eh? I actually played against him once, but that's none of your business.

"Anyway, Wilt was universally accused of being a selfish player whose individual scoring heroics came at the expense of his team's success. The Warriors were second-place finishers in the Eastern Division that season with a disappointing record of 49–31, and an even more disappointing playoff loss to Boston. Prior to the 1967–68 campaign, however, Chamberlain was determined to prove his critics wrong, and what better way than to lead the league in assists? So whenever Wilt captured an offensive rebound and found himself alone under the basket, he usually disdained the easy dunk and, instead, passed the ball out to the Warriors' best shooter, Hal Greer. The chance to register an assist trumped Wilt's opting for a never-missed dunk.

"Here's some more fodder for your horse-shit mind. . . . The pass that leads to the erstwhile assist pass is sometimes more significant that the assist itself. That's why hockey stats always include two assists for every goal. Why don't you bring this up the next time the league's bigwigs meet for tea?

"All the defensive stats are also FUBAR. Let me translate. . . . It's an expression commonly used in World War Two. You know, when the good guys fought the Nazis and the Japs? . . . Ah, good. I'm impressed. Anyway, it stands for "fucked up beyond all recognition." Let me explain. . . .

"These days, steals and blocked shots are cited as evidence of a player's prowess as a defender. Indeed, Larry Hughes was named to the NBA's All-Defense first team in 2005, solely on the basis of his snatching a league-best 2.89 steals per game. The votes were cast by the league's coaches, who obviously didn't care that Hughes was a mediocre straight-up defender whose perpetual gambles left his teammates in precarious defensive situations whenever his always-risky speculations came up empty.

"In truth, the true-blue defenders are those who concentrate on ball denial, endless hustle, precise and timely rotations, as well as chest-to-chest confrontations that force their opponents to unleash their shots under heavy pressure.

"I know that jackasses like you love to see shots swatted into the stands, but while it's a sometimes-useful skill, the ability to block shots is not always the measure of a superior defender. Too many long-armed, quick-footed, and high-flying big men are so eager to reject shots that they're liable to hastily abandon their assigned defensive positions to attack any shots in their vicinity, and are therefore vulnerable to biting at the merest head fake. I'm talking about guys like Dwight Howard, DeAndre Jordan, and Blake Griffin. Clever teams can maneuver the ball to deliberately sucker these block-happy dunces into leaving the basket unprotected. When the Lakers were coached by Phil Jackson, they were really good at this.

"Ball handling is next, and you'd be wrong—again!—to think that number of turnovers is an infallible measure here. Frequently, when one player zigs instead of zags, his teammate may get stuck with the ball in the wrong place at the wrong time and consequently try to force a pass or a dribble into rush-hour traffic—and get charged with the ensuing turnover. Also, point guards like Steve Nash and Deron Williams, who are required to totally monopolize the ball, usually will have a high assist-to-turnover ratio.

"Now we come to my favorite group of people. . . . According to Eddie Rush, the onetime supervisor of NBA officials, the calls made by the league's refs are correct ninety-two percent of the time. But that means that eight percent of the fouls called are erroneous. Plus, Rush offers no approximation of how many times the refs err by not tooting their whistles.

"The defensive game plan of both the Bad Boy Pistons—the NBA champs in 1989 and 1990—and the Boston Celtics—champs in 2008—was to commit a dozen fouls on every play, knowing that the three blind mice wouldn't call all of them lest the other team make a hundred-plus appearances at the charity stripe. Also, since refs are not robots, they each have their own personal interpretations of what they choose to see. Some let the players bang, while some are quick to make tickle calls. Many look to whistle their pet infractions—traveling, hooking on offense, going over the back in the battle of the boards, and so on. There are certain refs who tend to call charges instead of blocks, and vice versa. Some, like Bernie Fryer, were notorious homers. Some, like Violet Palmer, are obviously incompetent. Ms. Palmer remains employed only because of the NBA's misguided attempt to be deemed politically correct. Some overscrutinize the activities of certain players and certain teams. Bob Delaney habitually overreacted to every move made by Shaq. Jake O'Donnell was called "Jake the Snake" in Boston because virtually every questionable call he made went against the Celtics. Also, most refs won't let tall coaches leave their seats to lodge a protest. Bang! It's a sure tech. But small coaches can walk the length and breadth of the coaches' box and even step over the sideline onto the court. Some guys hug the sideline and start waving their arms whenever an opponent is double-teamed nearby, effectively forming a triple-team.

"For sure, given the speed, quickness, and super reflexes of NBA players—who are undoubtedly the world's best athletes—and because their lightning changes of direction are necessarily unexpected, refs are often forced to avoid being left in the dust by anticipating violations instead of reacting to them. But because so many of these assholes have their own distorted views of the game, statistics such as free throws attempted, fouls, turnovers, and even wins and losses are anything but objective.

"Now let's get down to what I know is your favorite statistic: points scored, which may seem to be a completely objective number. However, the points racked up by high-scorers on bad teams are relatively meaningless. Moreover, it's *when* a player tallies his points, not how many he registers that really counts.

"A case in point is Chamberlain's famous 100-point game against the Knicks on March 2, 1962. I assume you've seen the tape? . . . Bullshit. There was none.

"The game itself was a blowout—Philadelphia won, 169–147—and in the last quarter the Warriors took to deliberately fouling the Knicks as soon as the ball was inbounded. They did this to prevent New York from stretching their every possession, which would limit both Philadelphia's possession time and Chamberlain's opportunities to generate more shots. To this day, several of the Knicks who played in that game—notably Richie Guerin—still feel that Wilt's performance was dishonest, unsportsmanlike, and artificial.

"Okay? Idiots like you reflect the culture at large in using basketball statistics to establish who are the all-stars, who are the also-rans, who are the celebrities, and who gets the humongous salaries. For the most part, numbers are easy to understand by every dimwit in Sports Amerika, and also provide the media with a constant source of material.

"Moreover, the belief that statistics accurately reflect game action is also the idea that drives the proliferation of fantasy leagues in all of the major sports. Unfortunately, this is not the only circumstance in which a fantasy generates millions of dollars, and also drains so many misguided sentient beings of so much time and energy.

"Wait! Wait! I'm not done. . . . What? Sorry, you'll have to either hold it in or piss your pants. Don't worry, I won't tell anybody if you do.

"Have you noticed that, except for Games and Minutes Played, and sometimes Personal Fouls, all of these numbers are recorded when a player is in the immediate proximity of the basketball? This explains several unfortunate situations.

"It explains why, for example, so many NBAers have sticky fingers and are so reluctant to make quick, snappy passes. And why so many young players, not to mention so many hoop-o-philes, are absolutely mesmerized by the ball. Why virtually every live-action shot on TV follows the bouncing ball. Why every basketball highlight on the news focuses on dunks, razzle-dazzle passes, shots, and blocks. Why blocked shots and steals are deemed to be the sole measures of individual defense. And why American hoopers have such brilliant ball skills and excel in one-on-one confrontations.

"Listen carefully now. This is the gist of the whole deal.

"Almost all of the stats that are recorded ignore the fact that the game is played with ten participants and only one ball. While guys like Nash and LeBron are required to personally orchestrate much of their team's offense, most players only have the ball in their hands on a limited basis. All things being equal, statistics only measure what happens in approximately ten percent of the game, that is, those moments when an individual is in control of or reacting to the ball. And that's precisely why basketball statistics produce and encourage rampant egotism and narcissism.

"And that's why jackoffs like you are so dangerous.

"I'll untie you and let you go only if you promise to do what you can to spread the righteous word. Do you so promise? Cross your heart and hope to die? And agree to what was, in the Bronx, the most sacred and ironclad oath: to swear on your mother?

"Oh, I see that you did wet your expensive trousers. Tell you what. Take them off and leave them here. That's right. Wrap your jacket around your waist and your modesty will be preserved. Should you fire me, I'll call a news conference to display this piece of evidence. They can do a DNA test like they did with Clinton's sperm on Monica's dress. But hold on, boss. Maybe I should also confiscate your whitey-tighties in case you also left a brown stain. . . . Nah. I'm the soul of compassion.

"So long, bro. Maybe I'll catch you at the lunch line in Mickey D's."

A loud buzzer ends my reverie.

What's going on down there?

Hey, it's a basketball game. And, hey, those guys are pretty damn good—especially the center and the point guard in the black uni's. Looks to me like they're all legit NBA prospects.

Damn! Did I drink all that beer?

I'm even more confused when my cell phone also buzzes. Is this the end of the game? Then why are they still running around?

No. It's Earl.

"What are you?" he asks. "Fucking crazy?"

"What?"

"Making Weiss look like a fool. Sounding like the arrogant prick you are and always were."

"Okay. Did he at least give me some severance pay?"

"He didn't fire you, asshole. Not this time. I convinced him that if he was surrounded by nothing but yes-men, then he could save lots of money by firing them all."

"Thanks, I think."

"Fuck you. Where you headed next? The Garden?"

"Yeah. Then Syracuse, then . . ."

"I really don't care where you go or where you are. Just stay the fuck away from here until all the air is out of the hate balloon."

"Nice metaphor. And thanks, Earl."

"Fuck you."

CHAPTER EIGHT

Unaccustomed as I am to drinking alcoholic beverages and eating disgusting food, and despite my constant belches, farts, and gut rumblings, there's a cork stuck up my ass.

Red Holzman was right.

Indeed, he's one of my favorite all-time basketball geniuses. Yes, he was a great player before he got into coaching—the starting point guard for the Rochester Royals championship team in 1950. After laboring as a scout for the Knicks for several years Holzman coached New York to the franchise's only two championships (1970, 1972). He was responsible for the Knicks drafting of Phil Jackson, and later served as PJ's guru. Counting their combined careers on the court and on the bench, Holzman and Jackson have been responsible for sixteen championship rings.

And my own experience in the CBL vouchsafed the truth of one of Holzman's more esoteric pronouncements: "It's hard to win on the road, but it's much harder to take a good crap in a strange bathroom."

So far, the two bowls of oatmeal I had for breakfast in the New Jersey Ramada Inn have not loosened my innards. But something indeed seems to be stirring down there.

Anyway, I like to get to the games early to see which, if any, of the players are on the court (and what they are doing) before the turnstiles are in full swing and before the coaches deliver their pregame spiels.

Four Dukies are out there. A bench-bound freshman working on his jump shot with one of Mike Krzyzewski's assistant coaches. Two other raw-boned big men rehearse their moves in the low post. As well as Jateik Murphy, a sophomore small forward, who, I think, is the best amateur player in the country.

Murphy goes six-eight, 225 pounds. I've seen him play in several TV games and I like his athleticism, his long arms, the quickness and size of his hands and feet, his high shoulders, his stroke, his brilliant on-court IQ, as well as his diligent defense. Only a sophomore, the young man has yet to decide whether or not to declare for next June's draft. The general belief is that if Duke wins the NCAAs, then Murphy will turn pro and be a lottery pick.

Assuming he does opt for the cash (his mother is dead and his father makes a so-so living as a plumber), he's the guy we should be trying to get. Not that lame-brain, arrogant DePee-on kid.

At the other end of the court, St. Paul's early birds are a pair of seven-foot freshman, one a starter the other buried on the bench. They laugh uproariously as they take turns launching stupid shots—lefty hooks from the baseline corner, heaves from the time line. Now they're both under the basket trying unsuccessfully to bounce a ball off the top of their heads and through the rim.

Uh-oh! The cork is about to pop!

I use public bathroom only in dire emergencies. This is partially a hangover from the home team's shameful locker room in Peoria. One wall was lined with ancient, dented lockers so flaked with rust that the players only stashed their street shoes inside. Spare towels, clothing, overcoats, and winter jackets were draped over the wire hangers that were hooked to a crisscrossed network of overhead pipes. The room was cold, dusty, and smelled of decaying mammals. There was one outside window at the far end so coated with gunk as to be opaque. A solitary brick was set on the lower right-hand corner of the windowsill to fill a brick-sized gap in the window glass.

But here's the most pertinent factor: The only available toilets and showers were situated down the hall in a public men's room. The bowls were routinely stained and/or clogged, and the urinals were foul smelling. If I had to take a whiz during the half-time break, several fans would surround me and ask questions. Why didn't I play so-and-so more? How come we never used the old give-and-go? What ever happened to...? Did I remember...? And if I did have to drop a load immediately before or after a game, I could count on some desperate soul trying to hurry me by pounding on the door.

On one occasion, I dismissed the team after my half-time talk, then removed the brick and pissed through the opening into a deserted alley.

Fortunately, I have enough sphincter control to allow me to climb a short flight of stairs and gain admittance into the John F. X. Condon Media Room, named after the late public announcer for both the Knicks and the Yankees, whose recital of starting lineups and substitutions sounded like the voice of God. Knowing the room is swarming with just the kind of media Muppets, fellow scouts, and moochers I want to avoid, I hug the near wall and zip unseen into the bathroom.

Ah! The pause that refreshes!

Unfortunately my attempt to make an invisible exit stage right is foiled by someone loudly calling my name. "Rob! Rob! Over here! Come join us!"

It's Bill Kramer, veteran scout for the Detroit Pistons, an affable man in his late sixties who knows where everybody's skeletons are buried. Handsome in a weathered way, he has a full head of stark-white hair, a dark-pink face, sparkling blue eyes pinched to the root of a long, hooked nose, and teeth so white they might glow in the dark. Kramer is afflicted with rheumatoid arthritis and he stoops like a hunchback. It is rumored that there's a long, thin sword blade hidden within the length of his ever-present black oaken cane.

Also at the table is Joey Sforza, a dark, frowning man who scouts for the Boston Celtics and never voices an opinion about anything, much less player evaluations. This putz thinks that he's the Einstein of the profession and that everybody's out to either steal his information or his job. Plus Mike Fleischer, a clean-headed, fat-faced, part-time regional scout for the LA Clippers and, like Kramer, another amiable guy.

Hello. Hello. Hello.

Yes, they all agree that the available food is awful—meat loaf, lumpy mashed potatoes, and BB-hard green peas.

Say, isn't it terrible about Greg Oden's latest knee surgery? Can anybody dethrone the Lakers? Who will be the first NBA coach fired this year? Would Kwame Brown be getting a hands transplant in the off-season? What about a new heart for LeBron James? Isn't it a shame about the sudden passing of Shameer Elliot, one of the best players ever to wear a St. Paul's uniform?

Yes. So young. Such a tragedy.

As always, it's Kramer who commands our interest with his ready store of rumors, gossip, and wisecracks. He hears that Speedy Claxton is going to be traded for Shawn Bradley, a seven-six white hopeless.

"With apologies to Uncle Remus," says Kramer, "here's how I'd characterized that deal. . . . Zippity for doo-dah." Everybody laughs heartily, except for Sforza, who squeezes out a thin grin that looks like a grimace.

Just then the lights in the room dim for a moment and, on the TV mounted on the wall closest to us, we can see the players from both teams abandoning their warm-ups and clustering around their coaches.

"Time to get to work," says Fleischer. "Good to see you, Rob. Give my regards to Rachael."

"Umm . . . Sure. Will do."

Sforza merely nods before joining the exodus. I'm about to follow suit when Kramer puts a hand on my arm, saying, "Keep me company, Rob. I don't like to fight the crowds. Besides, you can miss a few minutes without missing anything."

"Sure. So how are you feeling, Bill? And when are you going to give it up?"

"Probably after the draft, but that's between you, me, and the lamppost."

"Of course."

The TV closes in on a head shot of St. Paul's coach Jerome O'Shaughnessy, and Kramer clucks his disapproval.

"I don't like him either," I say. "He's as phony as a three-dollar bill."

"You don't know the half of it," Kramer says as he grabs my arm and pulls me closer. "Now hear this. . . . We all know that O'Shaughnessy prides himself on controlling the game and that, in fact, he controls it too much. If one of his players doesn't follow the dotted lines, oops, the poor bastard gets an immediate hook. It's white-man's basketball, Rob, which is why so many of the really talented local black high school guys stay away from Saint P's like it was a leper colony."

This is no news bulletin, but what he says next is.

"So how does he recruit the black players that he does? Because he runs a crooked program. Take the housing. . . . It's no secret that there are no dorms at Saint P's, right? So what does the little fucking leprechaun do? He's got a list of rich Saint P's alums who are big players in real estate. Then he makes arrangements for three of these players to share some top-of-the-line furnished Park Avenue apartment that has three bedrooms, three shitters, a large balcony, the whole nine yards. Let's say the rent is six grand, right? Which the NCAA says is acceptable to house three players. So Saint P's athletic department, all on the up and up, gives the three guys the six grand supposedly to pay the rent. But guess what? There is no rent, and the players split the cash."

"No lie?"

"If I'm lyin', I'm dyin'. But here's more,"

We lean a little closer.

"All of the players have lucrative no-show jobs: at some Wall Street firm that's swarming with Saint P. alums. Or at a real estate office. Or whatever. And check them out after the game. They wear more gold chains and diamond earrings and dress better than most of the millionaires in the NBA. And get this. . . . Guess who sponsors the summer-league team that the Saint P's players play in? . . . You give up? . . . Clarence Manfred, who happens to be the biggest drug dealer in the city."

The game is under way, but I want to hear more. He reads my eagerness and continues. "Here's the kicker. . . . The late Shameer Elliot? He was a heroin junkie."

"What?"

"My sources are always impeccable. Remember how good he was at Saint P's, a first-team All-American, and what a bust he was in Cleveland? That's because one of the Saint P's boosters had a connection with Manfred and kept the kid supplied with all the junk he needed. But there are random drug tests in the NBA, so the kid was screwed. In fact, he didn't die of a heart attack like it was said. He died from an OD."

"Whoa!"

"So stay away from O'Shaughnessy's players 'cause you never know what you'll wind up with."

With a mighty grunt, Kramer uses his powerful arms to push against the table and climb to his feet. "Time to go punch the clock. Hey, don't wait for me. Anyways, so good to see you, Rob. Make sure that prick-with-earflaps who signs your checks doesn't force you to draft a junkie."

One of the press-table protocols is to separate the NBA scouts, presumably so they can't peek at one another's notes. So I'm sitting between a smiley-faced young man who's proud to be wearing a light "Carolina blue" V-neck sweater with "UNC" embroidered in large letters over his heart, and a crusty old man in a wrinkled gray suit whose desk tag simply says "Madison Square Garden." The former is there to chart all of Duke's plays and formations, and he initially flashes me a howdy-grin but ignores me for the duration when he sees my tattered notebook. The latter is more interested in fingering his iPhone and largely ignores the game.

None of the St. Paul's players interest me, and Duke takes control of the game from the get-go. There's O'Shaughnessy in his hideous trademark green-and-white plaid jacket, hopping, skipping, and dancing from one end of the coaches' box to the other—calling out plays, exhorting his players to hustle, and begging the officials for favorable calls. Making his usual public demonstration that he's coaching his ass off.

Meanwhile, every time one of his players misses a shot, mishandles the ball, or "lets" his man score, he glances at his coach as he runs downcourt. During time-outs, O'Shaughnessy yells, gesticulates, and pokes the most grievously offending players in the chest. When the game resumes, he turns to one of his assistants, shrugs, and shows his open palms to heaven. If only they would follow his orders, Duke wouldn't be 20 points ahead.

O'Shaughnessy is a prime reason why, despite the ravings of shills like Dick Vitale, college coaches are vastly overrated. Their boring, carefully scripted offenses seldom generate any shots that aren't available within five seconds after the ball crosses the midcourt line. This is especially true against zones. The big men are so poorly coached that they all have the same low-post moves—power dribbles one way, then jump hooks the other way. In any event, the short 3-point arc mandates bunched zone defenses and severely limits pivotal play.

Whereas the playbook of the average NBA team contains perhaps fifteen offensive sets and well over a hundred plays and options thereof, college teams usually have three or four sets and maybe two-dozen plays. Similarly, pro defenses are much more numerous and complicated.

For the most part, college coaches are really snake-oil salesmen. Their primary jobs are recruiting blue-chip schoolboys and sucking up to athletic directors and influential alumni. Even the worst NBA coach has more expertise than virtually every college coach.

With the notable exception of the visiting coach, Duke's Mike Krzyzewski.

His guys are totally unselfish, set sturdy screens, rarely force either shots or passes, make terrific entry and drive-and-kick passes, and always play hard and smart. While Krzyzewski shows a smiley face to the media, he's a vicious martinet behind closed doors. Which is okay by me.

As for Jateik Murphy, his shot is soft, quick, and on-target—even his misses are slightly long, a much better deal than front- or side-rim misses. He can pull and shoot with accuracy both ways, and he has a nifty step-back move to get his shot off under extreme pressure. His off-ball cuts are precise and decisive; his crossovers are tight both left and right; his passes are crisp and accurate; he can play with finesse or with power; he digs in on defense and makes appropriate rotations; he can find a space to shoot in heavy traffic; he's both fast (up and down the court) and quick (within a small radius); and he has great court awareness.

While on the run in a semibreak situation the kid responds to one of Coach K.'s barking directions by saying, "Yes, sir"?

If Murphy is a bit slow sliding to his left on defense, if he attacks a right-handed jump shooter's release with his cross-body right hand instead of his left hand, if he moves the ball too much in gathering to shoot free throws, all of his flaws are correctable.

Overall, there's no question that Murphy deserves to be a top-three pick next June.

Coach K. does prepare his guys for NBA action, which isn't necessarily the mark of a premier college coach. Among the current crop of pros, Coach K. has tutored exceptional scorers (Luol Deng, Mike Dunleavy, Corey Maggette, Kyrie Irving, Gerald Henderson, and Elton Brand, before the big fellow's wheels fell off). Shane Battier and Dahntay Jones are defensive stoppers. Josh McRoberts is a ruthless banger. JJ Redick is a thinker. Chris Duhon, Shelden Williams, and Nolan Smith are savvy role players. And Grant Hill can do everything.

All these, plus the several NCAA championships he has won, make Krzyzewski the best of his peers. But that doesn't mean he could excel in the NBA.

Those who disagree point to his success in coaching an NBA all-star aggregation to a gold medal in the 2008 Beijing Olympics. Big-time players like Tayshaun Prince, Michael Redd, and Carlos Boozer readily accepted sparse playing time, and everybody was admirably unselfish and on their best behavior.

However, coaching top-flight NBA players for six weeks for the glory of the red-white-and-blue is much easier than directing a team for nine months and dealing with the inevitable discontents over daylight, shots taken, contracts, and so on. His Dukies may respond to his criticisms with "Yes, sir," but hardened NBA vets with long-term guaranteed contracts are liable to react with "Fuck you." Which is why Krzyzewski has wisely turned down highly lucrative offers from several pro franchises.

Indeed, Coach K. is the exception that proves the rule.

In any event, I file my report in the morning, then decide to cancel my flight, keep my rented Buick, and drive the five hours to Syracuse. After all, it's ninety minutes to Kennedy in morning rush-hour traffic, then a cramped flight in a prop-driven sardine can, followed by a half hour's drive to the hotel, and a half day to kill in one of the dullest cities on the circuit. Plus, just in case of a change in plans, I always pack a batch of jazz CDs to keep me company and make the miles zip by. And I do love the chance for some time alone with my own wishful fantasies and neurotic musings.

CHAPTER NINE

Inserting six CDs into the player, I press the Mix button, make sure my bottle of water, my two roast beast sandwiches, and half dozen chocolate-covered doughnuts are within reach—and I'm off. Carefully navigating the impatient traffic on the West Side Highway and crossing the George Washington Bridge. There's still a hard shelf of ice clinging to the Jersey shore and, in the steel-colored river, each uncrested wave glints razor-sharp even as the feeble winter sunshine bronzes the long, swooping cables overhead.

Erroll Garner grunts, bounces, and bops his way through "I'll Remember April." I mean, the guy was a genius! He couldn't read music, and often stated the beat with his left hand like a rhythm guitar while his right played chords slightly behind the beat. The sheer joy of his playing always makes me feel good.

And why not? I've got a well-paying job without having to punch a clock. My immediate superior is my best buddy. My work demands every shred of expertise I can summon, plus it's at least theoretically important.

Right?

But here's Joe Williams singing "A Man Ain't Supposed to Cry" in his deep, vibrant voice.

How will I react if (or when?) Weiss completely disregards my reports? Then trades our best players so we can draft DeLeon Johnson—who's already trademarked "DLJ" as a brand name.

Maybe I should take John Ballard as my model. Just file my reports and not care what becomes of them. Don't make waves, and smile when I cash my checks.

Trouble is, I do care!

On the Palisades Parkway—where its fifty-mile-per-hour speed limit is universally ignored—headed for the New York Thruway.

Ella Fitzgerald sings "Falling in love with love is falling for make-believe."

That's me! That explains my attraction to Rachael—although I still can't figure out why she wanted me. To be perfectly honest with myself—which is a difficult task, since I'm such a glib bullshitter—I never really loved her. Convenient sex, meal preparation, house cleaning and tidying . . . that's all I really required of her. Jack/Jacques/Rob/Robert.

But have I ever truly loved anybody? That is the question of the moment.

Although I did empathize with my father's illness, his arbitrary wielding of his belt on my young, innocent flesh also made it easy to hate him. How many times did I pray to a god I didn't believe in for him to die? Quickly, painlessly, and neatly—with no blood on the floor for my mother to clean up. This prayer was always succeeded by a pall of guilt, which lasted until the next time he beat me.

My mother? I pitied her more than loved her.

Does the several beats my foolish heart skips whenever I see a beautiful woman count?

Was I, am I, then, incapable of love? Maybe so. As Bob said to Ray, "More the fool, me."

Even so, and despite myself, I desperately want to love, to be loved. Perhaps that's it. . . . I can't love until somebody (besides my mother) loves me. You first. Then me.

As I switch into cruise control on the Thruway, next up on my hit parade is (ha!) "When I Fall in Love" by the Miles Davis Quintet.

Back in 1956, Davis was eager to escape the contractual clutches of the Fantasy label, but he owed them four more albums. So he brought the young John Coltrane (tenor sax), plus veterans Red Garland (piano), Paul Chambers (bass), and Philly Joe Jones (drums) into Rudy Van Gelder's studio in Hackensack, New Jersey. With absolutely no rehearsals and no additional takes, they laid down four sensational albums—*Steamin'*, *Workin'*, *Relaxin'*, and *Cookin'*. For me, these represent the best music that Davis ever recorded.

Coltrane was, however, somewhat of a problem, simply because he habitually indulged in long, thirty-minutes-plus solos. Before the recording sessions began, Davis warned him to have more discipline. But how could Coltrane adjust his soulful, inspired playing to the dictates of the clock?

Davis's answer was simple: "Take the fucking horn out of your mouth."

Taking the toll ticket at Harriman, setting my cruise control at precisely seventy-two miles per hour—an allowable seven over the posted limit—and here's more Miles from the same Van Gelder sessions: "It Never Entered My Mind."

But what do I really know about love? What the fuck do I know about anything?

Miles blowing through his mute. 'Trane conjuring up mystical sounds. Garland's distinctive block chords. Chambers with his crying, melodic bowing. The soothing fire of Jones.

Ah! That's it!

Five guys playing together in perfect harmony with two main and one secondary soloist, and two players laying out the foundation that frees their teammates.

Like the perfect basketball team. A pair of go-to scorers to exercise their one-on-one skills. The point guard as piano man, supplying ideas and lead-ins for the franchise players, and taking an occasional lead to maintain balance and keep the defense honest. The bass man rebounding and playing fundamental defense, while the unsung power drummer adjusts his chops to whatever is necessary at any given moment.

Yes! I love basketball!

The quest for perfection!

Starting with the perfect play: any programmed backdoor cut or back screen leading to a nifty pass, and easy score. Like several specific options in Phil Jackson's evolution of Tex Winter's triangle offense.

The perfect shot: Like MJ's pull-and-fade jumper over Craig Ehlo to close out Cleveland in Game 4, thereby sweeping the series in the 1993 Eastern Conference Semifinals. Or crippled Willis Reed's jumper at the beginning of the seventh game of the championship series in 1970 that took the heart out of Wilt Chamberlain and the LA Lakers.

Or Rick Mount's normal jumpers. He was an All-American out of

Purdue who could do nothing but shoot during his brief and unsuccessful NBA career. However, I once saw a video showing Mount unleashing dozens of long jumpers from various spots. The kicker was that he used only one ball, had no rebounder feeding it back to him, and instead adjusted every shot from every spot so that the ball hit the far rim just so and bounced right back into his hands.

The perfect game: Villanova's nearly flawless performance (making 78.6 percent of their field-goal attempts, including 90 percent in the second half) in upsetting the heavily favored Georgetown Hoyas to win the NCAA title in 1985.

The perfect player: His Airness, who could do everything. And also Bill Russell, who could run, rebound, and turn the blocked shot into an art form. Although his overall skills were somewhat limited, Russell changed the game more than any other player in hoops history.

The perfect team: the 1995–96 Chicago Bulls, who won seventy-two games and went 15–3 en route to the championship.

More Errol Garner. After playing "Erroll's Theme" to end a live gig, as recorded in *Concert By The Sea,* he's called to the mic to let the audience hear the sound of his voice. In a hoarse and raspy grunt, Garner said this: "It's worser than Louie Armstrong."

Since my own voice is firm and clear, why shouldn't I chase a career in the over-the-airwaves media? I'd be a terrific in-game analyst, but not for telecasts, because I have a radio-face, that is, crooked yellow teeth, beady blue eyes, and a large, oft-broken nose.

As Miles plays, the miles fly by. Saugerties, perhaps named after an obscure Greek philosopher? Coxsackie, with the maximum-security prison visible to the east and which my players referred to as "Cocksuckie." Albany, a paper city inhabited mostly by lawmakers and lawyers. Rome, where at least half of the certified lunatics in town surely believe themselves to be the pope.

Munching my goodies in time to Thelonius Monk, aka Melodious Plunk.

Stopping to take a whiz in the Herkimer-Mohawk Travel Plaza, saddened at the fatties lined up to buy Shit-Burgers at Mickey D's. Also marveling at how, with the exception of the most dire emergencies, anybody would be willing to perch on the public toilet bowls.

Satchmo singing "Tenderly," with his lovable malapropisms: "The evening breeze *erase* the trees tenderly."

As far as I know, I'm still a long way from the evening of my life, but as I ponder my forthcoming thirty-sixth birthday, I can't help continuing to obsess about my short- and long-term future.

Perhaps DLJ will wind up in jail or in a coffin, and Weiss will follow my advice and draft Jateik Murphy or Kevin Love.

Perhaps Weiss will suffer a fatal heart attack and his dad will name Earl to succeed him.

Perhaps some distant and unknown relative will die and leave me millions.

Perhaps that monstrous machine that I'm passing and that's carrying a dozen new cars will blow a tire, or the driver will blow a gasket, and I'll be killed before I get to Syracuse.

Since my father died so young, death is also always nigh.

Anita O'Day singing "The Sunny Side of the Street."
Seriously. What do I really enjoy doing?
Watching a competitive ball game no matter how low the teams might be in the standings. Reading. Listening to jazz. Eating fast food. Dreaming of feminine body parts, then bursting with joy into a Kleenex via my own merry fist. Having absolutely nothing to do with the media.

Of course, I could do all of these in my cozy cabin, but I'd soon get bored.

Perhaps I could wade into the swamps of academe, get an MA and a PhD, then teach at some college in a sweet rural setting. If I lived even more frugally than I do now, I could easily stash enough cash to make this come to pass.

But, no. All teachers must necessarily be actors and professional geniuses.

Herkimer. Utica. Then finally Syracuse, where the toll is $11.60, and there's still no cures for my brain farts and fevers.

CHAPTER TEN

The campus sprawls over two hundred acres and is host to twenty thousand students and about fifteen hundred faculty. Somewhat smaller in area than my new home, the village of Woodstock, but containing more than three times as many denizens. Every building here is unique—ranging from huge Romanesque structures topped by gabled towers to gleaming steel-and-glass edifices.

There's freshly fallen snow at least twelve inches deep on the lawn spaces, but all the pathways have been meticulously cleared. And a knife-edge wind cuts around every corner and swirls the snow into sparkling white dust. The occasional tree is a white-boned skeleton. A line of shrubs fronting the library is stunted and leans away from the keening wind. Several outdoor sculptures look like large white teeth.

Here come two coeds bundled in fur coats, their faces swathed in gaily colored mufflers as they desperately clutch each other's hands to keep from falling. Laughing lightly, they exude an air of entitlement, and well they might, since someone's shelling out nearly twenty-seven grand for this semester's tuition, room, board, fees, and books. Or else they'll be saddled with enough debt to last them a couple of lifetimes. Imagine . . . over two hundred thousand dollars for an undergraduate degree. During my tenure at Hunter College I admittedly lived at home, but, stili, the sum total of my tuition and books for five years was about two thousand.

For some reason—carelessness? impatience?—I frequently misalign the buttons and the buttonholes on my navy-blue peacoat, so there's a flap instead of a tight seal at my neck. In passing, the girls glance at my lopsided coat and my ragged watch cap with palpable disdain.

Here's a freshman fledgling, books in one hand, his other hand holding an orange-colored beanie to his head as the wind spins the tiny cap-top propeller and threatens to send the poor schnook flying up into the sky. What other tortures will he have to endure to become part of the snotty in-crowd? Wearing a dead fish around his neck? Having to eat a can of worms or a loaf of shit? Carrying a paddle to facilitate getting his ass whacked by any passing frat bro? What fucking nonsense.

There's a muscular dude wearing cutoff jeans and a varsity letter jacket. Young blood runs hot. He's too buffed to be a hooper. Probably a football player or a wrestler.

Whereas the average Syracuse student is not exactly renowned for his or her brain power, the school is indeed celebrated for the excellence of its athletes. Most notably Jim Brown and the tragic Ernie Davis in football. Dave Bing and Carmelo Anthony in the NBA. Overall, the school has won several national championships in such diversified team sports as men's crew, football, and basketball. Not to forget Jim Nance, who won a pair of individual NCAA championships as a heavyweight wrestler before becoming an all-star fullback for the New England Patriots. In addition, the Orange have always fielded powerhouse lacrosse teams, winning fourteen NCAA titles. And guess who is universally celebrated as the best lacrosse player in the sport's history? . . . Jim Brown.

Just out of curiosity I ask a passing student where the English Department is situated, and I'm directed to a high-columned Doric building just ahead. Swept inside by the wind, and in the company of a small group of harried students, I search for and locate a list of English faculty members. And lo, I quickly find the teacher whom I suppose I was looking for. Dr. Tillman Breedlawn, noted medieval scholar and author of *The Hidden Chaucer—The Religious Subtext of "The Canterbury Tales."* Published, of course, by the Syracuse University Press. The very same dense but erudite tome that served as the main source for my Master's essay—"Christian Allegory in 'The Canon's Yeoman's Prologue and Tale.'"

His office is nearby, and the schedule posted on the closed-door reveals that his class in Renaissance poetry has already commenced in Lecture Hall 5, which is also just a few doors away. Ah, am I still an academic at heart? Dr. Robert Elliot Lassner, I presume?

Inside the room, several curving rows of seats form a semicircle that faces a modest blond mahogany desk and a portable black-board on a slightly raised platform. There's a door behind the desk where—I imagine—young lovelies audition for As and Bs.

Perhaps fifty students are seated—about half of the room's capacity—scribbling furiously into the same kinds of notebooks that I use. Even though I crouch and slink into a seat in the last row, Breedlawn notes my late arrival with a quick glance of his lively gray eyes as well as affecting a slight but dramatic pause in his discourse. His knife-thin nose and fleshless lips give a first impression of an imperial perfectionism, suggesting that, despite the imagined talents of the imagined be-couched coeds, he rarely dispenses any higher grade than a C.

He wears a brown corduroy jacket with black leather elbow patches. His bow tie is brown, his white shirt collar is starched, and so is his neck. The professor sits behind his desk, tapping his right hand on a teetering, chit-marked stack of books. A sheaf of Breedlawn's thin brown hair has fallen from grace, and his bony right hand strokes it back into place. And the great man speaks: "As I was saying before I was so rudely interrupted . . ." And there's the hint of a playfulness in his voice that betrays his stern appearance. Indeed, as he lectures, a tight smile widens his face as though he has a ribald joke in mind that he'd love to relate under less professional circumstances.

"The significant tool here is allegoresis . . . which is a nifty way of saying that something really means something other than it appears to mean. 'Allegoresis.' The very word has a persuasive ring to it. Like 'Marlovian.'

"Even though he wasn't Jewish," he goes on, lifting his eyebrows to indicate his gentle sarcasm, "Faustus of course was a lawyer. But he says that the law 'is a mercenary drudge,' concerned only with 'paltry legacies.' Marlowe takes pains to bag philosophy as well, 'To dispute well is logic's chiefest end.' Big deal, says Faustus. But the Bible, Jerome's Bible, is 'hard,' says Faustus. 'The reward of sin is death.' Yet Faustus resists, and chastens God's omnipotence by not permitting Jesus to save him. And finally, Faustus turns the world 'upsodoun' and sodomizes the devil. . . . But as to Marlowe's poem,

'Hero and Leander,' the subject of today's assignment . . ."

Breedlawn selects a book from the pile on his desk, and opens to a chit-marked page.

"The pivotal figure, of course, is Hero herself. Marlowe gives it away when he refers to her as 'Venus' nun,' Elizabethan slang for a whore. Along the same lines, Marlowe also likens her to a mermaid, also considered to be a licentious creature. Sometimes Marlowe gets carried away and writes pure burlesque . . .

She, overcome with shame and sallow fear,

Dot . . . dot . . . dot . . .

Being suddenly betrayed, dived down to hide her,
And, as her silver body downward went,
With both her hands she made the bed a tent.

Dot . . . dot . . dot . . . dash . . .

Yet ever, as he greedily assayed
To touch those dainties, she the harpy played.
And every limb did, as a soldier stout,
Defend the fort, and keep the foeman out.

"Hot stuff, ain't it? The moral being for you damsels out there to protect your dainties. . . . That's all for today. Next time we'll do the form and content of Shakespeare's sonnets."

He sits silently, staring at them, daring any of us to stir. Then he arises and, without further explanation, writes the names of several books on the blackboard, which the students diligently copy. Then he walks briskly out the rear exit and slams the door behind him.

Everybody else hurriedly gathers their books and departs. Alone in the silent room, I stand up, applaud, and shout, "Bravo! Bravo!"

Right here and right now I want to be Tillman Breedlawn when I grow up.

After taking a brief nap in an uninhabited corner of the library and then inserting four quarters into a vending machine for a lukewarm paper cup of bitter coffee that I sip once and toss into the nearest trash can, I'm ready to go to work.

I still can't get used to the sheer din that accompanies college games, but I love the time-outs, when I can scout the cheerleaders. However, the opportunity to horn in on a full-breasted honey is rare, only because bouncy boobs are automatic disqualifications.

Anyway, there's a leansome six-nine freshman on Georgetown who might develop into a useful player. If, that is, he spends some time in the weight room and also develops a semidependable jumper. As of now, though, he's certainly not draftable. Otherwise, the Hoyas' point guard is super quick and can shoot the lights out, but overpenetrates, gets caught off the floor among the trees, and then makes dumb passes. He's a junior and a certified second-team All-American. Rumor has it that he beat up his girlfriend a few weeks ago, but that the athletic department bribed the victim and goosed the cops, so the kid skated.

When Jerry Krause was the general manager of the Jordan-Pippen-Jackson dynasty in Chicago, he stated unequivocally that—all other considerations being somewhat equal—the Bulls always drafted for character. I tend to agree. Yet Krause also said that he could tell how good a player really was by looking at his nose and the shape of his face. Whatever the fuck that means.

Anyway, Georgetown's hotshot triggerman may be worth a gamble in the dregs of the second round. Or at least, an invite to the Nets' summer-league team.

Syracuse has three guys who should, and will, be drafted. One of them is a power forward with good vision, quick hops, and a deliciously belligerent attitude at both ends of the court. Too bad he can't shoot himself in the foot—but if Mike Riordan could learn how to bury jumpers, anybody can.

The Hoyas' point guard is a stumpy little fellow, but he can sky, shoot, pass with both hands on the run, and get underneath bigger players and snipe at their dribblings. At best he'd be a twelfth man who'd only play in dire emergencies. Also undraftable.

The first few minutes of the game demonstrate the superior talent of the home team. The only offense they need is a few screen/rolls to complement some drives-and-dishes, and every semiorganized set winds up with somebody going one-on-one. On defense, coach Jim Boeheim's traditional 2-3 zone that shifts into a 2-1-2 formation depending on the quickness of its practitioners.

Georgetown isn't especially well coached, so its zone offense consists mostly of perimeter passwork and jacking up treys. The way to overcome Syracuse's zones is to dump the ball into the low post, then have the weak-side wing make a dive cut. Another successful ploy would be to have a power forward roam the baseline to get behind the overeager defenders.

It constantly amazes me how many Division I coaches get stymied by zones. But, after all, most of these guys can stay employed by recruiting ostensible blue-chippers, and bullshitting the media, athletic directors, and alumni.

Anyway, the game is a wall-to-wall blowout.

Ah, here's a successful steal by the Georgetown point guard, leading to a breakaway dunk that's preceded by an under-the-asshole pass from his left hand to his right hand. Then the dunker flexes his right bicep and pounds the left side of his chest as the crowd howls with delight.

But, hold on, there's more to come: An Orangeman hits a 3-ball, then cocks his right hand to simulate a gun and blows invisible smoke from the tip of his extended index finger. Another dunk is followed by the player pulling the top of his jersey away from his chest with both thumbs. Here's another guy at the foul line, bouncing the ball three times as the fans loudly count along, spinning the ball on one finger, flipping it up in the air, then catching it and releasing his shot. For the game he's 7-for-11 from the stripe, and the game notes have him at 72 percent for the season.

Grrrr! With the kid's super-smooth jump shots, he should be at least an 85-percent shooter from the foul line. But with all the spinning and flipping, he never winds up with the same grip prior to his release. That means he has to make slight adjustments every time he shoots.

Bah!

Both the white and the black players indulge in similar celebratory nonsense.

And what's with all the slapping-dapping-hand-jive after free throws? Congratulations for making a one-on-none fifteen-footer. Congratulations for missing. All in the name of "family."

And here's another jackass waving to the crowd and cupping his ears to encourage them to raise the decibel level beyond the deafening point.

But, hey, NBA players are guilty of the same look-at-me bullshit.

Back when I was playing, anybody who went through any of these shenanigans would be knocked on his ass at the first opportunity. But too many of today's hoopers and hooplings are as obsessed with being celebrities as they are with playing basketball at such elevated levels of competition.

Syracuse wins by 23 points, and as ever, the winning coach pats the losing coach on the back and says, "Good job, Coach." The acceptable response is "Thanks, Coach. You, too."

What does the losing coach really want to say?

"Fuck you, asshole. If I had the same slush fund that you have and the same bottomless admission standards, I'd run you off the fucking court."

I scribble my report, then hightail it back to the hotel. I have an early-morning flight to Chicago, then a ninety-minute drive to Rockford to witness the CBL's all-star game.

A chance to visit with familiar compatriots and players, and to eyeball a *serious* ball game.

CHAPTER ELEVEN

During my tenure with Peoria, the CBL's game of musical franchises temporarily featured teams in such far-flung places as Portland, Maine; Sarasota, Florida; Albuquerque, New Mexico; and Yakima, Washington—as well as dozens of cities scattered between these extremes. Accordingly, over the course of any given season I spent innumerable hours and at least fifty thousand miles on planes. Aside from safely transporting me (and my players of the moment) from game to game, these journeys offered little that was enjoyable, or even pleasant.

One reason was that we were always booked into the earliest flights, simply because they were the cheapest. So, after finishing a game at, say, nine thirty, leaving the arena an hour later, then either gobbling a quick meal at some stomach-burger joint or returning to the hotel and ordering pizza and beer, we wouldn't get to bed until about one a.m. The wake-up calls, a mere four hours later, shocked everybody.

After single-handedly checking in everybody's baggage and seeing to the boarding passes, I'd try to get aisle seats for all of us—or at least any seat in an exit row. Unfortunately, the seats with the most leg room were at the bulkhead and were routinely given to little old ladies, two of whom could have fit into each seat, and whose feet seldom reached the floor. I certainly don't begrudge them the comfort of easing their arthritic joints and the security of being so close to the first-class cabin's rest rooms. For myself, I'd seek a seat far enough back in the cabin so that I could reconnoiter the doings of the players. Discouraging them from ordering booze en route no matter what the hour (a frequent occurrence), or sticking a hand up a stewardesss's skirt (more often than I could have previously imagined).

Wherever we were positioned, the coach seats were much too cramped for power forwards, centers, and me to rest comfortably, so us bigs had to be totally exhausted if we wanted to snooze once we were aloft. Of course, there were always some party fools who had been awake throughout the night and slept soundly even when we hit an air pocket and the plane suddenly dropped a few hundred feet. As for me, I could usually nod off with my chin resting on my chest in the hanged-man's position.

Another situation that made sleep difficult was the inclination of whoever was sitting in front of us (me) to fully recline his seat back, thereby painfully jamming our knees. My personal remedy was to force my knees into the back of the seat while the plane was still taxiing on the runway, hoping to make my erstwhile tormenter think that his seat back was broken. Occasionally, though, some jackass would try to force the issue, and I'd say, with as much sweetness as I could muster, "Excuse me, but I'm six-eight and there's not enough room for me back here if you recline your seat." Usually that would do the trick, but sometimes the jerk would persist, and we'd have an argument. Frequently when, or if, I did achieve some snooze time and my knees relaxed, he would suddenly force his seat back and awaken me with a start. My only remedy then was to bang my hand against the rear of his headrest every few seconds until he retreated. In any event, sleeping on a flight was only a means of passing time and never resulted in even the slightest degree of refreshment.

One might think that fifty thousand miles per annum would at least rack up beaucoup Frequent Flyer mileage. They certainly did, but not for us. That's because it was legal before and until shortly after 9/11 for all of the plane tickets for both players and coaches to be purchased in the names of various employees in the CBL's administration, from the commissioner to the lowliest secretary.

Anyway, the Nets always fly me first-class, even on puddle jumpers from Syracuse to Chicago. Ah, room to stretch, edible food, and cushy seats. Yes, there is life after the CBL.

Despite a heavy rain, my big-ass Buick-of-the-moment makes for an easy ninety-minute drive to Rockford. Just as I exit the highway, my cell phone breaks into a chorus of Cheech and Chong's "Basketball Jones," and a push of a button reveals that Earl is on the line.

"Rob, this is Condition Red!"

Jeez! Here comes another of Earl's imaginary hysterias. "Let's hear it."

"It's Weiss. He's going ape-shit. He wants to make sure you'll wear a tie and jacket to the game. He says if you dress the way you normally do, you'll embarrass the franchise and the NBA as well. He says you're a slob."

"What the fuck? You know that I travel light. I never pack a jacket and a tie. I do have a sort-of okay shirt, but the only pants I brought are jeans."

"Shoes?"

"Sneakers. But they're clean."

"Oh, shit. Do something, Rob. Go out and buy some presentable stuff."

"Will do. There's bound to be a place at one of the malls that has size-sixteen dress shoes, triple-X jackets, and extra-long pants that can fit me off the rack, right? Maybe in Chicago, but not in Rockford."

"Then drive back to Chicago."

"Earl. Be serious."

"I am serious. What with the way you faced him up the other day, your job could be at stake."

"My job at stake for a pair of shoes and a pair of pants?"

"Rob."

"Earl."

"I'm the one who hired you, so when you fuck up, it always comes back to me."

"All right. I'll see what I can do."

For a moment I'm absolutely determined to return to Chicago, locate a tall men's shop, and buy what Weiss would consider to be an appropriate costume. But the rainfall shows no sign of diminishing—and here I am, already within the Rockford city limits.

Rockford is tightly wedged into the very buckle of the rust belt and was once rated the worst city in the country by *Money* magazine. The Windy City's poor (and resentful) cousin features the emptiest libraries in the Western Hemisphere, only two decent restaurants, a highly advanced mall culture, and scores of rabid basketball fans.

Since the CBL's all-star game is to be telecast on ESPN, the league's bigwigs have determined to put on a show that will impress everybody concerned. Past and present, several NBA head coaches have served their respective apprenticeships in the CBL—Phil Jackson, George Karl, Flip Saunders, Bill and Eric Musselman (aka "the musselpeople"), Herb Brown, John Lucas, Dave Cowens, and Tom Nissalke—plus literally dozens of assistant coaches. The call went out to have as many of these and other CBL-to-NBA success stories as possible to parade before the cameras as part of the half-time festivities. That's why I'm here, but I have no idea what other CBL graduates will show.

Once I get settled in my semiluxurious room at the Clock Tower, Rockford's most prestigious hotel, I consult the local Yellow Pages. Upon not finding a single clothing store that caters to normal-sized guys like me, further investigation reveals that a Salvation Army Thrift Store is only a five-minute drive from here.

I love these musty, dusty warehouses of not-so-good goods frequented by middle-class folks (like me) slumming and seeking bargains as well as poor people desperately looking for necessities on the cheap. Sadly, so many of the down-and-nearly-out customers are either obese or pitiably thin. Sallow-complexioned women with their hair in curlers, sporting missing teeth, and dosed with nauseatingly sweet perfumes. Yowling infants and tattooed adolescents. Carefully inspecting the worn furniture and wondering if the detached hinges, the splintered edges, and/or the dark red stains could possibly be healed. Black-and-white TVs that look long dead. Bookcases filled with shabby copies of *Reader's Digest* Condensed pap at ten cents a copy. Records and CDs by the likes of Pat Boone, Doris Day, the Four Seasons, and Julie Andrews. Schlock jewelry. And aisles and aisles of clothing.

All for the glory of Christ and Christian charity. Hallelujah!

I bought a somewhat stained cushioned rocking chair for my Woodstock den at the thrift store in Kingston. (I put a towel over the seat cushion.) After all, it's well-known that the Salvation Army did more for the GIs in World War Two than did the Red Cross. So at Christmastime I always drop at least a fiver in the omnipresent SA kettles.

After a diligent search of the secondhand apparel, I find exactly what I need: a blue blazer with gold buttons with a large patch above the heart -pocket saying "St. Mark's Varsity Wrestling." It's a mite too short in the sleeves and too large in the chest and shoulders but still A-OK. At $1.50 how could I go wrong?

Also a pair of beige khaki chino pants secured at the waist with a frayed drawstring. So what if the cuffs are ragged, it only costs two bits. Then, to draw my outfit together, for a mere dime I purchased a slightly ketchup-or-bloodstained fish necktie in shades of gray and white with the tail near the topknot spreading to the head at the bottom. The same design made popular by Don Nelson when he coached the Golden State Warriors. (How interesting that Nelson's son is named Donn. Perhaps any subsequent grandsons will be named Donnn.)

In lieu of shoes, I'll simply paint my white sneakers with black shoe polish.

Voilà!

After a nap, some delving into another novel by Paul Horgan (*The Last Trumpet*), munching a too-dry cheese-and-mushroom omelet in the dining room, and taking a shower, I'm ready to face the camera's bright red eye as well as the bloodshot scrutiny of my boss.

The gala affair takes place in a cordoned-off and ribbon-bestrewed concourse room at the Rockford Airport. A stumpy old man in an all-purpose gray uniform eyes me with belligerent suspicion as I approach the only gateway.

"You some kind of basketball player?" he asks with a dubious squinting of his watery green eyes.

"No. I'm actually an elephant jockey."

"Say what?"

"Never mind. Don't you have a list?"

"Nope."

"Okay. Let me ask you this . . . Why would I want to get in there if I didn't have to?"

"Says you."

"Says me. Says the commissioner. See him over by the podium? The fat little guy stuffed into the gray suit? Go ask him."

"And leave my post?"

"Trust me, pops. I work for the New Jersey Nets."

"Who're they?"

"Just unhook the rope and let me in, okay?"

As he does so, he says, "I'm still gonna keep an eye on you."

Balloons adhere to the high ceiling, and a large banner stretches above a podium in the rear of the gray-aired, soulless space. There are perhaps two dozen round tables clustered together, each draped with a worn off-white linen covering and loaded with the requisite dishes, silverware, napkins, glasses, floral centerpiece, basket of puffy rolls, and gold-foil-wrapped pats of butter. Every place setting also comes with a small plastic gift basket that's overflowing with colorful strips of tissue paper and crepe-paper curlicues. Several gray institutional folding chairs ring each table. The overall impression is of a tawdry junior high school prom with no discernible theme.

Several of the chairs are already occupied, yet several men in smart business suits stand in small groups cheerfully chattering as they delicately sip their drinks. There's a brightly lit alcove off to the left where camera crews of the three local network affiliates take turns interviewing various attendant luminaries. An attractive young woman, wearing a busty blue sweater and a short black-leather skirt, buzzes around the room recruiting blue-chip interviewees. Here comes a sweaty sportswriter for the *Rockford Register* whom I vaguely recognize in his creased brown suit and black shoes. But he dismisses my presence after a furtive glance. Above the hubbub a scratchy mechanical voice announces the last boarding call for Continental Airlines Flight 128 to Des Moines at Gate 12, and the arrival at Gate 8 of Southwest Airlines Flight 17 from Columbus.

I wander over to the cash bar and order a ginger ale that costs four times as much as my pants, when I'm approached by a familiar face. Beefy, big-nosed, thin-lipped, with ultra-white tombstone-shaped little teeth that would surely glow in the dark. He's Dr. Jim Schwartz, a proctologist who has owned several unsuccessful CBL franchises, his current one being in Binghamton, New York, -and who's infamous for not having paid his league dues in recent memory.

"Congratulations on your new job," he says as he squeezes my hand in an almost painful grip. Then, without skipping a beat, he tells a joke: "Did you hear about the proctologist who used two fingers? . . . He wanted to get a second opinion."

Ha-ha and ugh. Are there brown stains in his cuticles?

"But seriously, Coach. It's good for all of us in the Crazy Basketball League to have one of our own make it into the NBA."

"Umm. Thanks."

"By the way, if things don't work out for you in New Jersey . . . I mean, it's no secret that Weiss is hard to deal with . . . you could coach for me anytime."

"And in any place?"

He chokes out a dry laugh and says, "We're solid in Binghamton. We have plenty of corporate sponsors, an enthusiastic fan base, and a nice situation for the players. Really."

Even though Schwartz has operated red-ink franchises in Easton, Pennsylvania; Columbus, Ohio; Albany, Georgia; Hartford, Connecticut; and Wichita Falls, Texas, I say, "I'm sure."

"Anyway", he says vaguely even as he spots some minor CBL functionary he'd rather speak to. As he turns away, he says this over his shoulder, "I'll check out the daily sports transaction, and when your name turns up, you won't have to call me because I'll be calling you."

"I can hardly wait."

I exchange tentative waves of mere recognition with the three or four current CBL coaches I recognize, but as far as I can determine, I'm the only NBA hireling on hand. The owner of the Peoria Stars smiles brightly in my direction and is on the verge of approaching me, when he changes his mind, does an about-face, and dialogues with someone I don't know. The blue-sweatered brunette comes over to say, "You're Rob Lassner, right? Who used to coach Peoria and is now with the Nets?"

"Guilty."

Extending her hand, she says, "I'm Bonnie Macklin, the Rockford Lightning's director of media relations."

How old could she be? Midtwenties? Indeed, her green-flecked blue eyes sparkle with youthful hope and vigor. But her plump smile is older, more enigmatic. At first glance it communicates a stern, demanding nature, an unmistakable sense that she's all business. Yet there's the slightest quivering at the right corner of her mouth that betrays what? Secret vulnerability? Subdued passion? I'm flooded with a strong urge to connect with her in some way. To discover her.

"Just a heads up, Mister Lassner. Before the game tomorrow night ESPN wants to do a short interview with you."

"Sorry, but I don't do TV interviews."

"Why not?"

"It's a long story. . . . My boss wouldn't appreciate . . . Ah, never mind. Let's just say that I have a radio face."

She frowns, saying, "Nonsense. You're a good-looking guy."

"Either you need glasses, or I need a better mirror."

Her trilling laugh lights her face, and I realize how beautiful she is.

"Think about it," she says.

"Okay. I'll also think about you."

Now she gives me a more serious look. "And vice versa," she says as she turns to chase down another celebrity.

The commissioner—Gerald Lee (née Levine)—who used to be the longtime public relations tout for the World Wrestling Federation, is waddling toward the podium. The perfect opportunity for me to make a pit stop.

An otherwise empty bathroom means that there's no pressure on me to wash my hands when I'm done pissing. Really now. . . . Mandrake is hermetically sealed inside my whitey-tighties, while it's my hands that are out in the bacteria-laden world. The truly logical thing would be for men to wash their hands before unzipping and then wash their penises afterward.

"Announcing the arrival of American Airlines Flight Seventeen from Akron at... SQWAUCK! BUZZZT! "... for taking your seats so we can begin the festivities..." BUZZZT! "... to Cedar Rapids at Gate Nine."

Upon returning to the scene of the promised "festivities," I see that virtually every chair is already occupied. But there's someone beckoning to me from the far side of the room, then pointing to a pair of vacant chairs next to him. I can't make out who he is but, even as the Commissioner blathers on about the wonderful world of the CBL, I wend my way toward my welcomer.

Too late I recognize the guy as George Morrison, a CBL referee who must have tossed me out of at least a dozen ball games. Indeed, the last game I ever worked under his jurisprudence he double-T'd me for merely calling him "a cocksucker."

Oh, well.

He's lean and mean, a proud gym rat with a shiny red face, light-gray eyes, a *goyish* button nose, and a grim smile. My other table-mates ignore us as they busily whisper sour nothings to one another.

"Sit down," Morrison urges. "Rest your bones."

As we shake hands—his are wet and appropriately slimy—he says that he's here to ref tomorrow night's all-star game. He's saving one of the empty seats for his partner in crime, who may not arrive on the scene until the morning.

A native of Georgia, Morrison speaks with a slightly lilting twang. It's ignorant of me, I know, but I seem to persist in feeling that nobody who speaks thusly can, by definition, have anything more than a modicum of intelligence.

"Tomorrow's game is an owdition for the players and for me, too," he drawls. "Anyway, it's so good to see y'all, and congrats on your new gig."

"Thanks."

Then his eyes blink rapidly as he says, "By the way, I've got me a kinfession to make."

Uh-oh! I wouldn't be surprised if he was a serial killer. Or a Satanist. A pedophile. A heroin junkie. Or a (gasp!) Republican.

"Just wanted to let y'all know that I shore did appreciate your constant complaints when I worked y'all's games. It forced me to bear down and kincentrate even more than I usually do. It's true. Y'all made me a better official."

Hmmm. I certainly saw no evidence that my grousing did anything but make him more antagonistic and more likely to turn every questionable call against me.

"That's really interesting."

At the podium, a nameless spokesman for NBA commissioner David Stern is reading a prepared message from his boss: *"If success is a barometer of toil and hard work, then the groundwork and foundation of success for many individuals past and present in the NBA is established in professional basketball's premier training ground, the Commercial Basketball League. The NBA is delighted to continue its long relationship with . . .*

"You know, Coach, that officiatin' is a whole lot harder than most people think. I mean, look it . . . the players are so big, so quick, and so creative, and everythin' happens so fast that we got to have lightnin' reflexes jest to keep up. If we want to take a real hard look at a play, why, then, it's already too late 'cause somethin' else is already happenin'. So sometimes we've got to kind of half anticipate what's gonna happen. But then these guys do some totally unexpected dipsy-doo, and we're left blowin' a phony whistle."

"So, is that when you do a make-up call?"

"Not me, Coach, 'cause that would be makin' two bad calls in a row. That's like if a student screws up a math test, then in his next class deliberately screws up a history test. Y'know? Makes no sense. But the thang of it is that NBA officials make the right call over ninety percent of the time. That's a pretty good deal if y'all's askin' me."

". . . produced a number of key players, coaches, executives, and officials who have made a major impact on professional . . ."

"Okay, I'm impressed with that. But what about the calls that aren't made? Most of the time those are the most important."

"We can't call what we can't see, and not even three of us can see everythin'. Especially with alla those big bodies in the way."

". . . development . . . partnership . . . excitement . . ."

"All right, but here's something that's always bothered me. It's that refs are not aware of the beauty of the game."

"It's true. When a ref is workin', he has no time to admire the beauty of what's goin' on out there. This here reel-izashun is a mighty problem for ex-players who try to become officials. Like Ernie DiGregorio, remember him? He'd get so caught up in the action that he'd forget to blow his dang whistle. The right time to enjoy a game is when an official is reviewin' the video. But that there's a luxury that workin' officials don't have."

"... more accessible to local fans ... excitement created by the innovative quarter-point system ... one point for winning a quarter, three for winning the whole ..."

"Okay, let me ask you this.... How and why did you become a referee? Why does anybody become a referee?"

He smiles, and no matter what he'll say, I already believe him.

"When I was in high school in Savannah, I played baseball, football, and basketball. Even though I liked basketball the very best, I wadn't any hot shit as a player, maybe the third man off the bench for the varsity. I mean I youster get splinters in my ass. My basketball coach youster earn extra money by officiatin' in local high school and small college games. He tole me that since I was a gym rat and obviously had no future as a college player, I might be interested in officiatin'. And durn if he wasn't right. And since I been a player of sorts myself, I had developed what we call an official's athletic-competition IQ. Anyway, soon's I discovered that I liked officiatin' better than playin', I figgered it was a opportunity to connect to the game in a totally differnt way. Bein' in the middle of the fray was sure 'nough a good time, and it was a challenge to boot."

"What kind of challenge?"

"Well, just challengin' your own self to do the players right and officiate the perfect game."

"... here in this wonderful city ... an opportunity to display their talents before a national audience ..."

"But if referees must focus on mistakes and misplays, then what's a 'perfect' game? One where there's no mistakes? No fouls? No turnovers? One where every call and every no-call is totally accurate?"

"Ha! Mistakes can never be eliminated. By nary a one of us. Not the players, the officials, and not even the coaches, too. Our job is to choreograph an athletic event, like a fancy high-speed dance, don't you know. To give the world's greatest athletes an even playin' field where they can show their skills. If we get alla that right, then *that's* a perfect game."

Hmmm. Perhaps I've had too jaundiced a view of these guys. Fuck me!

"But how about . . . ?"

Our dialogue is interrupted by the abrupt arrival of Elliot Charles, the coach of the Rockford Lightning. He's about my size, with slightly more hair topside than me, a gray-and-white short beard, and weary blue eyes set closely to the root of his oft-broken nose. Apparently his two front teeth were broken sometime during his playing days, and the continuing whiteness of the caps contrast dramatically with the yellowing of the other visible teeth.

I've coached against him for several years and have formulated this scouting report: Runs mostly either a flex or a box offense that features isos by his best scorers. His defenses are simplistic with an occasional wing trap, and all of his double downs come from the top. If he's not an accomplished X's-and-O's guy, he can read a game well and make effective adjustments. Will quickly trade blatant assholes, which is why his holdover players dig him. Personable and approachable off the court, but a foul-mouthed ref baiter once the lights are switched on. I admire his game-time passion and the loyalty he inspires for his good-guy players.

He's snarling as he drops himself into the empty seat beside me. Neither the coach nor the referee make any move to acknowledge each other.

"Fucking Mickey Mouse league," Charles says. "Look at the prick, sucking up to all the league's big shots."

His chin points where Kevin Shepherd is sitting at the table nearest the podium, wearing what is obviously a tailor-made natty black-and-white pinstripe suit, and eagerly schmoozing with the adjacent team owners and CBL executives.

"Just because he coached in the NBA for almost two years," Charles bristles, "he thinks he's the fucking king of the coaches. Even though he lost about twenty more games than he won at Golden State before getting his ass fired. Check this out. . . . He's coaching the league all-stars, right? And three of them are on his own team. But he refuses to have anything to do with making sure these guys are taken care of. I mean, there were no arrangements made for any of their meals. Or even to give them any per diem. I had lots of trouble convincing Rockford's owner . . . You both know him, right? Sol Jucker? Who gets his cash from producing low-budget soft-porn movies? Like the one with the Japanese chicks that's playing downtown—*Nip on These*? I can get you a free ticket if you want. Anyways, he let me argue him into comping my players' dinner at one of those buffet joints in the mall, right? So Shepherd says that since I'm coach of the home team and this is my turf, I'm responsible for feeding his team. And the commissioner couldn't care less if the guys starve. So I had to go back to Jucker and get him to foot the bill for all of the players. Then I had to make sure that my most responsible player had the key to the big van, and then follow them over to the restaurant with the Lightning's credit card, and then hang around until everything got settled. You know what it's like, Rob, with this fucking league."

Evidently the official introductory speechifying has concluded, since an obviously exhausted middle-aged waitress wearing what looks to be a used nurse's uniform sidles up to us to record our individual selections of the available entrées.

"You got two choices," she says. "Chicken or meat."

"Meat?" I inquire. "What kind of meat?"

She shrugs. "Dead meat, I suppose."

Everybody opts for the chicken.

"I wish I'd stayed with the players," Charles moans.

"Tell you what," I say. "If you could bring me some more rolls and butter, I'll be fine."

"What the fuck is in here?" Charles says as he tears apart the chintzy decorations of our gift baskets. Imagine our gleefully disgusted response when our prizes turn out to be small packages of locally manufactured potato chips.

"I'm outta here," Charles says. "You coming, Rob?"

Why the fuck not?

We wind up at the bar of the Clock Tower Inn. After a few drinks, Charles unloads the rest of his complaints: the Lightning's general manager spending money budgeted for the team's road trips on weekend excursions with his mistress; the owner forcing the team to undertake a six-hour bus trip on game day to save a night's lodging and a day's per diem.

"You know what the owner gave me for a Christmas bonus?" he says. "A small jar of fruit preserves. No lie."

"I know how it is, man. You've got to be coach, travel agent, scout, traveling shrink, and gopher. I still have nightmares. But remember what Kevin Loughery used to say."

"Yeah," says Charles. "'Coaching is better than working for a living.' But for what that Scrooge motherfucker is paying me, I'm not so sure. Check this out. . . . I'm on a base salary of twenty thousand, which is chicken feed. And the kicker is that I get an extra twenty-five bucks for every quarter point we win in every game. So if we win every quarter, I get an extra hundred and seventy-five. If we lose every quarter, I get zilch. And for every tied quarter? I get twelve dollars and fifty fucking cents."

After I fill him in on what a moron Weiss is, Charles says, "Hey, putzo, what the fuck do you care who he trades or who he drafts? It's his money, his team, and his responsibility. Just nod your head and collect your checks. . . . Excuse me, Rob, got to take a leak. I'll be right back."

But after waiting for fifteen minutes, he doesn't return, so I check out the man's room. Nada.

Oh well. At least I'm sober enough to find my way to my room and finish *The Last Trumpet*—another of Horgan's superb novels, at the conclusion of which the protagonist, a cavalry officer in the late nineteenth-century Indian wars, sacrifices his career for a point of honor.

Then I hotly fall asleep still wearing my Sunday go-to-meeting clothes.

CHAPTER TWELVE

In its own version of an all-star game, the CBL has frequently abandoned the usual procedure of pitting the best players in the various conferences against each other. Instead, in hopes of attracting a larger crowd, the games are sometimes scheduled in cities populated by rabid fans, where the hometown heroes contend against a league-wide all-star team chosen by the coaches. The trouble is that the all-star teams almost always win—the only exception thus far being Phil Jackson's Albany Patroons in 1983. So it is that Elliot Charles can prove that lightning can strike once if his guys can beat Kevin Sheperd's elite squad.

The phone bleeps at ten a.m., rudely awakening me from a recurrent dream that has me driving a strange car through a strange city while fruitlessly trying to find my way to some vague yet ultimately strange destination.

"Rob, wake up. It's Elliot. You've got to hustle your bustle if you don't want to get fined for being late to the shootaround."

"What? Where? When? Why?"

"What're you . . . writing a newspaper article? My team's shootaround at the MetroCentre. When? At noon sharp, and why? Because what else is your lazy ass planning to do this morning?"

"Yeah. Okay. As long as I don't have to wear a necktie. By the way, where'd you go last night?"

"That's none of your business, and probably none of mine."

Midway through the 1955–56 NBA season, Bill Sharman invented the game-day shootaround, a development that earned the enmity of countless players and coaches yet irrevocably revolutionized the way the game was played. Sharman was in his sixth season as Bob Cousy's backcourt mate for the Boston Celtics, and was always fidgety the day of a game. He'd simply pace around his house or his hotel room until it was time to leave for the arena. A high school was situated only a few minutes away from where Sharman lived in the Boston suburbs, so at ten o'clock on one fateful morning he decided to go over to the school just to dribble around and take a few shots. This happened just about a year after the NBA had implemented a new official ball, one without laces, which he was still slightly uncomfortable handling. During that night's game, Sharman felt looser and quicker than he ordinarily did, and even his shooting touch seemed to be enhanced. So he returned to the gym on the morning of the Celtics next home game, and was pleased to experience the same results.

Sharman soon developed a routine: Practicing only those kinds of shots that he'd normally take in a game, and not finishing until he'd made five consecutive buckets from each of his favorite spots. When his teammates noticed how much better he was playing, several of them started going to the gym with him.

In his initial five NBA seasons, Sharman was an 86 percent free-throw shooter. In the five post-shootaround seasons, his marksmanship at the stripe increased to 92 percent.

From then on, through stints coaching the Cleveland Pipers in the American Basketball League, and NBA teams in San Francisco and Los Angeles, the "shoot" became an essential part of Sharman's pregame plan. NBA watchers castigated him for unnecessarily wearing out his players and therefore making them increasingly susceptible to injuries. In truth, the early-morning activity forced the players to get out of bed (and presumably cut short their previous evening's partying), break a sweat, and avoid the logy feeling that often afflicted them at the start of games. Also, Sharman was convinced that the shoots developed the visual image, positive reinforcement, and muscle memory of the ball going through the hoop.

After Sharman led the Warriors to the NBA finals in 1967 (losing to Philadelphia), and then won the championship with the LA Lakers in 1972, shootarounds became de rigueur.

So, reverting to my normal civilian attire of jeans, a generic gray sweatshirt, and sneakers (albeit dyed), I arrived on the sidelines of the MetroCentre's court five minutes early. To my surprise and delight, all of the players were already dressed in official practice gear and ready for action, some of them playing one-on-one, others playing H-O-R-S-E, and everyone enjoying both a mild sweat and one another's company.

None of these guys were in the CBL when I was still coaching, but, figuring that there must be a compelling reason why I was there, many of them grace me with welcoming nods. If they don't know me, however, I've scouted most of them, judging that perhaps one or two might be good enough to fill out a summer-league roster.

Here's Charles making his appearance, wearing jeans and a Rockford Lightning jacket. On a dark-blue background, there's a small patch over his heart depicting a red-and-white ball poised over a yellow bolt of lightning under which "Rockford Lightning" is inscribed in white block letters. The same logo occupies most of the back of the jacket. He's unshaven, lacks a whistle, and is constantly clearing his throat.

"Hey, Rob," he says moistly. Then shouts, "Yo!" to catch is players' attention. "Let's go! Ten-and-twos!"

Without any further instruction, the players run through a series of three-man weaves with a lay-up at each end. Two up-and-down sprints are succeeded by four, then six, then eight, and then ten. A missed lay-up negates the sprint, which must be repeated.

The only encouragement voiced by Charles is this: "You gotta love it! Or else you'll hate it!"

The "two" requires a pair of full-court weaves to be climaxed by acceptable dunks, whose legitimacy depends on a voice vote by the players and is an excuse for some good-natured kidding among them.

"Nah! If the rim don't quiver, then it's not a real dunk!"

"That fingertip shit don't count! It's wrist-high or nothing!"

A water break ensues. Then the squad splits into two five-man teams, and they dummy through their offensive sets. All the while, Charles tries to relax beside me on the home team's bench, but must constantly clear his throat with loud gargling sounds.

"A dripping sinus," he says. "The doctor claims it's because I eat too much dairy and don't get enough sleep. But that's bullshit, because I don't change my diet or get more sleep in the off-season and it never bothers me then. It's stress is what it is.

"I used to get perpetual muscle spasms in my neck, but only during the season. Nothing helped. Not massage, or swimming, or some kind of chill-out pills. And they got even worse in the playoffs.

"Yeah," he says before suffering another near-coughing jag. "Anyway . . ."

Pity the poor coaches on every level of competition. Bench bound, they watch and bark orders and scream and curse and clap their hands and stand up and sit down and loosen their neckties and wish they could be out there communing with all that is meaningful and transcendent and viscerally exciting and beautiful about The Game—instead of being eunuchs at an orgy.

"Anyway . . . they look like a bunch of good guys, and you've got them well trained."

"It's not exactly brain surgery, but, sure, they're good kids. Fun to work with. Except that skinny guy with the fuzzy beard. I can't get him to stop gambling on defense. His idea of playing D is to make a steal, run out, then do some kind of fancy dunk. I mean, he's a nice kid, and he might even have an NBA future, but he watches too many hoops highlights on *SportsCenter*. If I could, I'd take away his TV privileges. But the kid always does play hard. I'm just afraid he's gonna be a CBL lifer."

My feeling is that even if the kid learns how to play sound defense, he's way too soft to ever reach the NBA.

"And what about you, Coach?"

"Me?" he says as he stands up. "Shit. My agent's angling for me to get some cozy D-Two job somewhere in South Carolina. He says if we can win tonight, I'm a shoo-in. But fuck, this is these guys' game, not mine."

Another ringing "Yo!" signals his players to cluster around him. "Here's the game plan for tonight: The starters play the first quarter and the opening six minutes of the third quarter. The second unit gets the whole second quarter, the end of the third quarter, and the first six minutes of the fourth quarter. Then the starters finish the game."

He looks at a smallish, dark-skinned point guard. "Josh," the coach says, "You're the only college graduate on the team. So translate what that means to the high school dropouts among us."

"Everybody plays twenty-four minutes."

Several players nod at this information, then clap their hands with glee.

"One more thing before we get out of here and let the visiting team on the court . . . This here is Rob Lassner, who used to coach the Peoria Stars—for how many years?"

"Most of my entire adult life."

"Now he's a big-shot scout for the New Jersey Nets, and he wants to impart some words of wisdom to you knuckleheads."

"I do?"

"Yes, you do."

"Well, okay . . . Anyway, there are several ways to get that precious ten-day contract. You can score a lot of points, which will impress most of the pinheads who make personnel decisions. But if that's the case, then you probably won't last too long, because no NBA coach is going to piss off his players by calling your number and running plays for you. So all you'll get is hustle shots or leftover shots and, as you know, shooters don't shoot well unless they get lots of shots. So you'll be handicapped."

They restlessly shuffle their feet, but play close attention.

"Another way, the best way, is to be a role player. That means to figure out, with Coach's help here, exactly what skills you have that will carry over into the next level. Maybe it's rebounding, or defense, or passing, or setting screens, or simply executing whatever any given sequence calls for. I know this is a problem for some of you guys who are playing out of your natural positions. Small forwards playing a power position. Power forwards playing center. But that's the way it is.

"I mean most NBA teams are looking for guys to fill out the end of the bench. So you always have to be ready and you have to practice like your ass is on fire. And if the veterans get pissed because you're practicing too hard, well, fuck them, so long as you don't hurt anybody."

Again there's a unanimous nodding agreement.

"But remember this: You're only somebody else's torn cartilage away from big-league bucks and big-league pussy."

My little speech is rewarded with laughter and a burst of applause.

Charles and I stand by while most of the players linger to take extra shots. "You forgot about the politics," he says. "This guy gets called up because his coach was a teammate of that coach, or they both have the same agent, or that guy has a photo of this guy fucking a sheep."

"All this is true, but I didn't want to discourage them."

"Anyway, let's get out of here before that asshole gets here." Then he shouts to the few remaining players, "Don't forget to rack the balls when you're done."

Charles has several of what he calls "bullshit" promo appearances to undergo, so I'm on my own until game time. Ah, but there are other game times.

The concierge at the hotel directs me to the nearest basketball court, which is housed in an Erector Set building, auxiliary to Rockford's largest hospital. My room card gains me free access to a large space that's dominated by gleaming Nautilus machines, which are currently being used by a corps of dehydrated seniors who push only the most minimal weights. Although they shuffle from station to station armed with towels and plastic bottles of cleaning fluid, none of them sweat. Yet they laboriously disinfect each pad, each hand grip, only one step away from godliness.

Several of the oldsters also carry portable oxygen units slung over their shoulders like briefcases. Long plastic tubes feed the gas directly into their gasping nostrils. Poor bastards. A sign of things to come for me?

Situated along one wall is a fleet of stationary bikes, treadmills, StairMasters, and rowing machines. At the opposite side of the gym, behind a floor-to-ceiling fishnet curtain, an aerobics class slowly waltzes to the strains of a million strings playing "Moon River." And beyond all of this slow-motion frenzy, at the far end of the room, is half of a basketball court.

The wooden floor is old and bouncy, and there's a brand-new rubberized-plastic ball resting on the foul line. The ball is wonderfully tactile, and the rim yawns and invites me to shoot. One-on-none. Jumpers from near and far. Soft, feathery fingers flicking the pebbled sphere into the mystery of space and time. The ball, my hand, and the sacred hoop are connected. *Swish! Swish!* Even my misses are kind and forgiving. The ball spinning like a friendly planet through a benign universe, watched over by the great god, Basketball Jones.

Thou source of all my bliss and all my woe . . .

My physical-cum-spiritual reveries are rudely interrupted by four young men who bring their own ball, their own boisterous enthusiasms, and their plans for a two-on-two game.

"Do you mind?" I'm asked. "You can have next."

No, thanks. I've already received what I came for—a light sweat and a reconnection with reality.

Back at the hotel, a shower, a chef's salad, and a nap prep me for the all-star game.

The arena is swarming with fans, CBL execs, and media hounds. It's difficult for someone my size to be inconspicuous, but I try. Hugging the dark corners of the media room, keeping my eyes cast to my shoes (noting that the black polish is starting to flake off), I'm nevertheless discovered by Bonnie, the Lightning's beguiling media director.

"There you are," she says. "Do you mind if I call you Rob?"

"Please do. But I have a favor to ask."

"Anything," she says.

Is she flirting with me, or am I flirting with her?

"I'd really appreciate it if you could seat me up there in the mezzanine press box."

"Nonsense. You're one of our most honored guests, Rob, and you're going to be introduced to the fans and the TV audience before the game. I mean, you're quite the success story."

The only concession I can wring out of her is to be placed at the very end of the courtside media table—a seat immediately adjacent to the all-stars bench.

Then she waves over a crew from ESPN—cameraman, sound man with a fuzzy mic mounted on the end of a long pole, and a young kid carrying a directional lamp. Then her eyes flash at me with both a warning and a promise as she says, "I'll ask the question, but one of the anchor guys will dub it in for the half-time segment. Look at the camera, not at me."

"Not an easy task."

Without being asked my permission, I find myself squinting due to the sudden positioning of bright light, while the mic hovers menacingly overhead, the sound guy says, "Got it," the cameraman sets his focus, and Bonnie asks me this: "As a former coach in the league, Rob Lassner, what do you think of the CBL's quarter-point system?"

My impulse is to say "Nothing" and exit stage right, but her intimidating glance makes me feel like a naughty schoolboy. So, against my better judgment, I give her a straight answer.

"It's awful. Because the end of each quarter is so critical that you have to have your best players on the court, which means they get too many minutes. Also, for the same reason, you can't employ a normal rotation, which would be having your subs in for the last four minutes of the first and third quarters, and the first few minutes of the second and fourth quarters. The entire idea that each quarter is a game unto itself is unnatural and makes absolutely no sense. It's like giving a baseball team extra points for winning an inning. Whatever excitement it's supposed to generate is phony excitement."

"Thanks," she says sweetly, then pauses while the cameraman whispers something to her.

"Okay, Rob. The director says that what you said was way too negative. Do you think we could do it again with you emphasizing the positive this time?"

With her dimpled jaw thrust forward and her eyes slightly narrowed, along with that minimal shivering in the corner of her mouth, I couldn't tell if she was insisting or pleading.

"Sure. Why not? But I'd only do this for you."

Now she's all business as the crew rearranges their equipment.

"Go," she says.

"I really like the quarter-point system because it hastens the education of young players. By that I mean they're forced to concentrate at the end of a close quarter as if the entire game was up for grabs. It also teaches them that every single play is important. The drama, of course, is also very appealing to the fans."

"That's great, Mister Lassner. Maybe I'll see you later."

Mister Lassner?
Holy Shit!
What the fuck did I just do?
How could I be so easily conned?
What happened to my cherished integrity?
No is always no? Except when no is yes?
Am I really just a cynical, run-of-the-mill, pussy-deprived hypocrite?
Or was all this just a meaningless joke?
An absurdity?
What the fuck?!?

That's why I'm so glum and inattentive when the game starts. None of the Lightning are candidates to graduate from the CBL, and I'm already familiar with the six all-stars who have already dipped their toes in the NBA pool. And despite the exhortation I delivered to the Rockford guys during their shootaround, it's a chalk-eaters bet that the guys with the NBA experience will be summoned back to The League before the untested hooplings. That's because NBA general managers always look to protect their own asses by making safe choices whenever possible.

As part of the pregame hoopla, I'm introduced as a CBL success story. Staying glued to my seat, I respond to the desultory applause with a desultory wave of my left hand, while making sure to cover my VARSITY WRESTLING patch with my right hand.

Once the game commences, there's Charles, wearing a nondescript dark-blue suit and light-blue tie, sitting unobtrusively at the end of the home team's bench and using hand signals to direct traffic. Meanwhile Shepherd, resplendent in a perfectly fitted soft-gray silk suit, black shirt, and yellow necktie, never sits. Standing with his arms folded, or stalking the sideline, always preening, occasionally making shouting instructions, which his players ignore.

The Lightning execute their offensive sets with total conviction, moving the ball, cutting, screening, passing, generating, and making open shots, taking full advantage of the all-stars' disinclination to play defense for more than a few seconds at a time. Despite Charles's passive demeanor, all of his players—those on the court as well as those on the bench—are clearly upbeat. This game doesn't count in the standings, there's no winner's bonus at stake, and besides they are distinct underdogs. Also, the NBA is a dream that may or may not come true, but the joyous fever of the game at hand trumps every other consideration. They are players, and they are playing with exuberance, for fun and for pride and for the hometown fans and for each other.

The all-stars, on the other hand, are playing only for themselves. Their individual game plans are identical: Shoot first and never ask questions. Only passing fancies and surefire assists are acceptable reasons for willfully relinquishing possession of the ball.

No surprise, then, that Rockford takes command of the game early, causing Shepherd to rail at his players in their huddles.

"Hey! You guys are the all-stars! Those chumps are the no-stars! You're embarrassing yourselves and you're embarrassing me!"

When Morrison calls a charge instead of a block, Shepherd screams at him: "What game are you watching? You fucking asshole!"

Morrison merely laughs, waves away Shepherd's rant, and hustles to catch up to another Lightning fast break.

Just a few plays later, Morrison makes another questionable call, this one in favor of the all-stars. While the presumably fouled all-star gears up for his first free throw, Charles climbs to his feet, leans over the sideline, and whispers this to the ref: "Hey, Kevin, was that the right call? Did you get a good look at it?"

A suddenly outraged Morrison quickly tags Charles with a technical! A tech in an all-star game? The first ever! How humiliating!

The all-stars make a modest rally early in the fourth quarter, and Shepherd is manic. His own guys are on the court for all of the last twelve minutes, while only three other players rotate in the remaining pair of slots—none of them getting more than two minutes of daylight in succession. He berates the refs for every call that doesn't go his way, and acts as though this is the seventh game of the championship series.

Of course, his players are pissed. During a time-out, one of his own guys suggests that the brothers of the bench deserve to get in on the action. "Shut the fuck up!" Shepherd snaps. "I'm the fucking genius here."

The Lightning win, 110–101, and Shepherd stalks off the court without congratulating Charles.

After the crowd thins out, I hightail it to the hotel bar and order a pitcher of some kind of German dark beer, as well as some deluxe nachos. A conglomeration of chips, refried beans, melted Monterey Jack cheese, hot peppers, and ground beef, the entire mess topped with globs of sour cream and guacamole. My goal being to drink and to gorge myself until I forget my hypocrisy.

Maybe it's an hour later, maybe even more, when I'm much more inebriated than I want to be and only dimly aware of Shepherd sitting at a corner table and loudly lording it over a group of adoring cronies. That's when I'm fully cognizant of Bonnie, the media chick, walking over and perching on the stool next to mine.

"What are you drinking?" I ask as the bartender approaches..

"A mojito," she tells him.

I move the remnants of my gooey nachos toward her. "Here. Help yourself."

"No, thanks. That stuff gives me gas. . . . Anyway, you don't know how happy I am that this whole thing is over. I've been running around like a rat on a wheel."

She gulps down the delivered mojito and motions to the bartender for a refill. "Shepherd was a total pain in the ass. He had to have a couple of gallons of cherry-flavored Gatorade in the, what do you call it? The cooler near the bench? He also demanded Indian River oranges for half time. No other kind would do. And get this. . . . They couldn't be cut into quarters, no way. They had to be cut into sixths. And for his shootaround? He had to have ten brand-new balls. What a fucking joke this guy is. He thinks he's the king of shit. Did you happen to cross paths with him when the Lightning left the court this morning?"

"No, not at all."

"Well, you really missed something."

"Tell me."

"I will after I finish this. . . . Hey, man. One more time, please. . . . Anyway, he shows up in a fancy suit and tie, different from the ones he wore at the dinner and for the game. So one of the players asks him what he wanted them to do, and he says, 'This is a shootaround, ain't it? So go shoot around.' And they spent about an hour playing H-O-R-S-E, matching half-court heaves and just fooling around, while he's gabbing with the media. He should have put in some kind of offense or something, right?"

"For sure. Some screen/rolls with weak-side action, or cross screens for post-ups, or a UCLA . . . Just to keep them from running into each other. Simple stuff that these guys could do in their sleep."

"Then he felt insulted when he lost the game."

"Which I'm glad that he did."

"I second the motion," she says. "But at least the game was very entertaining. The ESPN people were delighted."

I can't help wincing. "Basketball games are all about competition, not entertainment."

She laughs lightly. "If the games weren't entertaining, they'd be played in empty arenas, and nobody who wasn't playing or coaching or reffing would care. There'd be no media coverage, no anything."

"But they're entertaining *because* they're competitive. I mean, the game is the only thing that really counts. All of the post- and pre-game analysis, the commentary, the interviews, the players treated like movie stars. . . . That's all bullshit. The game qua game. Period."

She downs her third drink like she's been wandering in the desert, and actually says "Ahhh!" after each long swallow. Now there seems to be some kind of woozy promise in her eyes. Something soft and inviting. Or am I just seeing what I want to see?

"So, Bonnie. What about my flip-flop on the quarter-point deal? How did that go down?"

"The director loved it, and so did I."

"Don't you think it was the height of sophistry? That I'm a complete bullshitter?"

Again her tinkling laugh. "There's no biz like show biz." Then after swallowing the rest of her drink, she asks a question out of nowhere: "Tell me, Rob, are you married?"

"Not any more. Why do you ask?"

"Then it doesn't make any difference."

"Any difference about what?"

"Whether we go to your room or my room."

My room, because, unlike a suspicious wife, should Earl try to make immediate contact for some reason or other (perhaps the public televising of my thrift-shop threads), he would understand if the switchboard was instructed to deny all incoming calls.

In a flash, we fumble on the bed until we're both naked and ready to engage in feverish sexual commerce—when suddenly I unloose a resounding, odoriferous flatulation. Mandrake immediately falls on the field of battle, and even as I jokingly say, "Now that I'm tuned up, do you have any requests?" Bonnie quickly gets dressed and leaves in a huff.

Egad! More the fool, me.

I wake up the next morning with a basketball hangover: My head comes loose, and some vast, mighty hand starts dribbling it around the room. Ouch. Now I'm slam-dunked. Ooch. Then passed cross-court and downcourt until I'm dizzy. Intercepted, rejected, pinned to the backboard. *Get that shit outta here. . . .*

Oh, well. After a breakfast of black coffee and three aspirins, it's on to the next stop.

CHAPTER THIRTEEN

Before I left for the airport, I re-donated my emergency wardrobe to the Salvation Army. Then . . . another car to return, another flight, another city, another car to rent, another light meal and cozy nap at another hotel. This latest hostelry sits on Temple Square, a busy intersection bounded by the famous Mormon Tabernacle, a municipal building, the Zions Bank, and a department store. In the middle of the square stands a statue of Brigham Young, the city's founding father and spiritual beacon. The huge bronze statue is positioned so that BY's back is turned toward the temple and his open hand stretches toward the bank.

The Energy Solutions Arena is SRO, with all the nineteen-thousand-plus fans clean and well dressed, but using cowbells, drums, trumpets, and lung power to raise a constant ear-blasting cacophony. Male and female cheerleaders for both schools are performing acrobatic flips and human pyramids in wide-eyed, red-cheeked ecstasies.

None of the players on either Weber State or Utah inspire more than casual interest. Perhaps the Utah Jazz might invite one or two of them as media-attracting roster fill during the local summer league. Otherwise, even the brothers played like white boys: hitting open shots, setting and using screens to perfection, and mostly moving in straight lines.

Ho-hum. It looked to be another waste of my time and Weiss's money.

However, the game was barely five minutes old when the previously vacant seat next to mine at the press table was occupied with a gasp, a moan, and even a thud by my all-time favorite agent, Mister F.

His real moniker is Freddy Fletcher, but he's also known as Fat Freddy and, in a reprisal of the nom-de-blues given to Jimmy Rushing, Mister Five-by-Five. Because of his eggplant-black skin, his hairless head gleams darkly and contrasts with his dazzling large-toothed smile. He's got a puffy fat-man's face; a flat, nostril-flaring nose; eyes that are hawk brown; and brows that are eagle white Although he's only about five-eight, he must weigh upward of three hundred pounds, and Mister F's massive, no-nonsense approach to everything makes all of my and Weiss's expenditures worthwhile.

I have dealt with him many times while trying to recruit his players to Peoria, but agenting has always been a hobby for him, and he is rumored to have some secret, marginally illegal source of funds. On one occasion I dialed his number to inquire about a player he represented who had just come back from France.

"Hello," came a phony falsetto voice that was clearly Mister F's.

"Freddy? Is that you?"

"Sorry, he don't live here anymore, and I don't know where he moved to."

"Freddy, it's me. Rob Lassner from the Peoria Stars."

"Oh, yeah. What's up?"

Whatever his shady gig is, it pays for his immaculately tailored suits that made him look at least fifty pounds lighter. His fondness for wearing wide, hand-painted neckties also suggests a 1940's Hollywood gangster. But having made a personal connection, I've found Freddy to be charming, intelligent, and often outrageously opinionated.

We share an awkward hug across our side-to-side seats. And we practically have to shout to converse.

"Mister F, it's so great to see you, but what are you doing here? I thought you worked out of Denver."

"Ha," he says, his brown eyes twinkling. "I had to get out of Denver after our divorce. Ellie has too many relatives, friends, and spies there."

"Sorry to hear about that. Divorces can be painful."

"It's okay. We never should have gotten hitched in the first place. I mean, we were together for fifteen years, but we never wanted the same things at the same time. It just took both of us that long to realize it. But it's cool. I like living in Salt Lake City. The streets are wide, the traffic lights are perfectly synchronized, and there's never any traffic. These days I'm out much more, up to Wyoming and

Montana, over to Nevada, and sometimes I even sneak back into Colorado."

He hums with interest as Weber's black center scores on a well-rehearsed step-under move.

"Sure," he continues, "the Mormons are crazy. What with Joseph Smith's behind-the-curtain translation of the secret tablets, the magic underwear, and the promise that each of them will be rewarded for his faith by becoming the god of his own planet. Silly stuff. But the players are nice kids. And since the Mormons opened the door to black folks about thirty years ago, they fall all over themselves trying to be polite to us."

Now it's my turn to laugh. "You know, Freddy, used to be that this was the favorite stop on the road for black players all around the NBAbecause the white chicks would fight each other for the chance to fuck the devil. I mean, it wasn't unusual for a brother to bed down three white chicks at the same time."

"Sex, man! Not just these blunt-nosed Mormons, but the entire frigging country has such a perverted view of it. They say, 'No, no, no.' It's nasty. It's immoral. But they can't get enough of the peep show."

Then he turns his attention back to the game where the same big guy out-muscles Utah's entire front line to snatch a rebound in rush-hour traffic. Freddy nods his approval, and asks me, "Who are you looking at?"

"Nobody, really. Just seeing what's out here, which in my opinion isn't much. You seem to like that kid, Weber's big man, Number Eighteen."

"Yeah. Well, he's supposed to be a wonderful young man, although he'll never come close to being an NBA player. I'm just doing a solid for a friend of mine. I could probably get the kid a gig in Germany or Holland for twenty grand a year. I mean, I do have seven guys currently in the NBA, but I mostly avoid big-time players and try to help out kids like him. And you want to know why?"

"Of course."

"Because I hate the NBA. Except for Phil Jackson's triangle offense, every team runs the same stuff. Here a pick, there a pick, everywhere a pick, pick. And they do this for lots of reasons: The young kids coming out of high school or their frosh season in college don't know shit from Shinola, so it's Keep It Simple, Stupid. Also, because there's two guys on offense and two on defense out there by themselves, the refs get a good unobstructed look at the action. Which works to benefit the offense, since the refs always look first to call fouls on the defense. Plus, almost all of the guys in the league are so arrogant and greedy that they're impossible to deal with. They have no frigging loyalty whatsoever. I've seen it a dozen times. . . . I bust my nuts getting a kid a nice contract, then he drops me and signs up with another agent who can get him another thousand bucks."

"I know what you mean. They think they're the center of the universe."

"I had a kid and his mother to lunch at a Red Lobster just the other day, you know? Gave them the whole deal. If other agents take fifteen percent, I only take five. And whatever contract we sign can be negated by either of us at any time for any reason. Right? But all the mother was interested in was if I was also going to pay for dessert. So then I go to take a leak, and while I'm gone, the two of them order a party- platter-to-go of a hundred shrimp, which they picked up at the cashier's, when it was too late for me to say anything. Did I mention that they wanted twenty-five grand up front before the draft?"

Meanwhile, Weber's center shoots an air ball from the stripe, but Freddy barely pauses. "Do know what pisses me off even more?"

"What's that?"

"The racism in the NBA and how it's destroying the game."

"Say what? You got to explain that one."

"Look, my man. I've been through all of that bullshit. The quota system that limited the number of brothers on a team, and then in the starting lineup. Red Auerbach was an asshole, but he freaked everyone out when he used two black starters, then three, and then four. Remember them? Bill Russell, K. C. and Sam Jones, and also Satch Sanders? And nobody said boo, because the Celtics kept winning and winning. I'm telling you, man, that was hot shit."

How old is this guy? It's impossible to tell, if only because the distended skin on his roly-poly face stretches out any possible wrinkles. He could be thirty, or fifty, or sixty, or beyond.

The game has turned into a route, and the deafening delirium of the hometown fans gets louder as Utah's margin mounts. Twenty points. Twenty-five. They apparently won't be satisfied unless Utah wins by a hundred. Then, after the subs play out the rest of the half, the buzzer suddenly silences the arena.

Normal protocol calls for the media freeloaders to hustle over to the hospitality suite, munch on popcorn, potato chips, and pretzels, and glug various sodas. But moving his heavy body is always a chore for Freddy, and besides, he's on a roll.

"Later on," he continues without missing a beat, "in the midseventies, when Stern took over the league? The NBA was what? Almost ninety percent black? I remember all of the twelve players on the Knicks were black. A sign of the times was that one of the New York newspapers used to call them the 'Nigger Bockers.' And that's when, and that's why, NBA teams started drafting white guys from Europe. Some of these guys were good, and some were not so good. But the whole pointwas to get more white faces into the league. So we wind up with a bunch of seven-foot palefaces who want to shoot three-pointers and want no part of banging around in the paint. I mean, really, look at how many of the take-no-shit-from-anybody post-up centers are black. Dwight Howard. That kid Bynum with the Lakers. Who else? Help me out here."

"Even though they're both ready for the glue factory, there's Shaq and Jermaine O'Neal. Ummm . . . Carlos Boozer, Tim Duncan, Roy Hibbert, Zach Randolph, Nenê, Kendrick Perkins. Let's see . . . Emeka Okafor."

"That's what I'm saying. Don't forget Yao Ming, who's halfway to being a brother."

"What about Pau Gasol and his brother Marc? And Luis Scola? They're all white."

"Yeah, the Spanish guys are different from the other Europeans. They tend to be cutthroat motherfuckers. Pau is a pussy and he's the exception that proves this particular rule."

The Utah Redskins are back on the court going through their regimented warm-ups. But the Weber State Wildcats remain in their locker room, no doubt being chewed out by their coach. And Freddy struggles to his feet. "I've seen all I want to see of this shit. I'm outta here. Hey, care to join me for some good grub and a few drinks?"

Absolutely.

As we ride the escalator up to the street level, he says something short and snappy into his cell phone—and by the time we exit the arena, there's a stretch limo waiting for us. The uniformed driver is a middle-aged white man who holds the door open for Freddy, then races to the other side to do the same for me. "Thank you," I say, and he responds by lightly tapping the brim of his hat in a mock salute.

Freddy squirms and wriggles until he's comfortable, and although he supplies no destination to the chauffeur, the vehicle moves quietly and powerfully through the empty lanes of the parking lot and into the light traffic. Freddy then lifts the lid of a small built-in refrigeration unit, extracts a bottle of peach-flavored vodka and a pair of iced glasses. Without bothering to ask my preference, he pours me a healthy dose, an even bigger one for himself, and as we clink glasses, he says, "To those us who understand that life is a metaphor for basketball."

We sip our drinks in delicious silence until the limo comes to a smooth stop in front of a modest yellow-brick building that's squeezed between a furniture showroom and a used-tire shop in a somewhat sleazy outlying commercial neighborhood. Outside the building in question, an orderly line of almost exclusively black couples extends for half the block—all of them apparently waiting to enter a large, elaborately engraved wooden door that would be appropriate for some modest-sized medieval castle. A doorman in an elaborate red uniform replete with gold-colored epaulettes, sashes, and braids rushes over to open the car door nearest to Freddy, bowing as he says, "Good evening, Mister Fletcher. So good to see you, sir, . . . and your guest."

Freddy reaches into an interior jacket pocket and peels what looks to be a twenty-dollar bill from a large roll, then hands it to the fawning doorman. "Good to see you, too, George. How's Lucinda? Over her cold?"

"Yes, sir. Thank you, sir. She's bouncing all over the apartment again."

"Good. Good. Teething can be a trying time for everybody."

Then I notice a blinking blue neon sign placed at the rooftop level of the yellow-brick building: FAT FREDDY'S RIB JOINT. Inside is a surprisingly large space walled by the same yellow bricks as the outside. The only sign on any of the walls specifies that $24.95 buys "ALL YOU CAN EAT." And there are dozens of customers sitting side-by-side on benches and wearing red-checkered bibs to match the tablecloths that are spread on the long trestle tables. It's a family-style deal—come with your own crew or sit with strangers. Waiters in black shirts, black pants, and black bow ties scurry around the room, replacing empty bowls and platters with full ones.

As I follow Freddy in his surprisingly light-footed weave through the crowded tables , hands and voices are raised in welcome.

"Freddy! My man!"

"The main nigger's in the house!"

"Yo, Mister F!"

He nods and shakes a few outstretched hands as a bowing, obsequious man in a gray business suit leads us to a large round table set in a solitary booth against the rear wall. Two settings await us, featuring gleaming silverware, crystal glasses, and translucent china, all placed on a white linen tablecloth. As soon as we are seated, a black-clad waiter energetically greets his boss and delivers a bottle of champagne set in a silver ice bucket. He shows the label to Freddy, who nods and motions for the libations to be poured.

"Thank you, Simon," says Freddy.

"It's my pleasure, sir."

After a silent toast to each other, Freddy says this: "I'll bet you're surprised, huh? To see a well-dressed, well-fed black man who isn't involved in drugs, or booze, or numbers, or prostitution, or something like that? It's okay. You don't have to answer. That's a rhetorical question. Just to let you know that everything's strictly on the up-

and-up with me. Well, almost everything."

Another waiter arrives with a tray full of food. Huge platters of barbecued ribs, chicken, brisket, sausage, pulled pork shoulder, augmented with heaping bowls of coleslaw, greens, corn on the cob, macaroni and cheese, and thick-cut fried potatoes, along with three bottles of sauce respectively marked "Mild," "Medium," and "Ooo-Wheee!." Plus two pitchers of iced tea, one marked "Sweet," the other "Not Sweet."

"Thank you, Joseph."

"You're very welcome, sir. May you and your guest enjoy your dinner, sir."

Freddy says, "No question" to the waiter, and then "Dig in" to me.

As expected, the food is scrumptious, and Freddy merely nods when I tell him so. We concentrate on eating for a while until I notice the background music beaming forth at a perfect nonintrusive yet satisfying volume from hidden speakers. Miles Davis playing the lead on "It Never Entered My Mind." And I sigh with appreciation of the sweetly brilliant tones he gets from his muted horn.

"You know that, eh?" says Freddy with a mouthful of meat.

"Sure. My favorites of Miles's tunes. Those four albums at Van Gelder's studio were the highlight of his career."

He stops eating and locks his eyes on me as though seeing me for the first time. "I agree wholeheartedly. I can't stand a lot of his later stuff—all that fusion nonsense. Yeah, an artist has to keep growing and experimenting, but jazz and rock, or whatever that other element was, just don't mix. . . . Good. That's good."

I can't tell if he's referring to the music, the food, or me.

When we both come up for air, I have something else on my mind. "I hope you don't mind my asking you what might be an embarrassing question."

He absolutely chortles, even as he holds his linen napkin over his mouth to keep me from getting sprayed with shreds of food. "Man, I'm way past being embarrassed. Just look at all the fat on me. If I'm not embarrassed and ashamed by that, then I'm cool with anything. So ask away."

"Okay. It must have been three or four years ago, when I was still at Peoria. I called you about one of your players and you answered the phone in a high-pitched voice and said that Freddy Fletcher didn't live there anymore. I've always wondered what that was all about."

A hearty laugh threatens to choke him and the waiter is momentarily alarmed. But Freddy coughs up a morsel, sips his iced tea, and says, "I thought you were Ellie's lawyer. He was only supposed to speak to my lawyer." Then he spreads his arms to include the entire room. "I mean, the bitch tried everything to get a piece of this. Fuck! She wanted all of it. But I had enough bucks to stall her until she couldn't afford to keep paying her thousand-dollar-an-hour lawyers. So we bickered and delayed . . . and I must admit that I greased some palms . . . and I only let her have the house, and told her to go fuck herself."

"One more question, if I may?"

"Shoot."

"How'd you get where you are?"

"Okay. We've got a few minutes before dessert. So . . . I was born in Denver, and my daddy left me and my mom when I was six. Poor woman. She tried everything to keep me and my sister together. Washing clothes. Cleaning houses. But times was bad. The only thing left for her to do was to sell her body. That's right. And I ain't embarrassed by that neither. In fact I'm proud of her for sacrificing herself for her kids.

"Anyway, I was a really good basketball player in high school. The star of the team. Good enough to get a scholarship offer from Virginia Union. But then I was driving to the hoop in the state championship game when some white dude undercut me, and I broke my hip. Man, I was in a cast from my knee to my chest. For a long time. So I dropped out of school and there was nothing else for me to do but eat my mother's good cooking. Which as you can see, I did."

He pats his belly with affection.

"After I recovered, I started out here in this very place as a dishwasher. Anything to get my mom off the street, you know? The place was a shit hole back then. But I worked hard, saved as much money as I could, worked my way up to cook, and then, after a succession of guys kept getting fired for getting arrested or for showing up drunk or not showing up at all, I wound up being the accountant. But I only stole what was within the acceptable limits. I also found out that the guy who owned the place, Ezzie Thompson, was skimming money off the top and gambling it away. Anyway, Ezzie got himself shot to death in a card game, and his widow put me in charge. After a couple of years, I had enough to buy her out. I mean, she was also so sick of the whole business that I got me a really good deal. The rest, as they say, is history."

"And your mother?"

"I bought her a house, and she's doing real good. She's almost as fat as me!"

"Your sister?"

"I bought her a beauty parlor down in Ogden. She's married and has three kids. . . . So what you're seeing, Rob, isn't a black Al Capone. Not at all. What I really am is a black Santa. I mean, I pay the bribes and protection money to the cops and the mob for just about every black business in town. The barber shop, the clothing store, even the junkyard. I also put up bail money and hush money for black kids who are rousted by the cops. I'll also pay for whatever abortion situation any of my knucklehead players get themselves into. And I won't mention the charities and needy citizens I help to support. Now, I sure as shit ain't no Christian, but I do believe that the more you give, the more you get. . . . Ah, here comes the strawberry shortcake . . . Now it's your turn."

So I give him a brief but uncensored version of my childhood, my playing and my coaching careers, how I got the Nets job, and what a buffoon Weiss is, concluding with "I love my job, but I also hate it."

When we've finally finished eating and drinking, we are presented with damp hand towels.

"Thanks, Joseph."

"Yes, sir."

Alone again, Freddy turns to me and says this: "Come and work for me? I mean it."

"Doing what?"

"A couple of things. I'm getting too old and too lazy to be dragging my fat ass all over the place to scout players. You could do that easy. But I also sponsor a bunch of teams for guys that I can't place right away. We tour the country playing preseason exhibition games against some of the top twenty colleges. We also play in money tournaments here and in Europe. Hey, you can even play if you want to. And I put a team of undrafted free agents in the Las Vegas and Salt Lake City summer leagues. Just so's they can be seen. Now, I don't know what you're getting with New Jersey, but I'll give you a shitload more."

"Eighty grand plus expenses."

"That's chicken feed. A hundred. A hundred twenty-five. Whatever you need. And you can live wherever you want to. And everybody always travels first-class. But there's no need to make a decision now, Rob. Wait until the season's over, or the draft is over. Whatever. There's no time limit on my offer. Just think about it. All right?"

"As Symphony Sid used to say, 'All right, all root.'"

We share a belly laugh, his belly shivering and shaking much more than mine, when we're approached by an absolutely lovely young black girl. Wow! She whispers in Freddy's ear, and they obviously make plans for a rendezvous.

He pulls his card from an inside pocket. One wiggle of his right hand sends George scurrying to give him a pen. "Here's my private cell number. Call anytime." Then he pokes his chin at the tight, swaying ass of the retreating girl. "Want some company tonight, Rob? But let me warn you, once you go black, you never go back."

"No, thanks. I'm too drunk to rise to the occasion."

"Ah, you're just out of practice."

I'm engulfed by his huge bear hug. "George will drive you back to your hotel."

A good shit, a satisfying night's sleep, and not a trace of a hangover. And a glorious fall-back plan!

Next stop, Los Angeles.

CHAPTER FOURTEEN

I'm zooming along eastward on my way to the hotel, bumper-to-bumper at seventy miles per hour, the traffic moving in the opposite direction just as swiftly—until just before the Pico Street exit, one of the westbound lanes is backed up behind a rusty gray VW van. Two young Chicano men are standing outside the van, stripped to their waists, their backs, chests, and arms displaying numerous tattoos of unfamiliar geometric shapes and symbols. Laughing all the while, both young men are blatantly peeing in the middle of the freeway as several of their friends cheer them on from inside the van.

With their penises dangling in the breeze and the sunshine glittering on the gushing streams of their urine, the young men's faces glow with power. *Here! Look at us! We're strong enough to piss where you live, and you can't do shit!* And the motorists stacked up behind them are indeed intimidated. Instead of leaning on their horns or shouting curses, they quietly try to change lanes.

The rage of these young men is frightening. At the same time, there is something gutsy about what they are doing. What would happen if some cops showed up? *Who cares? Fuck them too!* Their freedom is on the line, yet the act of inviting danger—*bring it on*—is a source of pride to them.

And I can't help but admire their spirited reaction to the racism and economic oppression that blight their lives.

Earl has left a message ordering me to call him ASAP.

"Rob."

"Earl."

"There's trouble in paradise again.... It seems that old man Ballard filed a glowing report on Kevin Love. The freshman center with UCLA?"

"Sure. Stan Love's kid."

"Right. So Ballard says this and that, and he claimed that Love is a modern-day version of Bob Pettit and should be our top priority in the draft."

"That's pretty high praise. But that's why I'm here, right? To check out Love myself?"

"For sure," says Earl. "But I must confess that I'd never heard of Pettit, and that I had to Wikipedia him to find out how great a player he was in the fifties and sixties."

"A Hall-of-Famer. So what's the problem."

"It's Weiss. He never heard of Pettit either, and he read Ballard's report before I had a chance to research the guy. And Weiss went ballistic. Ballard was a senile old fool. Didn't he know that Andy Pettitte was a baseball player? A pitcher for the Yankees? It was time to fire Ballard. I mean, smoke was coming out of Weiss's ears."

"Then you eventually set him straight?"

"Of course. But now he insists that no college freshman could be as good as Pettit was, so he's still ready to shit-can Ballard."

"I get the picture. . . . Weiss doesn't know about this conversation, so when I send in my report on Love, I'm to emphasize the kid's positives and even make the same comparison that Ballard did. Sounds like Mission Possible."

"To save the old-man's job."

"Got it."

"By the way, Rob, I didn't get any stuff from you from either the all-star game or the Utah–Weber game."

"Yeah. I'm a little behind. I'll get those reports out before I leave for the game."

"Good, good," he says.

"Earl, I worry about you. I think you need a road trip to get away from that jerk-off."

"I'm okay. I'm okay. He's the one who needs the road trip. To Siberia. . . . Oh, shit. That's him on the other line. What the fuck does he want now? . . . Get your report on Love in right after the game, okay?"

"A-OK."

The scene at Pauley Pavilion, especially with the Bruins facing their crosstown archrivals from USC, is more intense than most other intercollegiate games. This is Hollywood, after all, so the usual potpourri of painted faces, blaring bands, and high-energy cheerleaders are augmented by several show-biz sideshows.

An Elvis impersonator is sitting in a front-row seat straddling the time line and opposite the team benches. He wears a white jumpsuit, dark sunglasses, and a glitzy gold-colored medallion that hangs around his neck. His black hair is slicked back, and a pair of phony sideburns are glued to the sides of his face. During a time-out, he jumps into the aisle and starts gyrating his pelvis as he holds a LET's GO BRUINS! sign above his head. The crowd, used to much slicker forgeries, blithely ignores him. During every time-out, the ersatz Elvis repeats his act. No matter how many times he pumps his hands to encourage a response, his practiced hysteria is utterly disregarded. Undeterred, he repeats his routine perhaps two dozen times during the course of the game.

There's a hugely pregnant woman in a UCLA T-shirt wiggling her hips and clapping her hands. Upon seeing her image projected on the large four-sided screen above the scoreboard, she lifts her shirt to reveal an orange basketball painted on her distended belly.

In addition to all of the over-the-top Boola Boola hullabaloo, there's also an LA Lakers presence on hand. There's Jerry Buss ensconced in the Lakers box, the wrinkled old lecher sitting paw-in-hand with his latest young and dazzlingly lovely high-priced escort. The other half of the Buss sandwich is another idiot son, Jimmy, who (like Weiss, Jr.) can't tell a screen/roll from a Kaiser roll. He's the heir apparent, who will one day take the reins of the franchise. Too bad Jimmy dotes on numbers even more than Weiss does. And here's what Jimmy has to say about my current profession: "NBA scouts don't know much more than the average fan."

Hurray for Hollywood, or as Hart Crane described it, "this Pollyanna greasepaint pinkpoodle paradise."

Like the Lakers home court in the Staples Center, the crowd lights in Pauley are never dimmed, even while the game is in progress. This, so the ringside glitterati are always clearly on display. There's Penny Marshall, Denzel Washington, Kobe and Shaq, and Jack Nicholson.

Also on hand is Susan White, the songbird and movie star famous for her All-American wholesomeness. As a Hollywood wag once said, "I knew her before she was a virgin." Yet it's also uncommon knowledge among the cognoscenti that Susan loves to fuck black hoopers. Indeed, she's often stationed in her usual front-row seat opposite the Lakers' bench with her legs slightly spread to show the brothers that she's wearing no panties. Rookies have been known to deliberately throw errant passes during warm-ups that they can stoop to fetch at her feet.

As if the perpetual din and commotion aren't sufficiently insufferable, the screens above the scoreboard periodically, during breaks in the game, show a "Sound-O-Meter" that ostensibly measures the decibel level of the crowd noise. Egged on by the projected close-up of Mickey Mouse clapping his four-fingered gloved hands, the very appearance of the meter induces a Pavlovian response from the assembled multitude. And even though a full roar produces a decibel level of approximately 95, the Sound-O-Meter invariably tops out at "999.99," a measurement that, if it were real, would instantly deafen everybody in the building.

But now down to saving Ballard's job, and perhaps my own. (Can I really believe that the golden safety net Freddy has offered is a real deal? Somehow, I'm not as thrilled or as optimistic as I was last night.)

Anyway . . .

KEVIN LOVE:
Born September 7, 1988,
in Santa Monica, CA . . . 6-10/255

His A-Level Skills:

Extraordinarily high basketball IQ.

Great hands. If he can touch a rebound, it's his. Is a relentless offensive rebounder.

Passwork is safe and solid, but his outlets were always on-target, and greatly facilitated UCLA's running game.

Sets sturdy screens, and knows how and when to slip the screen.

When teammates penetrate the lane, is adept at moving into open spaces and being available for drop passes.

When his feet are set, he's a knock-down shooter with legit 3-point range.

Has a picture-perfect lefty baby hook.

Conscientiously and effectively boxes out his man on virtually every relevant situation.

Establishes excellent initial position on defense.

His B-Level Skills:

Uses his upper body (especially his off-arm) to establish and maintain post position. In the pros, he'll need to use his butt more.

Not a shot blocker, but manages to move into the body of any shooter he can make contact with.

Goes to hoop with power, but in straight lines.

His C-Level Skills:

Not particularly explosive in the pivot. His initial dribble down there rarely gains him any ground or forces his defender to move.

He does show in defense of high screens, but is frequently too far away from the action to force the ball handler to fan away from the basket.

As good as his hands are, he has limited retrieval range—at best, a two- or two-and-a-half-space rebounder.

His D-Level Skills:

Has to gather himself before he jumps and is therefore relatively slow off the floor. Compensates with his adhesive hands and the space he creates.

Likewise has to hump up before shooting a righty jump hook.

Has no change-of-direction moves.

Missed badly when pulling up and shooting on the move.

When an opponent turns and faces, Love's body was too erect to make the kind of quick lateral move that was required.

Made no attempt to deny incoming passes to any of his opponents who set up in the pivot. Was satisfied to belly-up and depend entirely on his strength.

Was often caught with his back to the ball and was beaten on backdoor cuts.

Defensive balance and lateral quickness are serious concerns.

His F-Level Skills:

Plods rather than runs, which makes him a liability in transition defense.

Once he's beaten on a play, tends to become a spectator.

NBA Projection:

Needs some razzle-dazzle in his offense, and to quicken his shot release. All of these are imminently doable.

Will need to have opponents well scouted to play adequate defense. Can see him as developing into a career flopper.

Needs two years of steady playing time under the tutelage of an experienced big-man coach. Also needs to work with a smart, unselfish point guard and be the locus of a Love-centric offense. But his work ethic is admirable, as are his toughness and general athleticism.

His intelligence and eagerness to improve should not be underestimated.

His peers and his coaches say he's an agreeable chap.

Under the right conditions, he has the goods to eventually become be an all-star.

Suggestion:

A mid-lottery pick whom we should seriously consider.

Final Evaluation:

Kevin Love is a stronger, slower version of Andy Pettitte.

I ignore the tinseled temptations of LA's night life in favor of writing up and e-mailing all of my overdue reports, soaking in a hot tub with a book (*The Peach Stone,* Horgan's selected short stories), a glass of wine, but with nary a "thou" in sight.

In the morning, it's on to my last stop on this trip—Oklahoma City.

CHAPTER FIFTEEN

I always suffer a minor fit of anxiety whenever I'm on a plane that either arrives or departs from Oklahoma City. Perhaps that's because, as far as I know, the Will Rogers Airport is the only one that's named after someone who died in a plane crash.

OKC . . . The wildest West, where even the shortest drink of water proudly wears a ten-gallon hat. Where the heat and humidity are so viscid that several pedestrians hold small, battery-powered fans in front of their faces. Where the tragic destruction of the federal building has made the citizens both jumpy and fraudulently cheerful.

Twenty years ago, the black gold was gushing hereabouts and the biggest hats would think nothing of chartering a plane, flying to Paris for lunch, and then immediately flying back home. Nowadays, the exploratory, seesawing oil rigs are still ubiquitous, pecking into just about every uninhabited parcel of land on the outskirts of town like gigantic metallic insects. But the big-time thrills and the big-time drills are gone, and displays of ostentatious wealth are now deemed to be unseemly.

My preference is to keep my computer in a coma while I'm traveling and my cell phone shut down when I'm flying, which is why Earl usually has messages waiting for me at the hotel. "Yo, Rob. We get in about six. Will call and get together for eats."

Yipes! I forgot that the Nets are playing the Thunder tomorrow night—and that Earl is with the team on his way to the NBA's all-star weekend extravaganza this weekend in Oakland. Fortunately I'll be up in Norman, scouting the Oklahoma–Kansas game so I'll be spared the agony of watching NJ versus OKC, two of the worst teams in the league.

Both the Sooners and the Jayhawks are powerhouse teams, but my focus will be on Blake Griffin, the home team's All-American power forward. The consensus is that either DeLeon Johnson or

Griffin will be the top pick in the upcoming draft.

So while waiting for Earl, I read, snooze, gobble a chef's salad in the dining room, and peruse the NBA box scores. It's relaxing, but boring.

Later, Earl's summons wakes me up. "Hup, hup. Get down here. I'm hungry."

We're both wearing shorts—his are red plaid, mine are cutoff jeans—sneakers with socks, and short-sleeved collared shirts sans any identifying logo. "How about barbecue?" he proposes.

But my belches and *grepts* still recall overtones of last night's repast, so I decline.

"Okay, then how about Mexican?"

"Never again!"

"Chinese?"

"In the desert?"

"Okay, Rob. You make the call."

"Downstairs in the lounge they have decent All-American food and very cold beer."

We squeeze into a pair of too-small chairs behind a corner table and study the menu as we listen to the Rodgers Family play surprisingly tasty country-western tunes: "The Streets of Baltimore" written by Gram Parsons, Charley Pride's "San Antone," then "Easy Chair" by Bob Dylan. Ray and Gayle Rodgers are better musicians than they should be, an attractive middle-aged couple wearing matching blue cowperson outfits with the requisite white fringes and white hats. Their tuneful guitar playing is artificially enhanced by a bass machine and a drum machine.

"So," says Earl, not lifting his eyes from the menu, "what'll you have?"

"More Dylan."

He looks up. "What?"

"Never mind. . . . Chicken pot pie and a salad. You?"

"I've heard about chicken-fried steak, but I've never had it. What do you think?"

"It's disgusting. A thin slice of meat, heavily breaded, then fried and smothered in a gooey white sauce. Goes well with an Alka-Seltzer cocktail."

"Sounds great."

These requests, plus two Coors drafts, are relayed to a buxom waitress. As soon as she leaves, Earl says this: "Weiss saw your report on Kevin Love before I could delete your Andy Pettitte zinger. I thought we were both in the shitter, you and me."

I shrug. With Fat Freddy's offer in the bag, what did I really care. "Earl, you were always a step slow on defense."

He's offended. "Really? Is that what you really thought? Was that the book on me? Really?"

"No, you dickhead. Defense was never your problem."

He's relieved. "Anyway, you won't believe how Weiss reacted."

"Do we qualify for unemployment insurance?"

"Always a fucking wiseass. . . . What he said was that he was happy to see that you never heard of that other Pettit guy either. So now you're back on his Christmas-card list."

Our meals are delivered, Earl takes one bite of his steak, and says, "Delicious."

After some noisy masticating, and beer swilling, Earl says, "What'll we do if we do get canned?"

"We? You're cool, right?"

"Yes, as long as Weiss gets Johnson. When do you see him next?"

"In two weeks in Chicago, but he is what he is. A selfish, extremely talented airhead."

"Whatever. Ours is just to do, or die."

"You surprise me, Earl. I didn't know you read Tennyson."

"Who? Oh, that? It's a snippet of something I heard on some public-TV program that my wife made me watch."

"Ah. It's reassuring to know that you're still only semiliterate."

"That's your trouble, Rob. You're too fucking literate for your own good."

"'Let ignorance talk as it will, learning has its value.'"

"Did you just make that up?"

"Jean de La Fontaine."

"Never heard of him."

"Not much on defense, but his offensive was truly offensive."

"Rob, what the fuck are you talking about?"

"When I find out, you'll be the first to know."

Shit! Am I going to get drunk again?

Earl wipes the plate with his fingers and sucks up every last bit. More beer arrives and is duly inhaled. "You know what I'd like to do if Weiss fires me?" he says "There's a health club on the market back home in Nevada City that I'd like to buy. Fuck! Maybe I'll quit and buy it anyway. You could be the greeter. The glad-hander."

Then I tell him about Fat Freddy's promise and my golden future, but he just laughs.

"Rob, I can't believe that you were taken in by that crook."

"What're you talking about? The guy's a straight arrow."

"Sure, and I've got a bridge to sell you. . . . Where do you think he gets his money from?"

"His barbecue joint. The place is crowded to the rafters and there's a line a block long. . . . I saw it last night."

"Sure, the restaurant makes money, Rob, bit not *that* kind of money. The big bucks come from a medical laboratory he owns in Denver that does work for Medicare and Medicaid. No lie. What they do is run more tests on the blood or urine or tumors or whatever than the doctors prescribe. Then he sends the bloated bills to the federal government. It's a scam, Rob. I'm telling you, the guy's a crook."

"Where did you hear this bullshit?"

"I played with a couple of his guys in France, and one of them comes from Denver. It's not such a big secret, Rob. And if *I* know, then the feds sure do. Sooner or later, Freddy's gonna lose a lot of weight in the slammer."

"Is this true?"

"I swear on my children's heads."

"You don't have any children."

"Okay. Then where's a knife? I'll write something in blood."

I'm devastated. Left without a wisecrack. Without a future.

"Rob, let the asshole trade the whole fucking team for the rights to Johnson. What do we care? All we can do is what we can do."

"Which is to be totally useless. To do or die."

"Too bad we can't rig the Ping-Pong machine in the lottery the way the corner of the envelope was bent so the Knicks could draft Patrick Ewing back in 1985. Hey, maybe Fat Freddy knows somebody who could get the job done!"

"Fuck you. Go ahead and kick me when I'm down."

"Hey, even when the ball is kicked, there's still fourteen seconds left on the shot clock. Don't worry, Rob. It's not a problem until it's a problem."

He staggers slightly as he stands. "How many beers did we have, Robbo, me lad?"

"Probably too many."

"All right, then. It's beddy-bye for me. I'll see you tomorrow morning?"

"For what?"

"Instead of a shootaround, Greg is going to have a video session. Their last game against the Thunder. Ten o'clock in his room. I'll buzz you about eight thirty and we'll have breakfast."

"Deal."

I am trapped inside my own skull. My teeth are shut and grinding. My nose is tornado alley and to be avoided. There is a painting of a snow-capped mountain hanging from my uvula. I take my meals from scraps of food lodged in the fleshy folds at the base of my tongue. My source of water is a chronic postnasal drip. I hear dim voices coming from my brain. Maybe it's some other poor wretch trapped in here too. So I crawl through my sinuses to investigate—to rescue him. As I approach my brain cavity, one voice becomes intelligible. "I am not a crook," it says. Again and again. "I am not a crook."

In the redly glowing darkness, I can discern a boxish shape perched on some kind of bony prominence where my brain is supposed to be. It's an old-fashioned voting booth, enclosed on four sides by black curtains, and the voice seems to be emanating from inside. "I am not a crook." I wriggle under the hem of the nearest curtain, and there, speaking into a large bullhorn ("I am not a crook!"), is Nixon's head on top of Freddy's fat body.

I've got to get out of here!

Yes, yes. I've heard all the rumors. There's supposed to be another opening at the very top of my skull, where a flowering lotus blossom grows and reaches into heaven. But the walls are slick with blood.

Then I hear a scream of pain.. Unmistakable. A somewhat human scream.

Is it Nixon? Or Freddy?

But of course, it's only me.

And I wake up a nanosecond before the phone rings.

"Hup, hup," says Earl. "Meet you in the coffee shop in fifteen minutes."

CHAPTER SIXTEEN

Earl is slopping his way through the goo of Eggs Ranchero when I join him for breakfast. He's also reading the financial section of *The Daily Oklahoman.*

"Caught in the act," I say, after ordering coffee to wind my clock and oatmeal to sweep through my bowels. "You're supposed to be reading the sports section."

He blushes. "I already did that. The Lakers beat Boston. Miami beat Chicago in OT. Neither one of us got fired.... Anyway, just checking out my portfolio...."

"You have a portfolio?"

"Yeah. So should you. My broker says to buy now when everything is low and then—"

"Hold on. You have a fucking broker?"

"Of course." He flicks a hand at the newspaper. "There's no way I could understand this shit on my own. Hey, you scout ballplayers. My guy scouts corporations. There's millions of dollars involved in what you both do."

Who is this guy? I've always prided myself on discovering the essence of someone's makeup by watching him play. And Earl was competitive, unselfish, intelligent, compassionate, a regular Joe who saw and played the game correctly.... But can he still be all these things and want to be rich?

"Is that what you want to be, Earl? A millionaire?"

"Why the fuck not? Isn't that the real American dream?"

"Let me ask you this, then.... What would you rather be? A millionaire? Or the general manager of a championship team?"

"To be honest, Rob? Yes, I'd like to be part of a championship organization, but Weiss has killed something inside of me. My passion for the game. My sense of loyalty. Of justice. I don't know.... I'd chose the money."

We both stare at the food that a waiter sets in front of me. Too embarrassed to look at each other. Earl's truthful admission pains both of us.

"What about you?" he finally says. "The money or the ring?"

"I know what you mean about how Weiss ruins everything good and pure about the game. The ring, for your sake. And for my sake, too, but only if I was allowed to make a significant contribution."

"The money, then?"

"I really don't know. I'm afraid of myself, of the money changing the way I see things. My priorities. Shit! Maybe even my politics."

"Money is power, Rob. The rich run the country."

"They sure do. That's why Uncle Sam's Ass, which is supposed to be a democracy, is really a plutocracy. . . ."

We're both increasingly uncomfortable and eager to change the subject, to return to our bozos-on-the-same-bus connection.

"That reminds me of something that I could never figure out," he says brightly. "If Pluto can talk and Goofy can't, what happens when they get together? Maybe Goofy is just playing dumb. Maybe he's an undercover spy in the people world."

"In the duck-and-mouse world."

He forces a laugh.

"It's okay, Earl. I forgive you for wanting to be a rich power monger."

"Fuck you, too."

"Anyway, I've been thinking—"

"Let me be the first to congratulate you, Rob."

"—about the future of this fucked up franchise, and I have a plan."

Now he's interested. "Let's hear it."

"Okay, here's what we already have: Rodney Betts, a center who can't do anything except score. Darrell Harman, a point who can penetrate but can't run an offense. Ralph Layne, a power forward who can rebound and defend. Tyrone Howard, a two-guard who can shoot the lights out but can't defend or create off the bounce. Kevin Brownbill is a slasher at the three-spot, but has no room to operate with Betts clogging up the middle. So here's what I propose: Forget about DeLeon Johnson. . . . No, no . . . I understand. Hear me out. . . . First of all, we have to see where we draft. If we can, even if it's number one, we go for Kevin Love or Blake Griffin. Now,

I've seen Griffin on TV and I'm going to see him tonight, but even though Griffin is a better athlete, Love is much more advanced in a lot of ways. Plus he can shoot the shit out of it. So, let's say we draft Love. Or if they're both gone by the time we pick, then we go for Jateik Murphy from Duke. Okay, in the second round we go for this kid from Saint Joe's, Isaiah Jones. Big, strong, shot blocker, great footwork, eats rebounds, has one go-to move inside, looks to have a decent touch, runs like a deer—"

"But Weiss will never—"

"Hold your horses, Earl. Let me finish. . . . Now we have a dominating front line. If we can get Love and Jones, we start them both. That's right, two rookies. Betts plays about twenty-five minutes and is the go-to scorer on the second unit. Howard starts so he can stretch the defense. With Betts on the bench, Brownbill can get up and go. Sign a free-agent wing who can create, and one who can defend. Preferably one guy who can do both. Pump up the pace on offense, which we can do because Love and Jones will wipe the glass clean. . . . And if we can run-gun-stun-and-have-fun, Brownbill will be an absolute bitch, and Harman won't have to struggle to facilitate a grind-it-out half-court offense. We'll also need a backup point who can play slowdown ball to maximize Betts in the low post. All the other guys we have are good enough role players. If we can put this scenario into action, we'll be a playoff team in two years and a legit contender in another year. Now, I don't know what the contractual situations are with these guys. That's your department."

"Betts is locked up for four more years. Harman for two years. Layne will be a restricted free agent. Howard an unrestricted free agent. The other guys in the rotation . . . Cooper, Mangorie, Brennan? We have team options on all of them."

"Good enough," I say. "The brothers of the bench will do for the meantime. . . . So that's it. My master plan."

"Sounds great, Rob, but as I was trying to say, there's no way Weiss will buy it. You know how daffy he is over Johnson, and signing the kind of free agents you're talking about would be pricey. . . . I mean, who? Tony Allen? Matt Barnes? Trevor Ariza? Rudy Gay? Caron Butler? Wilson Chandler? . . ."

"I really like Chandler."

"Me, too. . . . Who else will be available? . . . Baron Davis? Jamal Crawford? Willie Green . . . ?"

"I like Green, too. In fact, he's the guy I'd go hardest after."

"Maybe. . . . Who else? Anthony Parker?"

"Another guy I like."

"Chris Duhon can back up Harman and won't cost a lot. . . . I don't know. There's a shitload of possibilities and most of them would cost a shitload of money. But it all doesn't mean shit if Weiss won't sign off. Which he won't.

"Earl. What if we sit down with him? Just the three of us. And we put our jobs on the line. If he does what we suggest and we don't make the playoffs in two years, then he can fire the both of us."

"Fuck that. My contract is for three more years after this."

"So take a chance, Earl. You're gambling on the stock market for some bullshit reasons. Why not put your ass where your heart is? Have faith that the two of us know what it takes to win in this league. Don't be such a fucking chalk eater. I mean, he can fire you tomorrow anyway, right?"

"Right."

"Forget about Johnson. What does Weiss really, really want?"

"To win."

"And that's how we approach him. We've got the guaranteed blueprint."

"Let me think about it. . . . You finished eating that muck? Anyway, it's time for the video session. If I know Greg, he'll fine us if we come late."

In addition to a bedroom and spacious living room, Greg Dodge's suite includes a kitchen equipped with a half refrigerator, a microwave, a small two-burner electric hot plate, and a dinette set with four chairs. Not to mention the walk-in clothing closet and the sixty-inch TV with built-in DVR. In other words, standard digs for head coaches on the road.

There's Greg in his official Nets sweats. He stands about five foot ten, but has terrific posture and swears that he's a six-footer. His daily power walks and his avoidance of fatty foods have kept his belly flat at age forty-seven, but have failed to conserve what used to be a full head of jet-black hair. A short, bristly beard and 'stache surround his fleshy lips and are meant to divert attention from the long scraggly hair carefully combed over and secured with some kind of glop to his otherwise bald pate. Greg is a smiley kind of guy, but under duress he unsheathes a ruthlessly sharp tongue. To his credit, he's not afraid to verbally abuse even his best players.

Except for his stubborn nature and his insistence on calling each and every offensive sequence, he's one of the league's best X's-and-O's guys.

His SOP for scouting opponents follows the league-wide norm: Responsibility for composing scouting reports for the other twenty-nine teams is divided unequally among his four assistants (who study game videos and eyeball "their" teams once every two to three weeks and ASAP after a major trade), and is abetted by two advance scouts, who are always on the road. Once he receives the respective reports, Dodge devises a game plan, which he is about to divulge to his players, all of whom lounge on the cushy couches and armchairs in the living room, with the rookies compelled to sit stiffly on the hard-backed dinette chairs. Most of the players munch on fast-food breakfast sandwiches fetched for them by the rooks. As the saying goes, "That's why God created rookies."

Dodge ignores the players, as he does Earl and me, and clicks on the edited video of the most recent NJ–OKC game, a sloppy game won in New Jersey by the visitors. He keeps up a steady narrative as the game unfolds:

"Here . . . good job helping on that screen, Ralph. Extension, balance . . . See that, Rod? . . . Notice how Durant doesn't like to be bumped. See? The pass instead of the shot? . . . Here's Westbrook with another bad decision, another turnover. Overpenetrating and getting caught in the air with the ball. Instead of making that ridiculous pass that led to a runout. . . . Good hustle, Ty. . . . He should have stuck the ball up his ass. . . . Chin the ball after that rebound, Rod. Stick those 'bows out there. Nobody wants to play defense with his face, right? . . . Look it, Darrell, here's the same fucked-up mistake that Westbrook just made. What the fuck were you planning on doing with the ball in there? Blasting off into space and dunking on the way down? One dribble too many. Just come to a jump stop and see what's what. . . . There . . . Ralph was wide open, but you didn't even look. Should have been a dunk and two points for us instead of two for them. . . . Rodney, it's okay to pass the ball out when you don't have the position you want, but look . . . you get resettled and then pass it out again? I mean, do you want the fucking ball in there or not. For shit's sake, what're you? Four, five inches bigger than Collison? . . . Late on that rotation . . . Cut tighter on that screen . . . If you're gonna foul the guy, Brownie, make sure he can't get the shot off. . . . Box the fucking guy out, Rod. Giving up an offensive rebound on a free throw is a felony. . . . No, no, Coop. You're on the wrong side. . . ."

Meanwhile, several players yawn, sigh, fidget, and look everywhere except the screen. But they snap to attention when Dodge lets one sequence play out in silence: In a scrap for a rebound late in the first quarter, Thabo Sefolosha turns an ankle when he lands on Ralph Layne's foot. But we have the ball, so OKC can't call a time-out. Also they don't opt to stop the action with a deliberate foul since the score is still tight and they are over the foul limit. So Sefolosha manages to hop back across the time line and keeps hopping on his right leg. Since Sefolosha is guarding Enzo Mangiore, Dodge calls for a 1-4 clear-out to let Mangiore take advantage of his crippled defender. While Sefolosha keeps hopping, Mangiore is totally confused and merely dribbles in place. The appropriate play is simply to drive past Sefolosha, get into the paint, and either shoot or find an open teammate. A no-brainer. However, after bouncing the ball for a few more counts, Mangiore lets fly (and badly misses) a long 3-pointer.

Dodge shows the same play three times in succession, not saying a word. Until finally, he says this: "And that, Enzo, is why Italy has never won a war."

Several players are seized with such convulsive laughter that they roll off their seats and flop to the floor. When the hysteria simmers down into chuckles, Dodge clicks off the machine.

"The rest of the game brought me to tears," he says. "I'll spare you the pain."

Then he distributes the printed version of the game plan. "Bus leaves here at four thirty for rookies and five for vets. Remember, we're in the central time zone. Be ready, guys. Just one more game before the all-star break. Rod will be traveling to Golden State with Earl here sometime tomorrow. Congratulations, Rod, but make sure to connect with Earl for the details. And some advice, Rod? Don't you dare get hurt. . . . All right, see you guys later."

Since I'm rarely in the same place at the same time as they are, none of the players have any idea who I am. Sure, I was an interested spectator at the beginning of the preseason training camp—just another faceless civilian who couldn't do anything for them. I do get a few impersonal nods on the grounds that my being there must have some relevance.

Then, with Earl conferring with Rodney Betts, and Dodge laughing it up with his assistants—no doubt about the players' reaction to his comment on Mangiore's blunder—I'm on my own.

A stroll around the beautifully landscaped two hundred acres of the main campus reminds me that intercollegiate football has always been the number-one sport in Oklahoma. That's because Bud Wilkinson and Barry Switzer coached OU's football teams to a total of seven NCAA championships. A small statue of Wilkinson sits outside the football stadium, but there's the Barry Switzer Center, which houses a museum featuring many artifacts and honoring many personages that represent the school's innumerable athletic successes, as well as the most technologically advanced training facility in the country.

For sure, the OKC Thunder routinely play before SRO crowds, but that can be explained by the blood-lust rivalry between Oklahoma and Texas. Counting football, basketball, hockey, and baseball, the Lone Star State boasts eight professional franchises, while the recently arrived Thunder represents Oklahoma's first and only pro team. Accordingly, Okies flock to Thunder games to prove that they are big-leaguers.

For sure, OU's hoopers achieved considerable success under Billy Tubbs, reaching the NCAA championship game in 1985. Indeed, Tubbs's hot-footed game plan was designed to appeal to football fans who craved furious action. Tubbs once stated that he'd rather have one of his teams lead the country in scoring than win an NCAA title.

In any case, the campus is quite impressive. Tall, majestic buildings that Frank Lloyd Wright described " as the Cherokee Gothic Style." Incredibly beautiful coeds casually perambulating the maze of lanes, walkways, squares, and circles. Sturdy young men walking more purposely—most of them wearing some kind of pin or sweater linking them to one of the school's three-dozen fraternities.

I cruise through the Fred Jones Junior School of Art and Museum. I'm not much of an art maven, but I can't help being impressed by the collection of Impressionists—the Gauguins, Monets, Pissarros, Renoirs, and Van Goghs. Except for a handful of students making pen-and-ink copies of the masters, and a suspicious security guard who tailgates me, the solitude is bracing. At the same time, all of those vibrant colors and radical brushstrokes make me weary.

So I retrace my steps and find a quiet bench under a shady tree and amuse myself with one of my favorite fantasy games—improving the traditional nicknames of college athletic teams, what I like to call "rectifying."

The "Sooners" rushed into the Oklahoma Territory before the land rush officially commenced in 1889. They proceeded to prematurely stake claims on the prime acreage, patently illegal moves that were quickly legitimized by the new state's legislature.

Here's another shady historical note: The State capital was originally Ponca City, until a group of gunman forcibly removed all of the official documents and transferred them to Oklahoma City.

In any event, instead of being known as the Oklahoma Sooners, I propose a change to the Okla-Homa Sexuals.

More:

Brown Nosers

Coe Dependents

Beaver Lickety Splits
Baylor Elgins
Boston Massacres
Pennsylvania Six-Five-Thousands
Pace Mannions
Mercy Kevorkians
Oral Roberts Anals
Seton Hall Monitors
Duke of Earls
Fairleigh Dickinson Dickindaughters
Idaho Potatoes
Long Island Expressways
Marshall Dillons
Missouri Compromises
Northwestern Passages
St. Francis Sissies
St. John's Worts
U. S. Naval Academy Bellybuttons
Butler Didits

Then it's game time in the Lloyd Noble Center where the manic antics of the fans of both teams make the goings-on in Salt Lake City seem as docile as a senior citizens' picnic. Students shrieking, jumping up and down, shaking fists, the normal undergraduate drunken madness amplified by a red-eyed rage. Imagine a bloodthirsty mob of antagonists at spring break in Fort Lauderdale. I feared that some trivial event—a few blatantly biased calls by the officials—would instigate a murderous brawl.

Anyway, here's what Blake Griffin showed me:

An incredible athlete with an excellent NBA body—six-ten, 250. Quick, strong hands. A star-toucher who's unusually quick off the floor.

When given space, can catch, drive, and dunk with power. Executes quick, tight spins, especially when on the right box, where his go-to move is a stationary dribble with a head fake into the middle, then spinning for a baby hook over his left shoulder. This is an NBA-quality move.

Throws accurate outlet passes.

Reacts slowly but makes simple passes out of double-teams.

Loves to slip screen/rolls, catch lobs, and dunk. Rarely makes acceptable contact on his screens.

Is an authentic Dunkenstein.

Rarely fights off his defender to gain and maintain optimal position in the low post. When he tries to do so, uses his arms and elbows but not his hips, shoulders, and/or ass.

When he does seal his defenders, never moves to meet entry passes. Consequently, several of these are tipped away.

Is clearly discomfited when fronted.

Seems to make up his mind what move to make before he catches the ball. Winds up repeatedly trying to force his dribble in a crowd.

Passive on defense. Plays behind his man in the low post. Shows on screens, then wanders into no-man's land. Has absolutely no presence on defense.

Fails to hustle in transition defense. On one play, he drifted downcourt without attempting to locate the ball, and a lay-up was scored behind his back.

Poor footwork when shooting jumper leaves him off-balance and having to make release adjustments on every shot. Plus, his release is much too wristy. Can't hit two consecutive jumpers to get into heaven.

Quicker and infinitely more athletic than Kevin Love, but has a severely retarded basketball IQ. Will undoubtedly improve all of his weaknesses and probably has the goods to eventually become an all-star. But the odds are long that he'll ever be a winner.

The game is close, but with five minutes left I take advantage of a time-out to get the hell out of there. I even change my plans and get a red-eye flight back to Albany.

Looking forward to four days of peace and, hopefully, love in Woodstock.

HALF TIME

CHAPTER SEVENTEEN

Beep . . . Beep . . . Beep . . .
" . . . . "
"Hello? Freddy? This is Rob Lassner. . . ."
" . . . . "
"Hello? Freddy? Is anybody there? You told me I could call any—"
Click.

I sniff each item and stuff only the most malodorous ones into my gym bag, drive into town to combine a visit to the Laundromat with another time-killing exploration of the library across the road. The Woodstock Wash 'n' Dry is housed in a long, low white-shingled building streaked with black blotches of seasonal grime and shit-colored drippings from the rusted rain gutters. Laundro thyself.

Inside, a row of large, glass-eyed Cyclopean machines tremble as their insides surge, gurgle, and spin. A line of battered and unoccupied folding chairs sits opposite the washers and dryers. It's hot, damp, and noisy in here. I insert a dollar into a vending machine mounted on the near wall and purchase a small box of laundry detergent.

To my dismay, only one washing machine is empty. To my delight, guess who's gently placing her dirty dainties into the adjacent machine . . . Woodstock's poet laureate, Nancy Sanger.

She's wearing a bulky gray sweatshirt that bears this message in blocky black letters across the front: SWEATSHIRT. Blue jeans, red kneesocks, and black Birkenstocks complete her attire. Her grayish-almost-white hair is fashioned into the braids that I recall from the poetry reading, and as before she wears no discernible trace of makeup. Casual and comfortable as she appears at first glance, she also retains an aura of dignity, of self-confident beauty.

Be still my foolish heart.

She closes the round door, pushes the appropriate buttons, and walks past me as though I were invisible. Ah, but one of her garments is lying on the floor. A rather sizable black bra.

I am seized by equal measures of lust and intimidation.

I pick it up and hold it delicately by a clasp with my thumb and forefinger as though it were a dead, but still dangerous rodent. "Ummm . . . excuse me?"

She turns and affects a look of suspicion and annoyance, but a slight quivering of one corner of her mouth once again betrays a sweet vulnerability.

"Is this yours?"

"No," she says with a twinkle in her eyes. "It's actually a two-pack yarmulke with chin straps."

Handing it to her, I say, "It's not my size anyway."

"Thanks." She accepts the bra, pushes a Pause button, and places it gently in the machine. Meanwhile, I toss my stuff, gym bag and all, through the porthole opening.

She feels obligated to reward my good deed by finding something friendly and quasi-polite to say.

"You put your colored and your white together" is what she comes up. "You must not be married."

"I used to be, but my ex was even lazier than me."

She nods her head and shows me the slightest curl of a grin, before she bustles out of the building.

The library is a large white cottage with a spacious lawn that fronts on Tinker Street, Woodstock's main drag. While it services a very small population, its shelves are filled with a fascinating assortment of books. Inside, to the left of the front door, several patrons peck away at a half-dozen computers I deposit a few books on the return cart (it's a point of honor with me never to keep a book past its due date), then make a beeline for the New Books section in order to fortify myself for my brief home stand as well as my next road trip.

Well, lookee here. A new book by my favorite hoop-o-scribe. *No Blood No Foul* by Charley Rosen. Uh-oh. It's about a referee. Especially since Rosen coached in the CBL several years before I did and was infamous for not only routinely leading the league in techs, but also serving several suspensions for his over-the-top verbal abuse of the refs.

Okay. That's one, but I need at least four or five more. Novels, political histories, biographies, whatever.

Egad. There she is again. In the Fiction section, perusing the G-through-I novelists.

Ambling over, I say "Hi," with as much ease as I can muster. "The Poetry section is in the next room."

She's startled. "Oh, it's you . . . Yes. The Poetry section. I know."

"By the way, I really liked the poem you read last week. It was lyrical, accessible, and meaningful."

"Oh. You like poetry?"

"I used to read a lot more of it than I do now. Back in school, you know? But I always felt that poetry was meant to be heard and not read. Like Chaucer reading *The Canterbury Tales* at court. Which is why I enjoyed your reading so much."

"Wait a minute. What do you know about Chaucer?"

I was determined to show off..

> "'Whan that Aprille with his shoures soote
> The droghte of Marche hath perced to the roote,
> And bathed every veyne in swich licour,
> Of which vertu engendreed is the flour;
> Whan Zephirus eek with his swete breeth
> Inspired hath in every holt and heeth
> The tendre croppes, and the yonge sonne
> Hath in the Ram his halfe cours y-ronne,
> And smale fowles maken melodye,
> That slepen al the night with open ye,
> (So priketh hem nature in hir corages:
> Than longen folk to goon on pilgrimages, . . .'"

"I'm impressed," she says. "Where does that all come from?"

"I was an English major with a concentration in medieval English literature."

"So you're not just another guitar-playing, drug-dealing, solid citizen of the Woodstock Nation."

"Not me."

"Anyway," she says as she picks Graham Greene's *The Quiet American* from the stack, reads the back cover and the inside flaps, then replaces it.

Meanwhile, having expended my theoretically most impressive poetic tidbit, I have nothing left to say. But I don't want to leave, and I can't.

Next, she inspects and rejects *A Prayer for Owen Meany* by John Irving.

"May I make a suggestion?" I ask.

Once again I've startled her. Haven't I already been dismissed? But I take her silence for acceptance, and pluck *Death of the Fox* from the shelf. "It's by George Garrett and, in my opinion, is one of the two best American novels since Faulkner. It's about Sir Walter Raleigh."

"What's the other one? The other best American novel since Faulkner?"

"*Wild in the Country.* J. R. Salamanca. But they don't have it here."

She hefts the book and says, "Okay. I'll try it. It had better be good, because once I start a book, I have to finish it. I owe it to the writer. Even if the book is awful."

"I guarantee that you'll—"

She flexes her chin in the general direction of the book in my hand, so I show her the cover: a photo of a striped shirt, a lanyard, and a hand holding a whistle.

"What's that about? I don't understand. . . ."

"Basketball."

"Oh." She crinkles her nose as though I were about to hand her a dead skunk. "Sports. I hate sports."

"Why's that?"

We walk in tandem to the checkout desk, then she pushes open the outside door and holds it ajar for me. The day is frosty with steel-gray clouds promising snow as we walk slowly back to the Laundromat.

"Because ," she says, "it's the secular opium of the masses. A reason for boorish behavior. Much ado about zilch."

"It is indeed all of that, but only if you look at it from one perspective. To truly appreciate a sporting event, you have to ignore the fans and the media hype. A game qua game is an unscripted drama with real people in real time. A single-chance, spontaneous test to see which players have courage and which do not. Which of them can demonstrate grace under pressure. . . . . Hemingway."

"Of course."

"I mean, my particular sport is basketball. At the highest level of competition, it's played by the best athletes in the world. When it's played the right way, it's like ballet with defense."

Both of our wash loads are done, and I follow her lead in moving the clean, damp clothing to a pair of side-by-side dryers.

"What else?" she says.

"What else what?"

"Do you have a real job?"

"Yes. I'm a college scout for the New Jersey Nets."

"I don't understand. I've vaguely heard of the New Jersey Nets, but what is it?"

"They're a professional basketball team. I watch college basketball games and evaluate the players. Whether or not certain players can succeed as pros. If the Nets should draft them or invite them to be part of our summer league team in Las Vegas."

"What are you talking about?"

"It's complicated."

We sit mutely side-by-side until her bras, along with her other garments, are dried and fluffed. Meanwhile my drawers, socks, sweats, and jeans are still spinning and clacking.

Quickly folding her things and gently placing them in a large straw basket, she says this before she leaves: "Why don't you take me to dinner sometime and explain the complications. I'm at zero-eight-hundred. 'Bye."

"Yes. Nice talking . . ."

But she's already gone.

Beep ,,, beep ,,, beep ...   "............"

"Freddy, are you there? Is this the right number for Freddy Fletcher? Three-oh-one-seven-five-two-one-three-six-nine?"

". . . . ."

"Freddy, this is Rob Lassner. Remember, we . . . ?"

Click.

I finally figure out that the number Nancy gave me—0800—is prefaced by the 679 that covers all Woodstock exchanges. Now, about that "sometime" quasi dinner invitation . . .

Beep . . . Beep . . . Beep . . . Beep . . .

"Yes?"

"Ummm . . . Nancy? This is Rob."

"Who? Never heard of you. How did you get my number? Please don't call—"

"No, no. Rob Lassner. The tall guy? We met at the Laundromat? And the library?"

"Oh, yes. The medieval maven."

"That's me. . . . Anyway, you said something about my taking you out for dinner? And I was thinking that maybe—"

"Oh, I've thought it over and I've changed my mind."

"Oh?"

Shit! Piss! And fuck me!

"Yes, I really don't like being out in a crowd. I only do those horrible readings because, as I said, poetry is meant to be heard."

"Oh?"

"So I think it best if you come over here for dinner."

"OH!"

"Is there anything you don't eat? Maybe you're a veggie? Or a vegan? Or a macro-wacko?"

"No. no. Whatever you fix will be fine."

"All right. How about Sunday, then. about six?"

"Sounds great   "See you then. I'm at Three Ratterman Road. Right off Route 375, on the left just before the golf course."

"Right. But should I bring—?"

Click.

With a big yummy and a hearty *Yahoo!*

For the next half hour, I briskly pace the floor of my tiny shack shouting her name. "Nancy! Nancy! Fancy Nancy!"

Girl of my dreams! Sunshine and moonlight of my life!

Umm. Hold on there, big fella. There you go again. Falling in love with love. Falling for make-believe.

Right. I'll be calm but expectant. Bright-eyed but not bushy-tailed. Confident but not cocky.

Then it hits me!

Six o'clock Sunday is the tip-off for the NBA All-Star Game, a bullshit, three-ring circus that I now have a legitimatge reason for ignoring.

A brainchild of Walter Kennedy, owner of the Boston Celtics, the first ever was held on March 2, 1951, in Boston. Back then, most sports fans considered the fledgling NBA, with its rapidly folding and shifting franchises, to be strictly a curiosity—and its newfangled all-star game was dismissed as a paltry imitation of baseball's midsummer classic. The 10,094 who did witness that initial contest were part of a comparatively small coterie of pro-basketball die-hards. While the game itself wasn't very close (the East led 53–42 at the half, and won by 111–94), it was fraught with meaning.

Sure, there was the thrill of seeing the league's top twenty players (chosen by the coaches) on the court at the same time. The West's leading point makers were Alex Groza, Frank Brian, Dike Eddelman, and Bob Davies, while the East was paced by "Jumping Joe" Fulks, Dolph Schayes, Paul Arizin, "Easy Ed" Macauley, and "The Cooz." And the players competed with all their might, eager (and needing) to capture the hundred-dollar bonus paid to the members of the winning team. But what made that game so intense and so significant was that the two teams had historical reasons to try to best each other.

The NBA had been officially chartered in August 1949, when the surviving franchises of the Basketball Association of America absorbed the remnants of the National Basketball League. Pointedly, many of the East all-stars were BAA veterans, while most of the

West cagers were refugees from the NBL. As a result, the sharpest competitive edge of that pioneering all-star game was the reprisal of the rivalry between two defunct leagues. Although BAA franchises were anchored in several of the country's largest cities (including New York, Boston, and Philadelphia), whereas the NBL teams played in what were deemed to be backwater burgs (Oshkosh, Sheboygan, Toledo, Youngstown), it was generally believed that the NBL had the better players.

Thus was a real-live ball game, with both honor and meat-and-potatoes money at stake. That's why the defense was authentic, the cuts hard, the rebounding ferocious, and the game faces highly serious.

For the next several seasons, the game was considered by its participants to be so important that numerous all-stars were delighted to play forty minutes and more (George Mikan—1953; Jim Pollard—1954; Jerry West, Bill Russell, Oscar Robertson—1964; West, Robertson—1965; Nate Thurmond—1967). Imagine, these days, what a hullabaloo Mike Brown would raise should LeBron James play forty minutes on Sunday.

There were two crucial turning points in the devolution of the all-star game. One came in 1966 in Cincinnati, when the Royals' Adrian Smith was picked for the East squad to satisfy (and sell tickets to) the hometown fans. Okay, Smith was a fine ballplayer—the third-leading scorer on his team (behind Jerry Lucas and the Big O) at 18.4 points per game. But he was also the Royals' fifth-worst shooter (ahead of only the eminently forgettable George Wilson, Art Heyman, Bud Olsen, and Jay Arnette), who missed 59.5 percent of his field-goal attempts. More of a quasi than a legitimate all-star.

In any case, the game's MVP was to be awarded a brand-new automobile, and since the game was nolo contendere (the West prevailed 137–94), Smith was force-fed the ball for the entire second half. Encouraged by his teammates and the fans, Smith just kept firing away. He finished with 18 shots in 26 minutes, scoring 24 points and winning the car.

Oh, what fun! An all-star game turned into a shooting gallery.

The next violation came in 1972, when the fans were allowed to vote for the starting fives. Ever since then, the all-star game has been little more than a popularity contest. The rationale is that since the fans are paying the freight, why not let them choose to see whom they want to see?

As if the NBA really cares about the paying customers. In truth, since the NBA takes over about three quarters of the all-star-game tickets at any given game to distribute to their corporate sponsors, the loyal season ticket holders are routinely crossed out.

Since the politically correct attitude on defense is "Hurry up and do your thang so I can do mine," the NBA all-star game is only half a game. Imagine the baseball all-star game with one outfielder and two infielders. Or the NHL gala with no goaltenders. How about the NFL's postseason extravaganza sans linebackers? All of these phony competitions are just trivial gimmicks designed to attract ratings.

As it is now, the NBA all-star game showcases a parade of merry dunksters and passing fancies, whereas the only real "scores" any of the players care about have to do with the degree of difficulty of their shots. It's sloppy, flashy, trashy basketball.

So count me out. I'd rather watch the pitiful Nets play the equally pitiful Clippers in a game that counts for something.

And that's why Nancy's invitation to dine on Sunday at six constitutes the universe's blessing on our connection.

Beep . . . Beep . . . Beep . . .

"Freddy, is that you?"

"In person. Who's this?"

"Rob. Rob Lassner. Remember—"

"Rob! My man! What's going on?"

"Umm . . . I tried calling you a couple of times at this number and somebody picked up but didn't respond to—"

He lets loose a long, liquid laugh. "That's my nephew, Cordell. My sister's boy. Sometimes when I got to go out, I pay him a few bucks to answer my phone and take messages. But the dumb-ass kid smokes so much weed and does so much coke that he turns into a mummy. I mean, I do it as a solid for Thelma, you know? Family is family. . . . So what can I do you for?"

"Well, I was wondering if the offer that you made to me in Rockford was still good."

"Refresh my memory. I must have been drunk as a skunk."

Oh, shit.

"You said you were getting tired of all the traveling and you wanted me to take over most of it. Also, I'd coach your free-agent team and even play if I wanted to."

"Sounds familiar. What else?"

"You said you'd pay me more than the eighty grand I make with the Nets."

"Sounds doable, but also subject to negotiation."

"Okay, but . . . umm . . . There's one more thing. Something that I hope won't embarrass you."

"Hey, man. Didn't I tell you that somebody as fat as me can't possibly be embarrassed?"

So he *does* remember!

"Well, I heard from a reliable source that your drug-testing company is doing a lot of illegal things. Like padding the Medicaid and Medicare bills with extra tests. And that the federal government is hot on your trail."

Another gurgling laugh turns into a brief coughing spell. "That's old news, man," he says as he strains to clear his throat. "I had a crazy partner who was into that shit. Thelma's husband's brother. But he's long gone and everything's back on the level. Besides, I'm more of a silent partner these days. A ghost partner. So there's no possible way I can be connected to anything illegal that may or may not be going on there. . . . Who's this reliable source you mentioned?"

"Well, it's actually thirdhand information and I don't know the guy's name. Some ballplayer from Denver."

"It's that fucking Sebastian! I know it's him. I got the fool a three-hundred-thousand-dollar deal in France, even though he can't shoot himself in the foot. And he pissed all the money away before the season was over. Then he got pissed at me for not squeezing some more juice out of the team, even though he kept on missing practice and got two French girls pregnant, including the fifteen-year-old daughter of the owner. So he's been spreading his bullshit stories about me ever since—"

Beep . . . Beep . . .

"Wup, there's another call. Hang on. . . . Say, man, I got to take this one. Call me after the season, okay? I'm sure we can work out something then."

"Sure, be happy to. . . ."

Click

She lives in an old slouching, white-shingled farmhouse, up a long rutted and cratered driveway. She opens the door to greet me, and after I hand her the bouquet of flowers I'd bought from the Grand Union in Woodstock, she doesn't turn away when I instinctively plop a kiss on her cheek.

Both of us are dressed in jeans and baggy sweaters, but where I wear sneakers, she has on open-toed sandals. Plus she wears a bright-red apron that shows a slight yet conspicuous bulge in the single kangaroo front pocket. A derringer? A small can of Mace?

She still exudes that cool fire of intelligence mixed with passion that had initially attracted me. No lipstick or other makeup, her grayish-whitish hair woven into long, thick braids. As she turns to lead me inside, her eyes reflect the flames dancing off the logs burning in a fieldstone fireplace. Elsewhere in the great room are a sagging brown couch with matching armchair, several floor-to-ceiling bookcases, a small dining table surrounded by four ladder-back wooden chairs and adorned with place settings for two, and a cramped kitchen alcove. Set in front of an expansive picture window, a large desk overlooks another small pond. The desk supports a laptop computer as well as several thick reference books, and is busily littered with individual sheets of paper. Noticeably missing from the room is a TV set.

"I'll be just a moment," she says as she goes to fuss with something in the oven. "Make yourself comfortable."

Wandering over to her bookcases, I'm alarmed and, I must admit, frightened by what I see. *The Female Orgasm, The Erotic Mind, Passionate Sex, God Herself, Time for Magick, The Sea Goddess*, plus several books on numerology, the Tarot, alchemy, the Kabbalah, and palmistry.

Holy shit! She's a fucking witch! A sex witch!

"Okay," she chimes, beckoning me to the table. "Everything's just about ready."

Before she serves the food, though, she extracts a joint, a lighter, and a forceps from her apron pocket. Lighting up, she sucks up a double-lungful of smoke before offering it to me. "*In cannabis veritas*," she says as she exhales a cloud of unknowing.

I used to smoke plenty of this stuff in my undergraduate days. During the rest stops after long-distant away games, Ike and I would find a dark corner somewhere and fire up a doobie or two that he had brought. I used to get slightly (and sometimes shiveringly) paranoid when high, but now I feel open, safe, warm, and fuzzy.

"Hey" I blurt. "This is pretty good."

"Yes. Getting good weed easily and cheaply are among the primary benefits of living in Woodstock."

Our repast consists of somewhat dry vegetable whole-wheat lasagna, a bountiful salad, and tepid water. No bread. No beer. Not enough cheese on the lasagna.

"Delicious," I say. "Really. What's in the lasagna?"

But rather than discuss the ingredients, she grills me about my life so far. So I proceed through a remarkably candid synopsis of my childhood ("my father took out his despair at being so sick on me"), my school daze (including my "bullshit protector"), my undergraduate hooping ("all I wanted to do was to score points and be a bully"), my marriage ("neither of our individual dreams came true, so it was easy to blame each other, but if I was a schmuck, she was a bitch"), plus a detailed account and explanation of my job.

After she nibbles at, and I wolf down, store-bought brownies, we assume comfortable positions at opposite ends of the couch while we finish the half-toked joint and she tells me her story.

She grew up an only child in a suburb of Boston, where her father was a successful podiatrist. "He used to brag that he was saving lives one toe at a time." He was also "boring, arrogant, and totally self-absorbed." Her mother was mainly interested in gardening and in playing bridge. "The only time she really paid attention to me was when she taught me how to weed, deadhead, and water her darling flowers." Whatever problems Nancy brought to her mother, the proffered solutions were always the same. "That I'd outgrow them. So, after a while, I only shared polite and absolutely necessary communications with both of them, and cried myself to sleep almost every night. She wasn't aware of my getting my period until about two years after the fact." Nancy also recalls her parents citing the closets in her room that bulged with toys, dolls, and frilly clothes as proof of their devotion. "I was more like their expensive pet than their child."

She volunteers to having a 168 IQ and "cruising" through every level of her schooling. "I can identify with your 'bullshit protector,' because I hardly believed anything that any of my teachers ever said. From George Washington and the cherry tree to the rationale for dropping the atomic bombs on Japan. My real education came from the books I read outside of the classroom. Karl Marx. Howard Zinn. Edgar Cayce. Even so, she graduated at the top of her class "among the brain busters" at the exclusive Cambridge Rindge and Latin School, but dropped out of Brandeis after her freshman year. "I simply couldn't take any more bullshit." When her parents threatened to disown her if she didn't return to school, she hitchhiked to White Lake for the original Woodstock Festival, where, having been intimidated into taking her very first dose of LSD, she had "a cosmic experience in which I saw the connection of every living thing." She then thumbed her way to Woodstock, and has been here ever since.

And the work on her desk?

"I'm a copy editor," she says, showing the first signs of discomfort. "I spend about eight hours a day squinting at my computer screen, worrying over missing or misplaced commas, semicolons, dashes, quotation marks, all of the tiny ants that crawl across the screen. Fixing nonsensical clauses, sentences, and paragraphs. Keeping a style sheet to track every name of every person and place. I do everything, from cookbooks to books on horse racing, pop psychology, vapid novels, you name it. Meanwhile the sun is shining or a beautiful snowfall is making the world fresh and clean, and here I am wasting my precious life and energy on dull, totally meaningless junk. I mean, my stupid work has definitely dumbed me down. Like my brain is so full of sludge . . . Sometimes I think that I've even forgotten how to laugh."

Now she starts sobbing, but waves away my impulse to reach out and comfort her. "I'm an expansive person with almost unlimited interests—except for sports and the dumbed-down, glitzy fantasy life that's portrayed on TV. It's . . . it's . . ."

Now she's copiously weeping, using her napkin to wipe her eyes and blow her nose. "I mean I'm almost totally isolated here. And everywhere."

"Don't you have any friends?"

"I had a couple of boyfriends, but they all either got married or moved away."

Hmmm. What's the quantitative difference between "all" and "a couple"? But she's a good witch. A sad, lonely, and probably horny one, but a good witch nevertheless. I want to cuddle her. To take care of her. To rescue her from her mind-numbing work.

To love her?!?

She had also been "briefly" married. His name was Marvin, but he insisted on being called Monte and he wore dark sunglasses indoors. "That should have been warning enough." But he was oh-so cool, the half owner of an ultra-hip boutique in the center of Woodstock who used to snort his coke through rolled-up hundred-dollar bills. "I tolerated all that crap because he seemed to be soft and caring." And because they had so many passionate interests in common—poetry, foreign films, medieval music, astrology, liberal politics. "So much in common that we became competitive. Who was better—Keats or T. S. Eliot? Did monks chant better than nuns? Were British films foreign enough? We started pecking at each other until there was nothing left of anything."

He was also a sex addict. "This was fun for a while, until he insisted that he couldn't fall asleep until we screwed. When I began to turn him down, he would masturbate right beside me there in the bed, and then he'd start snoring immediately afterward. Then, one night, he tried to screw me while I was asleep, and when I woke up screaming before he got his rocks off, he slapped me in the face.

That was enough for me." Shortly thereafter, Monte took all of the money from the boutique and ran off with a woman whom Nancy had thought was her best, and only, friend. "A few months later, I received a notice that he'd been granted a Las Vegas divorce."

Her sadness has turned into an anger that makes her cheeks blush and her eyes sparkle. She suddenly looks capable of undertaking some kind of violent revenge.

"Friends." She spits the word out like it is a putrid morsel of meat. "What about you, Rob? Do you think you have any of them?"

"Well, I've got one real friend, one guy I can be totally honest with. I used to be his boss and now he's mine. But I'm on the road so much that we mostly communicate by e-mail or phone, which isn't the same as talking face-to-face. . . . Anyway, is that all you do is work?"

"No, to exercise my body, I like to take walks wherever and whenever I can. To exercise my mind and my soul, I write poetry. But I get tired of reading my poems aloud to myself. . . . Anyway, do you want another brownie, or something?"

"No, thanks. I'm good."

She stretches out a foot and suddenly, softly pokes Mandrake with her toes. "I think you are really good, Rob. You're obviously intelligent, but that's easy to be. More importantly, you seem to be gentle and kind."

"I probably am. As long as I'm not on a basketball court."

"I don't know what that means."

"I get very competitive and aggressive whenever I play basketball. It's something I've been dealing with for a long time."

"Why not just stop playing?"

"That'll come sooner rather than later. My left hip really hurts after I play, so my playing days are numbered. If I don't have a hip replacement by the time I'm fifty, that means I didn't play hard enough."

"I don't know what that means either."

"Nothing really. Just some macho posturing."

She pokes Mandrake again. "Ah, speaking of macho posturing I see that your little man is at attention. Let's go upstairs and see if we can put him at ease. Maybe I'll even let you tickle my fancy."

And so we do. My hands and my lips feast on her tight-soft body while she lightly licks Mandrake's helmet. Then she says, "Vaginal orgasm is a myth," and pushes my head down to her pussy, where I suck and slurp until she comes in a writhing, shrieking, laughing ecstasy. Now it's my turn to jab, jab, jab, and explode.

After which we fall asleep on opposite sides of her bed.

She nudges me awake shortly after midnight, saying, "You'd better go. Call me tomorrow."

"Umm. I have an early plane to catch to Chicago, so I'll have to call you later."

"Whatever," she says.

What the fuck do I make of all this? A delicious one-night stand? Am I using her, is she using me, or is it mutual? Could this be the warm-up to a for-real heart-to-heart relationship? For now, I'm too bewitched, bothered, and bewildered to come to any viable conclusion.

Let's see what happens later in the game.

SECOND HALF

CHAPTER EIGHTEEN

Las Vegas is the quintessence of America.

With the season over and the draft only a week away, I'm here to reconnoiter the Las Vegas Pre-Draft Combine. The blue-chip lottery guys are here only to get weighed and measured, but the other sixty players have been chosen by the NBA's official scouting department to be subjected to various drills, interviews, and nightly games in hopes of improving their draftability. That's why the hotels and casinos are swarming with NBA coaches (Greg Dodge's mother-in-law died the other day, so he's an excused no-show), assistants, GMs, and scouts, plus scouts from several teams in Europe, South America, and Asia. Also on hand are unemployed coaches, assistants, GMs, and scouts furiously trying to network, plead, and/or backstab their way into a gig. Dozens of agents are likewise on hand, but are not permitted entry into the Las Vegas High School gym complex.

I am thrilled to discover that.

During the four-hour interim between the drills and the games, I mosey around "the Strip" and am both fascinated and appalled by what I see.

The Stratosphere Hotel, for example, sports a 1,148-foot tower ("Twice the height of any other structure in Las Vegas") that houses several restaurants, luxury suites, and casinos—and, with its gigantic knobbed head, bears a close resemblance to a penis made of steel and glass. The nightly extravaganza in the Strato Theatre is a "sexy vampire production."

Untold millions of Americans, of course, would be eager to drink blood in order to live forever. This fantastical transformation would also make them potent seducers of innocent, luscious virgins.

Then there's Caesars Palace "celebrating the glory of Rome." But not, however, the slave labor, the bloodthirsty entertainment for the masses, the aggressive militarism, nor the deranged, villainous rulers. Certainly not the parallel between the fall of Rome and the decline of Uncle Sam's Ass.

The floor show at the Aria Hotel and Casino features a tribute to the music and life of Elvis Presley in what is billed as a "whimsical, powerful, sexy fusion of high technology and raw emotion." Elvis the Pelvis, who started his career as a white boy doing black shtick, and ended up as a bloated, drug-addled, paranoid, "hip" version of Wayne Newton. The continuing miracle of sad, frustrated people mindlessly obsessed with fatuous celebrities.

The entrance to Bally's contains eight miles of neon. Inside the nightclub, the main attraction is a re-creation of the sinking of the *Titanic*. After all, what's more fascinating than a show-biz version of somebody else's tragedy? Unless, of course, it's the nude pool that offers "an escape from the traditional pool experience."

What else is happening when the basketballs are not bouncing?

The "legendary Donnie and Marie bringing the house down" in the Flamingo. In the same neighborhood is X Burlesque, where equally legendary tits and asses are on display.

In Paris Las Vegas, there's a fifty-story Eiffel Tower containing several casinos and continental restaurants, where "the night is always young." Likewise does New York New York offer opportunities for gambling and eating in half-scale models of the Brooklyn Bridge, Grand Central Station, Ellis Island, and the Empire State Building. And lest we forget that we are still ostensibly alive and free, at the base of a 150-foot replica of the Statue of Liberty is a solemn tribute to 9/11.

The Golden Gate boasts of its gigantic shrimp cocktail that goes for only $1.99 at the San Francisco Deli. The Hooters proudly advertises its world-famous chicken wings. And both of these delicacies are indeed scrumptious.

Even the economically blighted among us can afford to shell out the thirty-five dollars or so that virtually all of these theme parks charge for one night's stay. What a bargain! Especially since the local chamber of commerce produces "scientific evidence" that a visit to their city "will actually improve your overall health and outlook."

Viva Las Vegas, where beneath the faux glamour, the phony, fleeting thrills, the perpetual hope that the next card or the next number will produce untold riches, and the cut-rate abundance, the bottom line is always the bottom line.

R.I.P. America.

Far more meaningful and congenial are the outlying wastelands beyond the crowded stucco houses north of the city lights. Out where the only visible life-forms bordering the highway are some mesquite bushes and bristling Joshua trees. The beginning of the world must have looked like this: a blazing sphere of fire spilling over mountain peaks. Dark stones and deserts howling in the wind. So will the end . . . with ancient seas sunken into the earth's saline crust.

Old News

The Ping-Pong balls swirled and bounced, and it chanced that the Nets wound up with the third pick in the upcoming draft. *Perfect, I thought. Johnson and Griffin will be one-two and we'll be left with the jewel of the draft—Kevin Love.*

Weiss thought otherwise. He cursed both the Pings and the Pongs, and instructed Earl to get on the hooper and "do whatever it takes to get the first pick." Thus far, Earl has had no success and, accordingly, feels that his job, his reputation, and his life are on the line.

By a near unanimous (and ignominious) vote, LeBron James was named the Most Valuable Player. Trouble is that I don't know what "Most Valuable" is supposed to mean.   The player who did the most to help his team? With a dismal record of 17-66, the Sacramento Kings were the NBA's worst team., but without Kevin Martin it's entirely conceivable that they never would have won a game.

The player with the best numbers? Which numbers? Scoring? Rebounding? Assists? Given that numbers are of minimal significance anyway, how is it possible to compare the stats of players who play different positions and have different roles? Like centers and point guards? In baseball, are pitchers and designated hitters evaluated by the same set of numbers?

The best player? How could this be determined without conducting a league-wide one-on-one tournament? And how meaningful would the result be if a center was marched up against a point guard?

To underscore just how nonsensical this whole business is, the MVP award is determined by a vote of writers and broadcasters. Except for the odd ex-player among this group, these guys don't know an X from an O.

Consider the following absurdities: In 1986, the media Muppets elected Alvin Robertson as defensive player of the year. Shortly thereafter, the league's coaches voted Robertson to the NBA's *second* all-defensive team. Dikembe Mutombo was the subject of the same ludicrous voting in 1995.

The prosecution rests its case.

But there's more. In 2011, the writers and broadcasters presented Jason Kidd with the coveted Sportsmanship Award, disregarding his having previously settled out of court a lawsuit charging him with beating his wife.

In truth, all of the postseason awards have a single purpose: to create a media buzz.

Down with all of them!

To my delight Phil Jackson coached the Lakers to still another championship. I just love the triangle offense! Originally designed by Sam Barry at USC, it was systematized by Tex Winter, and adapted to the pro game by Jackson.

Basically, the triangle is a "read" offense, where players react in a choreographed way to how the defense reacts to passes, cuts, and positioning of the ball. It demands unselfishness and a high basketball IQ. Virtually every other offense at virtually every other level of competition is an "execution" offense, where players generally follow the dotted lines and have two or three scripted options on every play.

The triangle formulates the way basketball is supposed to be played.

Whereas most folks, if they had their choice for an all-time schmooze partner, would pick Jesus or Elvis, I'd select Jackson.

Let me count the cities: Tuscaloosa, Tucson, Washington, D.C., Fayetteville, Waco, Cincinnati, Clemson, Storrs, Detroit, Pittsburgh, Gainesville, Tallahassee, Atlanta, Beaumont, Louisville, Baton Rouge, Milwaukee, Minneapolis, East Lansing, Albuquerque, Niagara Falls, Eugene, Houston, San Diego, Seattle, Palo Alto, Austin . . . and these are only the ones that I can recall offhand.

However, the only visit that turned up anything meaningful was to Chicago, where DeLeon Johnson competed against the top-rated high school in the country—St. Barthlomew's—which featured three seven-footers on the front line and an All-American backcourt. The game was close, and DLJ played brilliantly on offense . . . for about twenty-eight minutes. He never exerted himself on defense, but in the concluding four minutes, he simply stopped driving, stopped shooting, and stopped rebounding.

With St. Bart's leading 61–60,, the game was rapidly ticking down, and DLJ was aimlessly dribbling the ball above the key . . . 6 . . . 5 . . . 4 . . . 3 . . . Then he whipped a bullet pass to a teammate who was open in the near-side corner, but the ball bounced off the poor guy's chest and landed in the third row just as the buzzer sounded. And as he walked off the court, Johnson wrapped his arm around his downcast teammate and started laughing.

Several onlookers praised his unselfishness as well as his compassion. But what I saw was DeLeon deflecting the blame for his own late-game choke and putting the onus on the kid. Thereby confirming my conviction that DeLeon is a loser.

Here's the way I look at it: Not only are winners eager to take win-or-lose shots, they exert themselves to the max on every play in every game. After a loss (by whatever margin), they are physically, mentally, and emotionally depleted. Having risked everything, not even their identity has survived. This doesn't mean that they rant and rave in the postgame locker room—they don't even have the energy to do so. The difficult task is to rebuild themselves from ground zero in time for the next game.

On the other hand, losers never make a full soul-spending commitment to winning. Instead, they will protect the essence of their self-definition no matter how badly or how disinterestedly they have played. That's why losers can laugh, and blame somebody else after so egregiously fucking up.

Could I ever make Weiss understand this? Never.

By the way, that same fur-coated black man was waiting for DLJ after the game. Their joyful jive-five, back-slapping greeting indicated that they hadn't seen each other for a while. But then, after some private palaver, they shook hands again. A straight business-like handshake, after which Johnson folded his hand and put something in his pocket.

Looks like Earl was right on. An agent compromising the kid's amateur status by slipping him a fistful of money.

Oh, well. God bless them both.

New News

Meanwhile back at the huge Las Vegas High School athletic complex, the length of three basketball courts are separated by retractable floor-to-ceiling curtains. The team's nickname is the War Eagles, and there are assorted images of these angry-looking, open-beaked, sharply-taloned birds painted on many of the walls and also on both sides of all of the curtains.

The center court is the only one bordered by rows of foldout bleacher benches. The initial morning session of this three-day affair was devoted to various measurements. Height and weight without sneakers. Body fat. Hand strength. Wingspan. Standing jumps wherein each of the sixty invited players leaped to touch and displace swinging bars set an inch apart. Then one-step jumps using the same device. It's astounding how many of these kids can touch the forty-inch bar.

I was pleased to note that Isaiah Jones had not been invited. He's the six-eleven rebounder and defender from St. Joseph's who so impressed me while he was playing against Villanova back in Philadelphia. NBA teams can certainly request the presence of certain projected second-round picks whom they want to observe playing against top-notch competition, but apparently Jones has been overlooked by all of my competitors. That's unfortunate for the kid, since nobody here will get a chance to see just how good he is. Fortunate for us, though, since we can probably swing some kind of deal to get a low second-round pick to augment our higher one. Or, if not, and he goes undrafted, we could simply put him on our summer-league team.

The players on hand are divided into six teams, so there are three forty-minute games played on the center court every night. Similar to high school all-star games, the guards (especially the point guards) dominate the action. When a posted-up big secures excellent position on one box or the other, his hands can wave and his eyes can bulge until they threaten to pop out of his head, but chances are he won't get the ball unless an entry pass will guarantee that an assist would be credited to the passer. For the most part, bigs get to score only on put-backs, drop passes that lead to dunks, and by running themselves into more dunk (and assist) opportunities. There is, of course, no practice time for any of the teams so it's all free-lance bullshit, where guards and wings can go get the ball while front-court guys have to wait for the ball to come to them.

The teams are coached by otherwise unemployed onetime NBA players hoping to hook up with any team in any capacity. The pivot-bound players will be fed incoming passes only if their particular coach played center in the NBA and has forcibly instructed his guards to always look inside. I heard one such coach say this in his pregame huddle: "Part of what those dudes in the stands are looking for is how you little guys can get the big guys involved."

Being an average-sized guy myself, I love coaches who can relate to bigs. And, yes, you have to be a big to know how to coach bigs. You need personal knowledge of never being able to hide and of the humiliation of getting a shot blocked by some runt. Only a specialized big-man's coach can teach the unique footwork, offensive moves, physicality, and the particular angles of the game that big men must master. After all, NBA action is basically center-centric. It's the centers who are the first players to touch the ball to tip-off every game, and the centers who are usually a team's last line of defense.

Back when I was playing in highly competitive schoolyard games, I would stash a pin in one of my socks, then find a time and place to surreptitiously let some air out of the ball. The idea was to discourage the runts from endlessly and needlessly dribbling, and forcing them to pass the ball inside to me.

I mean, it only stands to reason that big men have more brain power than do the vertically challenged players. Bigger is better.

Even so, there's only one exercise specifically designed for bigs—the so-called Superman drill. A ball is placed on the floor just outside each of the two boxes situated on opposite sides of the foul lane and the man in the middle has to bend, pick up one of the balls, and either dunk it or make a lay-up, then do the same with the other ball. Meanwhile, two rebounders and ball replacers are on hand to keep the action going. Each player is graded on how many baskets he can score within sixty seconds. It's an excellent measure of a big man's agility.

At another basket, players are timed as they assume a proper defensive crouch and slide around the perimeter of the lane. Up, sideways to their left, backward, then sideways to their right.

They are also timed as they sprint the length of the court from baseline to baseline.

As I wander from drill to drill, I make an unobtrusive effort to eavesdrop on various conversations, mostly jobless guys jabbering to general managers and trying hard to get themselves hired. This intrusion is easier than expected because everybody has to raise their voices to be heard above the bouncing balls, squeaking sneakers, and shouted instructions.

At every station of the double-cross, I overhear nothing but criticism.

"... easy to see that he lost the team, right? After they broke the huddle, the players formed their own huddle out on the court to make their own ..."

Everyone from bigs to littles shoots ten jumpers from five designated spots on the floor, moving from left to right and then back again. That's a hundred shots to be carefully chartered and collated.

"... had the kid for, what? Three years already? And taught him, what? A crab step, power dribble, bump-bang, and then a drop step? Or the Georgetown Gallop into the middle for his righty hook? There's so much more I could ..."

The forwards and guards undergo the same shooting drill from five spots on the nether side of the 3-point line.

"... coach is preaching ball movement and unselfishness. Always making the extra pass. So what's his top assistant saying to Maxwell? That his teammates can't be trusted, so if he can see the rim, he should shoot. And the kid's all ears. How can the team go anywhere when there's such disharmony in the coaching staff? When Steve is being undermined by his own ...?"

Here's a full-court transition 3-on-2 drill. The defenders move into a tandem, with the lead man responsible for stopping the ball then sinking into the middle, while the lag man is responsible for moving to the first pass. Meanwhile, unless he can take the ball to the rim, the triggerman is supposed to pull up at the stripe while the wings make ninety-degree cuts to the rim. Bodies collide, elbows flash, but no whistles sound.

"... what I would do? Undo the trade and send Melo back to Denver for Chandler, Gallinari, and Mozgov. Ha! Since that's impossible, and since Melo's contract and Stoudemire's fragile body make them both untradeable ... But, you know, it's not that these two guys can't play together. It's that Stoudemire and Chandler can't play together because Chandler can't shoot, so his defender can clog the middle and make Stoudemire little more than a jump shooter. The answer is to put Melo at the power-forward slot permanently and have Stoudemire back up both Melo and Chandler. I know that would be a hard sell, but ..."

There's a full-court 2-on-1 drill. The offensive players avoid getting too close to one another, while the sole defender tries to fake the ball handler into stopping. The guy with the ball doesn't fall for the bluff and drives until the defender makes a full commitment to stopping him. The defender then turns so that his entire body is between the ball handler and the wing runner.

"... all about loyalty. C'mon, man. Remember the time you were so drunk and Coach would've fined your ass into bankruptcy? And I *took the hit when I told him that it was . . . ?"*

To test their individual skills on both sides of the ball, there are fiercely fought games of one-on-one.

". . . suddenly died. The coach that gave him his first break and made him into an all-star. So there he was, in the cemetery, the rabbi is blessing his soul or whatever those guys do, and everybody is crying, and meanwhile he's yapping away into his cell phone. Is that the kind of . . . ?"

To test execution of, and defensive reaction to, screen/roll situations, there are similarly combative games of 2-on-2 and 3-on-3.

". . . finally convince him to go. So all the kids go ape over him. Those poor kids with their heads shaved and looking like skeletons. All of them terminal, like I said. So he talks for about five minutes. How one day they'll come to see him play in person. How God loves all of us. Yackety, yak. He could have read them the phone book and the kids would have swooned. But he can't wait to get the hell out of there. So he says his good-byes and the kids limp over to him asking him to sign their casts, their medical charts, whatever. And you know what the asshole says? These kids are dying right before his eyes, but he says, 'I never sign autographs on game days.' Would you fucking believe it? And he wants to be on your staff? That's . . ."

Here comes Earl to say, "This is wearing me out. Let's go get some lunch back at the hotel."

"Okay. I'll meet you there."

A large sign in the main lobby boasts that Circus Circus is the "OFFICIAL HOTEL AND CASINO FOR THE NBA COMBINE." Outside, the carnival midway is jammed with tourists, gleeful tots, jugglers, beautiful ladies slowly riding though the throng while standing on the backs of white horses, an acrobat doing backflips, a pair of shapely tattooed ladies in bikinis, and a veritable congress of clowns. Clowns on unicycles, clowns on pogo sticks, clowns with red-flashing noses, tramp clowns, everywhere a clown clown.

There had been no traffic, and even though I'd made a pit stop up in my room, I have to wait a half hour before Earl sits down opposite me in the Big Top Restaurant, where scantily dressed maidens casually swing on the several trapezes that hang from the ceiling. Upon closer inspection, they are tethered to their perches by semitransparent nylon ropes. Because the morning drills are only now ending back at the gym, the room is sparsely populated and our service is virtually instantaneous.

Earl looks haggard indeed, but before we can begin to talk, a solicitous waiter hovers over us. He, too, is a clown. Actually more of a jester, with his jingling bells and his brightly colored motley.

A chef's salad for each of us. Earl will have sweetened iced tea, and I go for bottled water.

When we are finally alone, I say, "What the fuck, Earl? You look like something the cat dragged in."

"It's Weiss. He calls me every hour, and I can't get off the phone. That's why I was late."

"He wants Johnson."

"He'd kill to get him. And he's killing me. He still insists that the Ping-Pong balls were fixed so that the Clippers got the top pick. He says that the NBA doesn't give a rat's ass about New Jersey. He says they consider us a small-market franchise. He wants to know what I'm doing to get that pick away from LA. Now he'll trade anybody including his two 'pets,' Harmon and Betts. Shit, he'll add me, you, and his father. Plus, get this, our number-one picks for the next five years. Five fucking years! He says if we can get Johnson, every possible free agent would crawl through a football field of horseshit to come to New Jersey and play with him. And they'd be so horny to come here, we could sign them for next to nothing."

"So we wouldn't need to draft anybody."

"Right. It's so fucking ridiculous that I want to—"

Here comes our food.

"You want to what?"

"I don't know. Something violent or stupid."

"Don't worry, Earl. Stern would never let Weiss do anything crazy."

"I'm just so fucking frustrated." He stares at his plate and absently moves his food around with his fork. "And besides, there's absolutely no fucking way that the Clippers will make a deal for Johnson. Donald Sterling might be an even bigger fuck-up than Weiss, but he knows how much money the team can make with Johnson in LA. Ticket sales. Johnson jerseys. Higher TV ratings. More . . ."

"Eat, Earl. Eat something. It's healthy food. You can't let yourself break down."

"Yeah. Yeah. You sound like my wife. . . . I just wish he'd stop calling me every time he gets some dumb idea. You can't imagine how hard it is to be agreeable and polite and to make believe his ideas make any sense. Just now? He said, that in addition to Betts, Harmon, and a shitload of draft picks, he'd also make a million-dollar contribution to whatever charity or political party Sterling chooses."

"It's crazy, but there's only so much that you can do."

"Rob, I can't remember how many times he's threatened to fire me if I can't bring him Johnson on a silver platter. . . . Are you sure you're not interested in going halfies in that health club?"

"I'm not sure of anything. . . . Eat."

We munch away on our salads for a few minutes, but Earl could never stand too much silence. "What's next on your agenda?"

"I don't know. Look at some game tapes. A nap. Hopefully a good dump. What about you?"

The morning session is over and the coaches, scouts, agents, and ubiquitous NBA personnel begin to arrive. Hellos-at-large must be exchanged before he can answer.

"I've got a kid to interview," Earl finally says, "then I'm going over to the casino."

"A fool and his money . . ."

"Hold on, Rob. I've set a limit of two hundred bucks. If I lose that, then I'm done. And I only play the ten-dollar blackjack table."

"I'll bet you two hundred that you'll lose your two hundred. You can't beat the house, Earl. It's pissing against the wind."

"To lose slowly is to win."

He insists on picking up the check, then says, "Hey, come up to my room and check out my interview with Gary McDonald."

"Really? At best the kid's a low first-rounder. Why waste your time?"

"Maybe he'll slip down to us in the second round."

"I'd much rather go with that Jones kid from Saint Joe's."

"I'd rather fuck all of the chorus girls. But, speaking of hard-ons, Weiss has got one for this kid, too."

"Okay. Thanks for lunch."

"Don't thank me. Thank Weiss. And fuck you, too."

"What? I didn't say anything."

"Yeah, Rob. But I know what you want to say."

"Fuck you, Earl."

"Exactly."

Earl's room is no bigger than mine and has the same paintings on the walls: an elephant rearing up on its hind legs, a lion jumping through a fiery hoop, a tuxedoed ringmaster shouting through a megaphone, still another frowning tramp-faced clown.

We take turns pissing and washing up, when comes a loud knocking on the door. "Wait'll you get a load of this kid," Earl says as he moves to admit the interviewee.

Gary McDonald bursts into the room with the audacity of a cop entering a gambling den. He wears flip-flops, cutoff jeans, and a sleeveless red shirt that sports a black-and-green etching of Bob Marley.

"Hey, guys," he fairly shouts, and there's an awkward moment when he tries to manipulate Earl's proffered hand into a high-five, thumb-hooked, ghetto dap. He's easily six-nine, 260 pounds, and has obviously spent many hours in a weight room. "I'm G-Mac."

His head is as white, clean, and gleaming as a cue ball. The only hair on his face is a black soul patch under his thin lower lip. There's a long red spout of flame tattooed the length of his right arm. A ring of barbed wire has been inked around his bulging left bicep, and a small basketball leaves a jet trail from his left elbow to the wrist as it approaches his hand.

I'm introduced as the Nets' "director of scouting," and *we* engage in a much smoother version of brotherly hand-to-hand calisthenics.

He declines Earl's offer of water or soda and flops onto the only available couch, leaving Earl and me to squeeze ourselves into a pair of cramped wing chairs.

"Okay," G-Mac says. "What do you dudes need to know before you make me your first-round pick?"

Earl gets him to tell us his basic biography.

Born in Santa Clara, California, twenty years ago, McDonald was a first-team high school All-American. He accepted a "full boat" to UMass because he "wanted to see what winter was like" and because he wanted to learn what "Coach J-O" could teach him. After averaging 20 points and 12 rebounds during an otherwise disappointing freshman season in which the team failed to qualify for a postseason tournament, he made himself eligible for the draft because "I learned everything Coach J-O had to teach me, and I was also sick of losing."

"Tell me about your parents," says Earl.

The kid gives us two thumbs up as he says, "My dad is an electrician, but as soon as I sign my contract, he's gonna retire." Then he turns solemn. "He was a big influence on me. Always encouraging me, picking me up after I had a bad game. My dad is a real good dude for an old guy."

"And your mother?"

"She's one of them house-makers, you know? Cooking, cleaning, and that stuff. She's a good dude, too."

"Any siblings?"

"Well, I had a wart on my arm once, but I chewed it off."

"I mean any brothers or sisters?"

"Oh, yeah. My sister Merilee. She's two years younger than me, so I got to date lots of her girlfriends. She's really a cool chick."

What career might he have pursued had he not been a basketball player?

He flexes his massive right bicep. "A movie star. I really dig those action flicks."

What else?

He shrugs. "A politician, maybe. I'm not dumb enough to think I could be the president, you know? Just a governor or a senator. I mean, you got to keep it real."

Anything else?

"Maybe one of them enterprenners. You know? Rich business

dude?"

Which would he rather do? Score 30 points and lose the game? Or score 5 points and win?

He laughs. "Ain't happening. If I score thirty, there ain't no way we lose. And if I score five, there ain't no way we win. Do the math, dude."

What are his strengths?

"Everything."

And his weaknesses?

"Nothing."

One final question from Earl. "Let's say you're in a boat with your wife and your one-year-old son . . . or daughter. And you love them both. And a big wave comes and washes both of them overboard and they can't swim. And they're both going down so fast that you could only rescue one of them. Which one would you try to save?"

"That's easy, man. The wife, she's already had a life, but the baby is too young to have one. So I'd let the bitch drown and save the baby."

"Great. Thanks, Gary."

"No, man. Thank *you*. I'm gonna enjoy playing for you and I promise I won't disappoint you."

We share a laugh when the kid leaves,

"What do you think?" Earl asks.

"He's a 'white shadow.' He'd be thrilled to death if you called him a nigger."

"And your scouting report?"

"Terrific athlete. Good work ethic. Has a decent midrange jumper but only wants to drive and dunk. Good hands. Quick ups. Good lateral movement. Looks to block every shot he can see. He's a mistake-player and doesn't know how to play. Needs another couple of years in school. But he's right that Jerry O'Neil probably did teach him everything he knows. . . . But, hey . . . what's with that last question? About the wife and the baby?"

"That's just something that I stick in on my own to see if these kids have any long-term vision."

"And the correct answer is . . . ?"

"Save the wife, because she can have more babies. . . . So where do you project—?"

His cell phone comes to life with Dave Brubeck's unmistakable introduction to "Take Five."

"Shit," says Earl. "It's Weiss."

"I'm outta here. See you at the gym."

"Yeah," he says as he pushes the Talk button and carries the phone into the bathroom.

After a long nap and a shower, I aim to reconnect with Earl high up in the bleachers just as the first game is commencing. As I climb the rickety steps, there's someone already sitting beside him and yapping away at warp speed. Earl is vaguely nodding until he spots me and beckons me with a wiggle of his right hand. The monologuer turns, sees me, shakes Earl's hand, says something else, then beats a hasty retreat, taking care not to come within hailing distance of me.

"Wasn't that Henry Williams?" I ask as I sit beside Earl. "The guy who was fired from Minnesota's staff a couple of years ago?"

"That's him."

"What the fuck does he want?"

"Your job, my job, anybody's job. But don't get your bowels in an uproar, Rob. He's about the tenth guy who's been up my ass today."

"No shit."

"They've got a million stories: Ballard is retiring; Wallace is lazy; Plochman is taking big money from agents to pump up their clients; you dress like a Bowery bum, lack the proper decorum, and generally conduct yourself in an unprofessional way. One guy also told me that you fucked Rockford's PR chick at the CBL all-star game."

"I would have," I say, and he laughs uproariously when I spill the beans.

"Fuck all those vampires anyway. I just tell them to e-mail me their résumés, and then I delete them as soon as I get them. I can't stand—"

There goes Brubeck again.

"Guess who?" Earl says, as he leaves to find a more private spot.

Meanwhile, the players go at each other, vying for fame, glory, and money. Running, dunking, passing, banging, making shots, missing shots—the usual stuff. And I scribble a few observations in my schoolboy's notebook. I like this guy's lateral movement, that guy's quick hands, the other guy's court vision. But there's something peculiar about these games: The total absence of any crowd reaction. No cheers, jeers, or moans.

Indeed, most of the spectators are either conversing with somebody or talking into their cell phones. There's that worm Plochman tête-à-têting with the general manager of the Celtics. Another of my scout mates, Alonzo Wallace, is yukking it up with an ex-teammate. And Ballard is doing the same, except that his onetime playing buddy is in a wheelchair.

"Rob! Rob!"

Who's that?

"Rob! Over here!"

Ah, it's Taylor Pierce, the top man in the NBA's scouting department, dressed as ever in neat gray slacks and a blue-collared shirt with the official NBA logo patched above his heart. His job is to collate the field reports from his army of part-time scouts (who get expenses and about $250 per), and distribute to each team a brief predraft summary of the ups and downs of those players who are here and several who are not. In all, reports of over a hundred hopeful hoopers are included. However, since every NBA team has had their scouting staffs scouring this and other countries for lo these many months, Pierce's publication is mostly superfluous.

But Tay was once the GM of the Memphis Tams of the long-defunct American Basketball Association, so he has more than a passing acquaintance with the intricacies of the game. And he's a wonderful man, who likes nothing more than either a good book or an appreciative audience for his opinions.

He's sitting by himself on the uppermost bench about a long jump shot away. "Rob! C'mere!"

Right-o.

In his upper sixties, Tay is crunched and wrinkled. His face is pitted with acne scars that are barely hidden under a scanty gray beard, and his bright-blue eyes are the windows into a sharp intelligence. Too bad his fleshy, moist lips constantly spray a mist of spittle when he talks, which is why he's sitting by himself, no dout. But I like the old-timer, and as long as I can maneuver my head to avoid getting spritzed, his company is always invigorating.

Whenever we meet, his first question is always, "Read any good books lately?"

"Yeah. *The Heart of the Matter* by Graham Greene. He's a really good writer, and the book is fascinating. But he's such a virulent anti-Semite."

"It was fashionable in some circles to be an anti-Semite in those days."

"And you?"

There's a mischievous twinkle in his eyes as he says, "Some of my best friends are anti-Semites."

"Ha! But what I mean is what are you reading?"

"Fifty years later I'm rereading Hemingway. I thought maybe I was too young to appreciate him, you know? But I'm discovering that I like him even less than I did back then. His prose is flat and lacking in passion and intellectual depth. And he's so mucho-macho that he must have been in the closet."

"Maybe that's the real reason why he killed himself."

"Could be." Then he points the tip of his scraggly beard toward the court. "What do you think? Any sleepers?"

"I like that point guard from LSU. I think he's really helping himself here. Maybe moving up to a mid-first-rounder."

"Anton Hayes," he says, then recites the pertinent information as presented in his handbook. "Drives left, shoots right. Good crossover both ways. Sees the court. Finishes at the run. Quick enough to stay in front of his man on defense."

Turning my head slightly as he talks, I say, "That's about right."

Then he heaves a mighty sigh. "It used to be so different. This whole scouting process. Back in the day, teams had no scouts and not even any assistant coaches. Coaches and GMs would get tips on players from friends who were college coaches or sportswriters or radio play-by-play guys. Hell, I can remember some team making their first-round picks on the basis of those basketball cards that used to come packaged with bubble gum. Remember those?"

Bobbing and weaving, I say, "That was before my time."

"Basketball magazines were also a good source. *Street and Smith's* was the best. I can remember when the NBA draft was held in a meeting room in the Manhattan Hotel. It was open to the public, and a few die-hard Knicks fans would show up to attack the cold-cuts buffet. One GM, who shall be nameless, had to ask the opinion of one of the fans about a player from NYU. The fan gave a positive report, so the kid from NYU was drafted in the second round. What a difference these days, eh? With so much money at stake, if a team fails to perform its due diligence, it's a million-dollar disaster. Still, even with the best scouting, vetting, and background checks, the draft is not an exact science."

While imitating an agreeable laugh, I duck my head. I'm about to ask what he *really* thinks of DeLeon Johnson when his cell phone explodes into the well-known theme from the *1812 Overture*.

"Excuse me," he says with a conspiratorial wink. "It's David Himself."

David Stern, the Commissar of us all.

One game is over and another is set to begin. But I've had enough. Of Las Vegas. Of living out of a travel bag. Of meat-market basketball.

I'll change my flight and get the hell out of here tonight. If called on the carpet, I'll claim that my aunt, uncle, high school coach, college teammate, or better yet my ex-wife Rachael has died in a car accident.

Turns out, though, that nobody seems to be aware (or seems to care) that I've left before the final buzzer.

CHAPTER NINETEEN

As usual, the mail at the end of the driveway is stuffed with flyers advertising sales at several local stores, as well as with bills (electric, phone, cable TV, and on-line access). But there's also a small padded manila envelope that has my name and address typed on an adhesive label, with a Detroit postmark and no return address.

Inside is an inch of hundred-dollar bills that add up to ten grand! A typed note says this: "Everything is on the level."

It has to be from Fat Freddy.

Beep . . . Beep . . . Beep . . . Beep.
"Hello? Who's this?"
"Hey, Nancy, it's me. I just got home. Wazzup?"
"I'm going crazy with this job. A stupid, badly written, historical novel with a million names, places, and dates that I have to hunt down and keep track of. My fucking style sheet is already fifteen pages long and I'm not even halfway through this fucking disaster. The sonofabitch editor didn't do his job and just threw it all in my lap. . . . I'm sorry to lay all this on you, Rob. I know you must be tired."
"It's okay. Do you want me to come over later, or what?"
"Absolutely. I've got about three more miserable hours to reach today's quota. So about seven or so?"
"And dinner?"
"I'm too wiped and too pissed to cook, and I have no desire to go out. Could you bring some take-out? I know you like Chinese, even though it's greasy, made with the cheapest possible ingredients, and loaded with corn syrup, but I'm in no mood to be fussy."
"Okay. See you then."
"'Bye."

There are two reasons why I'm happy to fetch take-out food for dinner: It's true, I love Chinese food, even bad Chinese food, and the eats from the Wok 'N Roll in Woodstock are at least satisfactory. More importantly, I won't have to help Nancy prepare a home-cooked meal.

Ever since that initial at-home meal, I have become the washer, peeler, and cutter of the various vegetables. And many strange veggies they were. For example, something called burdock root, which took a laborious fifteen minutes to clean. Or daikon, fennel, and fiddlehead ferns. Plus, she's very precise as to how these vegetables are to be sliced. The carrots, for example, have to be julienned, and every morsel a similar size "so they all cook at the same rate." The garlic must be mashed before it's diced, "to bring out the flavor."

A stainless-steel wok is her utensil of choice, and stir-fries her fail-safe meal. Fortunately she's a wonderful cook. And, of course, all the ingredients are always organic. She laughs when I tell her that I've always wanted to die a naturally oganic death. Her laughter is always contagious.

Meanwhile, I cram for the upcoming draft by studying videos of dozens of players, mostly guys I've only seen once or twice. Kudos to the Nets' nerdy video man—Tom? Tim?—for editing the games so that only those plays involving the specific players I've chosen are included. His overnight packages include postage-paid return envelopes in order to save me the time and trouble of having to go to the post office.

Even so, many of the videos are inadequate—even those copied from televised games. That's because the camera usually follows the bouncing ball, thereby preventing me from tracking every move the targeted player makes. Like life, good jazz, and sex, live experiences beat the shit out of secondhand recordings.

She's still pissy when she greets me at the door with a half-smoked joint in hand.

"Are you feeling any better?" I ask, turning down the proffered toke with a slight shake of my head.

"Not really. This stupid book is making me seriously crazy. The characters are clichéd. The writing is clichéd. The hero is actually described as being 'tall, dark, and handsome.' The heroine 'melted into his arms.' There's an improbable plot twist in every chapter. Car accidents in foreign countries where all the victims in all of the cars just happen to come from the same small town. The hack who wrote this piece of shit thinks that Vienna is in France and that Brussels is in Germany."

"Who's the publisher?"

"Houghton Mifflin."

"How could a big company like that publish such a thing?

"It's the second in a trilogy, and the first one was a best seller. But I can't imagine who would buy this crap. Bored, semiliterate housewives? Frustrated teenage girls in Appalachia? Books like this are another sign that our culture is self-destructing."

Neither the pot nor the food can shake her despair.

"You know what I think?" she says.

"No, I never do."

"I think that throughout every level of the entire educational system, K through twelve, kids are basically being taught one thing: how to be good consumers. Everything is either dumbed down, blatant lies, or else pure propaganda. From George Washington and his cherry tree to the rationale for every military action the USA has taken since the end of World War Two. If a kid wants to go to college, he has to carry an enormous debt for the rest of his life. That's because he might accidentally learn something dangerous there. And with very few exceptions, such as Bill Moyers, Chris Hayes, and Rachael Maddow, television does the same thing. It's a conscious thing, Rob. There's nothing accidental about it. Corporations rule the airwaves, the media, and every aspect of politics. Just look at how many TV and radio stations are owned by the same conglomerates. They're so powerful they can even steal national elections. What do they call it when businesses totally control a county?"

"Fascism."

"Hello. We're about one generation away from being a full-fledged fascist country, populated by rich people, middle-class technicians, and serfs. My God, am I glad I don't have any children."

We eat in silence. Despite her distaste for Chinese food, she eats heartily—and with chopsticks no less! Afterward, we sit in silence at opposite ends of the couch while she lights up another joint.

"Nancy, do you want me to leave?"

"No."

"Then can I ask you something?"

"If you must."

"Why do you smoke so much pot? I know how careful you are about what you eat, and about all of your walking and your tai chi practice.... How can you be doing so much of something that's probably not good for you?"

Whoops! This starts her to softly weeping again..

"Maybe I should go."

"No!" she says, surprising me with her sudden vehemence.

After she finds a tissue, she says, "Here's why: because I hate my fucking work and I hate my fucking life."

"But . . ."

"Yes, yes, I know. I don't have to work nine-to-five in some sterile office and be chased around the desk by a lecherous boss. I live in a beautiful part of the world. I make enough money to live an otherwise fairly comfortable existence. But . . . But this work is deadening. So the only escapes I have are my walks, my poetry, and smoking pot. Yes, I'm somewhat ashamed of being such a pothead. But maybe that's why living in this particular place is so appealing . . . because pot is the official drug of the Woodstock Nation."

She stops crying and busies herself with drying her face with tissue after tissue.

Hmmm. I guess I don't qualify as an "escape"—though I wish I did. But I do feel an ache of compassion for her.

"Is there anything I can do to help you?"

"Yes," she says. "You are sweet, intelligent, and considerate. You know, I've never cried in front of anybody before this, so I guess I must trust you. I feel seen and heard by you. Plus you're fun in bed, and you make me laugh. Besides, you have a good job."

I flash her my gunfighter's glint. "You forget that I'm also a handsome devil."

"Yes!" She laughs. "Better that than an ugly angel!"

Could it be that I really, truly, honestly love her? Holy shit!

"So what can I do, Nancy? I'll do anything you want. Anything you need."

Now the corner of her mouth is atremble. "Anything?" she asks in a coy little girl's voice.

"Anything."

"Okay, then . . . marry me. But only if I can quit this work."

"Whoa. Is that a good reason to get married?"

"Well, I do like you. An awful lot. In fact, I think that I'm almost in love with you."

"You think? Almost? What the fuck, Nancy? Anyway, we hardly know each other."

She laughs again, but this time I'm not so thrilled. "Do you really think that people who have been married for, say, fifty years really know each other? I mean, do we even know ourselves? The Buddhists believe that there really isn't 'somebody' to know." She expands her arms to include the whole world. "Maybe this is all a dream. Maybe we really don't exist. Who's the 'I' that I think I am? The 'I' that you think you are?"

"I think," I say, "therefore I think I am."

"Exactly. Therefore I think that I love you, and you probably think that you love me."

"Are you serious, then? About our getting married?"

"Ah, you see? You use the possessive pronoun with the gerund. That's good enough for me. Besides, think of the money we could save on rent and utilities. What have we got to lose?"

"We need to discuss this more. Maybe we should move in together as a sort of trial."

"Okay," she says, then she's crying again. I move to put my arms around her, but she shakes me off. "I'm so lonely, Rob. I'm such an outsider. That's another reason why I like living in Woodstock. So many people here are so far out that they're in. But . . . you're an outsider, too. I know you travel all over the country and you mingle with a lot of people you think are your friends. . . . But you're still outdoors in the cold peeking through the window at a warm fireplace. If pot and poetry are my escape fantasies, basketball is yours."

Only half kidding, I say, "You mean, life isn't a metaphor for basketball?"

"There are no metaphors in life. Only in poetry. Life is always what it is."

"I don't know. . . ."

"Nobody does. But I have a feeling that two outsiders, outcasts like us, could make some kind of arrangement. Our own little world outside the tent of ignorance and greed and . . . anyway, let's go into the bedroom and find out."

"Just what I had in mind."

Back in my hermit's digs, I appreciate Nancy's forcing me to come to terms with myself, and with the rest of my ways and days. I just hope that I can eventually become as honest with myself as she is with herself. Because of her I'm finally developing a taste for real life.

So now, painfully, I'm forced to focus on the latest batch of specially edited game videos. Players three inches tall. The games cut into disjointed pieces to facilitate tracking the movements of specific players. This is one of the necessary evils of my profession, I feel now, after getting to know Nancy. Maybe I really want to play again; maybe I want to reenter real life with Nancy—whatever it is that I want, I'm clearly becoming increasingly weary of just being a professional witness.

Ah, me. If I could change anything about Nancy it would be her lack of interest in The Game. She doesn't appreciate the exquisite balance between offense and defense. The many decisions that have to be made on the run. She doesn't know how amazing it is that, unlike players in other sports, every basketball player at every level needs a certain mastery of *all* the basic skills. For example, catchers don't pitch, defensive tackles don't throw forward passes, and goalies don't score goals. Nor does she get the uniqueness of the constant nonverbal communication that's essential among teammates during a game. A meeting of the eyes, a seemingly casual glance, can lead to a backdoor cut or a lob pass. Furthermore, basketball is the only sport where the distinction between a player who's selfish and one who's not is clear.

If she knew more about the game, she'd surely appreciate its transcendent virtues. For example, the awareness it takes for each player to accept his own strengths and weaknesses as well as those of his teammates. The fact that each player must sublimate his own ego for the sake of the group. Righteous basketball players are righteous people.

An essential part of knowing one's teammates and knowing thyself is being able to trust. Look at Michael Jordan: Before Phil Jackson became the Bulls' head coach and implemented the triangle offense, MJ would most often try to win ball games by himself. In a pair of playoff series against the Celtics in the mid-1980s, Jordan filled up his stat sheet with 56 points, and then 61 points—and Boston *still* prevailed. Flash ahead to the finals between Chicago and Phoenix in 1993, where, with the sixth and potentially clinching game on the line and the clock ticking down to zero, Jordan passed up a slightly contested jumper and delivered the ball to the wide-open John Paxson, who connected on the game (and the series) winner. Even Michael Jordan, arguably the greatest basketball player who ever lived, had to learn that he was unable to impose his will on most games.

Unselfishness. Teamwork. Trust. Self-knowledge. Physical, emotional, and mental resourcefulness. Respect for all participants (except referees!). The awareness and enjoyment of the living moment. No metaphors needed. How zen can you get?

All these things are much clearer and therefore easier to attain within the boundary lines of the game than they are in the so-called real world. We can know the rules of basketball. We can understand what the various markings on the court signify—the time line at midcourt, the stripe at the foul line, the delineations of the three-second lane, and so on. There's no mistaking the scoreboard and the clocks.

Outside the boundary lines, however, the rules are confused and often contradictory. The scoreboard of civilian life is difficult to decipher. Nobody knows when their own game clock will expire.

So, then, like every other possible undertaking—like fetching water, chopping wood, baking cakes, ad infinitum—basketball can be a meaningful way of life, something that's infinitely more important than the mere winning or losing of ball games.

At least that's the way it *should* be.

Ah, but here's the kicker: There's only one way to truly experience the heart of anything. In basketball, coaches, video guys, general managers, and scouts are *all* strangers in paradise. To live The Game, one must be a player.

Which makes Fat Freddy's offer to be the player-coach of his touring teams not only attractive but absolutely necessary.

What abut the Nets? DeLeon Johnson? Earl? Weiss? Nancy? *Me?*

CHAPTER TWENTY

Beep . . . Beep . . . Beep . . .

"Hello?"

"Rob, it's Earl."

"Okay, let me say this now so I won't have to say it later . . . Fuck you."

"Tell me when to laugh. Seriously, Rob, I've got good news, medium news, and bad news. Which do you want to hear first?"

"I guess the good news."

"You know how teams bring in guys who weren't in Las Vegas to work out?"

""Okay."

"Well, in his finite wisdom, Weiss put the kabosh on us doing that. 'What for?' he says. 'Why do we have to spend the money to look at a bunch of flunkies that the scouting staff has supposedly already seen?' So that's the good news, Rob. You don't have to get down here for the workouts."

"Goody. The medium news?"

"He says the only summer league he wants us to enter is the one in Orlando. And only because he has some business interests down there. Hotels, I think. And only because he wants to show off to his cronies. 'But,' he says, 'we better win it all down there.'"

"Win what? There are no standings and no league. It's just a place for last season's brothers at the end of the bench and maybe some rookies to get some experience."

"Yeah. Yeah. I know. The guy makes no sense at all."

"All right, I'm ready for the bad news."

"Well, he's unhappy because I still can't swing any kind of deal to land Johnson. Believe me, Rob, I've tried everything. Number-one draft picks up the wazoo. A million bucks under the table. Plus their pick of any two players on our roster. I even went up to any three players. No go."

"That's stupid of them. Watch, you'll see that the kid's a fucking loser."

"You just might turn out to be right, but that doesn't matter before the fact. Anyway, as a last resort, I suggested that Weiss call Sterling and try to get something done owner-to-owner. But he said he wants nothing to do with 'that Hollywood jock sniffer.' I think the real the problem Weiss has with this is that he doesn't want to take personal responsibility if nothing happens. It's easier to blame me."

"I can guess what the bad news is."

"Right. If I can't get Johnson, he promises to fire me."

"Fuck. I'll quit."

"You won't have to, Rob, because he also said that he'll fire you, too, if only because I hired you to begin with."

"Not Ballard or Wallace or Plochman?"

"Nope. You were the only one who told him he was full of shit, remember?"

"Well, fuck us." Then I tell him about the ten grand I got from Fat Freddy.

"Sounds like a nice safety net for you, Rob. Does he need another hit man? Anyway, Weiss said he wants you in the draft room next Monday."

"So he can fire us face-to-face."

"Maybe he'll hire Donald Trump to do it."

"Oh, well. Tell me this, Earl. . . . How come we're such good buddies and our phone calls always end with a hearty fuck you?"

"I'm fucked if I know."

"That's better. Say good night, Gracie."

"Fuck you."

Nancy's plan is for us to take a "little walk." But first she drives over to check out my cabin. "I like the location and the privacy," is her verdict, "but it's too small, and it smells like there's a dead animal somewhere in here. No, I could never live here. If we did decide to live together, it would have to be at my place."

"Okay."

Then I squeeze into the shotgun seat of her twelve-year-old blue Subaru and she drives slowly up the steep and winding Mead Mountain Road.

"What we're going to see," she says, "is another reason why I like living in Woodstock."

As we near the summit, she points to an old wooden structure off to the left. "That's the Church on the Mount. It was mostly hand-built by a guy named Father Francis, certainly the only human being who lived long enough and traveled widely enough to have made the acquaintance of both Rasputin and Bob Dylan. He was the American bishop of a branch of Christianity called Old Catholicism, which claimed direct descent from Saint Peter. They believe that their practice is divorced from all of the historical decrees promulgated by popes and synods and is the purest form of Christianity. Father Francis died about twenty years ago, and there was a lot of infighting about who was to succeed him. These days, there must only be five or six members of the church left."

Perhaps a hundred yards higher up the road, several huge buildings loom over and shadow the church. As she pulls into a small parking clearing, she identifies this cluster of structures across the road as comprising Karma Triyana Dharmachakra. "A monastery that's the American center of the Kagyu lineage, a Tibetan form of Buddhism. That white-walled building with the red-shingled roof holds the main shrine room."

The peace and tranquility that one would expect of such a site is obliterated by the noisy working of backhoes, small excavators, and the hammers and pneumatic drills of dozens of workers.

"They're tearing down some of the older buildings and putting up some new ones It's a vision and a plan that's been in the works for many years."

A middle-aged man dressed in neat chinos and a collared shirt paces back-and-forth in front of the entry arch, carrying a sign that reads, "KTD's EXPANSION IS DESECRATING THE SACRED MOUNTAIN." I'm lured to the picketer, but Nancy points to the beginning of an uphill jeep trail opposite the arch. "That's where we're headed."

"Okay, but what's with the 'sacred mountain' stuff?"

As we start to climb the dusty, stone-littered trail, she refuses to let me shoulder the stuffed backpack she's brought. "The native Americans who lived here before the white man thought this place was holy," she reports. "So we have the aborigines, the Christians, and the Buddhists all sharing a spiritual vision of the mountain. By the way, from here on up it's called Overlook Mountain. And this, more than the art colony that was established here a hundred years ago, more than the festival, is why Woodstock is a special place."

Where I grunt and labor with every step, she breathes easily, gliding along. The road is so bordered by thickly clustered trees and vegetation that there are no compensatory views to reward my exertions.

"Do you ever go there? To the monastery?"

"No. They do have public teachings in the shrine room, but it's much too foreign for me. Their patriarchal tradition is another put-off. Like some kind of Asian Catholicism. No, I get what I need by reading Western Buddhist writers like Pema Chodron."

"How long is this climb?"

"About an hour. Don't worry, you'll get your second breath and survive."

We meet a couple moving down the path, who must be in their sixties. Both of them with strong, reedy bodies and white hair, they're moving rapidly along with the aid of walking sticks.

"Good morning," they chime. "Great day for a stroll."

"Be careful," the man says in passing. "We came across a rattler in the old ruins up there."

"Thanks."

My back hurts, my knees throb. "Rattler?" I ask Nancy.

"Don't worry. They're supposed to be afraid of people."

"'Supposed to be,' eh?"

Chugging along, ever upward, with no change in the scenery, I decide to go into my chamber-of-commerce spiel. So I tell her about the whys and wherefores of the inevitable loss of my job. And about the cash-backed offer from Fat Freddy. "So, now we have to consider the virtues of living in or near Boulder, Colorado. . . ."

"Say what?"

"Shush, Nancy. Just hear me out."

Situated in a bucolic valley and surrounded by incredibly beautiful snow-capped mountains, Boulder is only twenty-five miles from

Denver. An elevation of 5,432 feet insures a pollution-free atmosphere. Within Boulder are thirty-six thousand acres of open spaces and nature preserves, all readily accessible through many miles of world-class hiking trails. "And get this, Nancy, Boulder is rated among the top-ten cities in the country in such categories as livability, best-educated, brainiest, and healthiest and happiest population. Plus, it's one of the greenest cities, and the most hospitable to artists. It also has the reputation of being among the most liberal cities in the USA. The population is just over ninety-four thousand. . . . Wait! Wait. There are health food stores galore, an annual outdoor Shakespeare festival, and the University of Colorado presents numerous other cultural events. And within ten to fifteen miles of Boulder are small, hip towns like Lyons and Nederland. . . . So, what do you think?"

"Okay. Here's the halfway rock. Let's take a brief rest."

"Wonderful."

Before she can respond to my presentation, we hear a referee's whistle, followed closely by a pair of young men zooming down the trail on mountain bikes. They both share quick, energetic greetings with Nancy.

"Tommy and Rennie," she tells me in the wake of the dust they leave behind. "Friends."

Then she explains why she has no desire to emigrate from Woodstock: In addition to the unavoidable number of assholes, a lot of creative people live here or used to live here. Musicians like Jack DeJohnette, David Bowie, Carlos Santana, Thelonious Monk, and Bonnie Raitt. Writers like Francine Prose. Heywood Hale Broun, and Ed Sanders. Actors like Ethan Hawke, Lee Marvin, and Uma Thurman. Plus talented carpenters, cooks, plumbers, electricians, you name it. There's a reason why Bob Dylan lived here for so many years. And why Van Morrison and Jimi Hendrix loved to come up here and jam."

"Impressive, but there are more creative people in Hollywood and New York."

"The thing is that it's not so strident, so competitive, or so glitzy in Woodstock. Then there's the natural beauty of the forests, the fields, and the mountains Hey, where else can I make believe I'm a teenage hippie until I croak? By now I've gotten my second-wind and I'm starting to enjoy the mulelike uphill push. We resume the climb.

"Really, I can read my one poem every week, and do my shitty work without anybody bothering me. . . ."

"How come you only write one poem per week?"

"A good question . . . Want a slug of water? Here. You never drink enough."

"Sure." I greedily gulp the warm, fish-smelling water from an old-fashioned metal canteen.

"I'm a perfectionist, which is why I'm such a good copy editor. So I work on a poem for the entire week. Sometimes I'm still working on it while I'm walking from my car to the reading."

"I've just heard the one, but I really liked it. Have you ever tried getting them published?"

"There are a number of small presses in the area, and I did get an inquiry from a small press in Albany. But I'm too afraid of having them published, where they can be criticized or simply ignored. I'm not nearly as self-confident as most people think. . . .

"Just around the turn up there we'll see the remains of the once-famous Overlook Mountain Hotel."

And there they are . . . an empty-eyed two-story skeleton of a building. White-bricked and roofless, ligamented with green vines and leafy branches. A staircase leading to nowhere. Footed with rubble, red powder, and weeds.

"Be careful," Nancy advises. "Porcupines like to scrabble around in there."

"What is this place? Or what was this place?"

"One of the most luxurious hotels in the state. It was considered a miracle of engineering when it was first built back in the early nineteenth century. Just imagine horse-drawn wagons carting all these bricks up the path, and later, once it was built, transporting the guests. There were a couple of fires over the years, but they led to equally miraculous rebuilding jobs. It remained a popular resort until one final, really destructive fire finally wiped the place out, . . . No, no. Don't get too close, Rob. You might step on a rattler."

I quickly step away from an imaginary snakeas she provides another historical tidbit. "Sometime in 1921 there was a secret organizational meeting up here of what eventually became the Communist Labor Party. You see? Overlook is holy even to Communists."

We trudge ever onward and upward, though the road is less steep now as it winds through a small field of shaggy grasses and dull-colored, low-lying wildflowers.

Up ahead on the summit is a tall, spidery transmission tower, as well as a rickety fire tower with a small room at the top. We next pass a small log cabin that has thick wire screens over the windows and a large padlock on the front door.

"A forest ranger is supposed to live there," she says, "but nobody I know has ever seen him. I wouldn't risk climbing up the fire tower, either, because so many of the steps are either broken or missing C'mon. *Excelsior,* as we say in Latin."

We take a fork in the path through some tangled bushes, then we're treading carefully along and through a rocky road. She's about a midrange jump shot ahead of me and I can see her stop and unload her backpack. I catch up to her on a wide stone ledge at the edge of a sheer cliff, and the view is astonishing.

"There's the Kingston–Rhinecliff Bridge over the Hudson. Way off in the distance are the Berkshires in Massachusetts. Over there's the Ashokan Reservoir. Just down there you can make out the Woodstock dump. You can't see Woodstock itself because it's just around the bend there."

I've never been in a place like this. Sure, Denver is the mile-high city, but the most expansive view of so much greenery I've ever experienced was from the last row in the right-field grandstand at Yankee Stadium.

She boldly moves to sit at the edge of the cliff and lets her feet dangle into space, but I hold back. In fact, just staring up at some hawks riding the thermal currents makes me so light-headed that I have to sit.

Nancy rummages in her pack and holds out a stuffed plastic sandwich bag. Then she pats the space next to her. "C'mon."

"No, thanks. All tall guys are afraid of heights."

But I do make a nifty one-handed catch of the sandwich. Avocado, Cheddar cheese, lettuce, tomato, and mayo on a crusty roll. "Delicious. . . . By the way, what's the elevation up—?

"Shhhh. Be quiet. Be still. Just breathe and treasure all of this."

The blue, cloudless sky. The crystalline sunlight. Just being up here at the easternmost prominence of the Catskill range, the oldest mountains in the country.

Peace. Beauty. And even possibly, most likely, love. This is indeed a holy mountain.

The perfect place to build a basketball court!

Eventually we hear a faint squeak of laughter. Shrieks and giggles getting closer, louder. Until a gaggle of teenagers swarm into view, blithely ignoring us as they gabble and cluck, while simultaneously fingering their handheld gizmos with incredible speed.

"Hi," one girl says in our direction, and when I turn, she flashes me the split-fingered peace sign.

Nancy smiles at-large, but says nothing as she rehitches her canteen to her belt, stuffs our soiled sandwich wrappings into her backpack, springs to her feet, and steps onto the downhill path.

Finally we are taking large, almost leaping strides that kick up pebbles and wisps of dust. In silence. Remembering the silence of the breeze, the hawks, and the sunshine. Not until we drive down past the Church on the Mount does Nancy say, "I really liked *Death of the Fox*. You were right about how brilliant it is. What are the next two novels in the trilogy like?"

"If *Fox* is a ten, then *The Succession* is an eight. It's about Queen Elizabeth. The third is *Entered from the Dark* and its subject is Christopher Marlowe, one of my favorite period playwrights and poets. I thought it disappointing. A grudging six and a half."

"Interesting," she muses. "I think I'll read them all."

Not another word passes between us until she drops me off at my cabin.

"Are you as tired as I am?" she asks.

"At least that."

So our lips meet above her transmission lever, where we terminate our latest adventure with a sweet kiss.

SCOUTING REPORT

NANCY SANGER:
Born January 18, 1978, in Boston, MA . . . 5-5/140

Her A-Level Skills:

Beautiful in a totally unique and natural way.

Like Lucky Strikes used to be, her body is round, firm, and fully packed.

Enjoys sex, unlike Rachael, who, just like Maimonides said of his wife "laid there like a lox."

Honest, dignified, extremely intelligent.

Talented poet.

Appreciates good literature, i.e., the novels I recommend.

After many years of various types of counseling, knows her self better than I know myself.

Thinks the Beatles are overrated.

Adores Monk, Miles, and most ballad-tempo jazz.

Has an expansive view of the world.

Always has positive, healing intentions.

Her B-Level Skills:

Gainfully, if unhappily, employed.

Has a sly sense of humor.

Is a perfectionist, but always has a rational reason why everything (cutting veggies, making the bed, washing the dishes, and on and on) must be done in such-and-such a way.

Is basically shy.

Her C-Level Skills:

Likes medieval music.

Constantly nags me about drinking enough water to keep me healthy.

Only moderately well organized.

Her D-Level Skills:
Knows herself better than I know myself.
So intelligent that she wins every argument.
Smokes too much pot.
Thinks the wondrous Errol Garner is "too bouncy."
Like the shiksa she is, puts ketchup on hot dogs.
Makes no distinction between a "little walk" and a strenuous hike.

Her F-Level Skills:
Hates Bob Dylan, Neil Young, and the Grateful Dead.
Loves classical music.
Doesn't consider Chinese food a fail-safe meal.
Detests sports.
Does not own a TV.

Projection:
If a magic metaphor could be found that would convince her to move to Denver (highly doubtful), she'd make a superb addition to the team..

Suggestion:
A high lottery pick.

Notes to Myself
Although we could live off my accumulated savings for about a year, I would need to find some type of agreeable employment hereabouts.

Petition Freddy to let me work out of Woodstock.

Threaten to break Earl's legs if he can't make a deal for Johnson.

Blackmail Weiss with a photograph of him fucking a barnyard animal.

Marry Fancy Nancy and live happily ever after.

CHAPTER TWENTY-ONE

Beep . . . Beep . . . Beep . . .
"This is Earl."
"This is Rob."
"Hi. Howzit?"
"Assuming that we'll both be out on our respective asses, what kind of job possibilities are out there?"

"None that I know of right now. Especially since Weiss will be badmouthing both of us from Atlanta to Washington. Probably better prospects for me only because Jerry Hart—remember him?—still has lots of contacts in the NBA and also on the college scene. Believe me, Rob, if I wind up on my feet, I'll find some way to squeeze you—
Beep . . . Beep . . . Beep . . .
"Got another call. Still trying to get Johnson. Maybe this is the deal that will save us. See you tonight. Dress nicely."

I say "Fuck you" into a dead line.

[[line space]]

We're in the same small-grained, oak-paneled conference room in which I essentially told Weiss that he couldn't find his ass even if he used two hands. There are a dozen cell phones on the long table, and a gigantic TV set placed at the end of a side cabinet adjacent to the same greasy-spoon buffet as before.

All hands are on deck: Earl sweating as he speaks sharply into one of the phones. Alonzo Wallace constantly reconnoitering the room as he speaks into another phone. John Wallace blissfully stuffing his face with free food. Evander Plochman in a whispered conference with Weiss. The video guy eyeballing some handheld new device. Greg Dodge gabbing with somebody I don't recognize.

And me, sitting by myself, defiantly wearing jeans and a sweatshirt, ignored, superfluous, waiting for the ax to fall.

The actual draft is being conducted in the Felt Forum, a three-thousand-seat amphitheater annexed to Madison Square Garden, where I witnessed my very first New Riders/Grateful Dead concert. Now there's an empty podium on the stage, and there are NBA logos displayed here, there, and everywhere. The TV camera cuts to a four-man panel of experts who are unanimous in anticipating that the Clippers will initiate the gala proceedings by selecting DeLeon Johnson.

". . . a franchise player . . . makes LA an instant championship contender . . . ushers in a new dynasty . . . modern-day Michael Jordan . . . can't possibly miss . . ."

Their chatter and the murmuring in New Jersey's draft central fall silent as David Stern emerges from behind a curtain at the rear of the stage, steps to the podium, adjusts the microphone, smiles benignly at the loud jeerings of the crowd, and welcomes one and all to the NBA's draft. He reminds us that each team has five minutes to make its pick. "Now on the clock," he says, "are the Los Angeles Clippers." Then he disappears through the curtains.

Earl puts down the phone, looks at me, and sadly shakes his head.

Stern makes a sudden reentrance with a paper in his hand. "With the number-one pick in the draft, the Los Angeles Lakers select . . . DeLeon Johnson! From Crescent City High School!"

There's Johnson, a fashion plate in his puke-yellow double-breasted suit, black T-shirt, and black porkpie hat, kissing his mother and his girl friend and shaking hands with others of his crew, including the black-garbed pimpy-looking gangsta.

An official NBA usher finds Johnson, presents him with an official LA Clippers cap, and leads him to the nearside of the stage, where the NBA's newest super-duper star towers over the diminutive Stern as they shake hands and pose for the media hounds.

Back to the experts, whose energetic approval is drowned out by Weiss's loud temper tantrum. He slams a bloated hand on the oak table, then points an accusing finger at Earl as he shouts, "You're a useless do-nothing!" Then he turns his wrath on me. "And you're a useless know-nothing!"

He literally stomps his right foot as though killing a gigantic cockroach., then gestures at the official Nets logo banner hanging on the wall, and says, "Enjoy this while you can, boys. Because when your contracts run out on July first, both of you dunderheads are fired!"

He turns to storm out of the room, but Dodge grabs his arm to say, "Who should we draft?"

"I don't give a fuck!" Weiss bellows. "Ask these two geniuses!"

And he slams the door behind him.

Everybody is stunned, except for Plochman, who nods his head and smirks his approval.

After Charlotte drafts Blake Griffin, Earl sidles up next to me. "Rob, should we draft Kevin Love?"

"Why don't we fuck Weiss over and pick some nobody from nowhere?"

"Then we'll never get another job."

"You're right," I say. "Don't forget Isaiah Jones in the second round. That rebounding, defensive demon from Saint Joe's."

"Got it. He's at the top of my list."

"Okay. I've had enough of this. Call me when you can."

And I'm out of there like the devil escaping from heaven.

On the long, frantic, melancholy drive back to Woodstock, I sing along to some tunes on a couple of Anita O'Day CDs.

"What's Your Story, Morning Glory?"

"Just One of Those Things."

"From This Moment On."

"What Is This Thing Called Love?"

I click on ESPN to discover that in the second round, the Nets picked Marcus Ross, the shooter with the too-slow release from Villanova. This, despite Isaiah Jones's being still on the board. Indeed, the always-clever and well-prepared San Antonio Spurs traded up (undisclosed cash and a salary-cap exemption) to nab Jones immediately after the Nets tabbed Ross.

I immediately call Earl on his cell.

"Hello?"

"Hello, yourself. I thought Jones was at the top of your list."

"Hey, Rob. You weren't here, and Plochman was hounding me. He even said that Weiss wanted Ross, which sounded like bullshit. But I figured, screw it. Let them do whatever they want to do."

"I understand. . . . I'll bet the kid has signed with Plochman's agent."

"Could be . . . And I wonder who's gonna be the new GM."

"Damn! You're absolutely right. That little shit!"

"Hey, Rob? You know what?"

"Tell me."

"Fuck them."

OVERTIME

CHAPTER TWENTY-TWO

Beep . . . Beep . . . Beep . . .

Jesus! It's four o'clock in the fucking morning. Who the fuck is this?

"Yes?"

"It's Earl. Wake up."

"This better be good."

"I've got bad news. Really bad news."

"Oh, fuck! What is it?"

"DeLeon Johnson is dead. It looks like a drug overdose."

"No, shit!"

"Yep. He was celebrating with a gang of friends at some nightclub when he collapsed. By the time the ambulance got there, the kid was already gone."

"Len Bias dies again! Poor fucking, stupid kid."

"But this is good news for at least three people."

"What're you talking about, Earl?"

"Well, first there's Weiss, who's the one who called to tell me what happened. He's as happy as he can be. He's ready to suck my dick and eat your shit in Macy's window. He wants to give us each a big raise and a three-year guaranteed contract."

"I can't fucking believe any of this."

"Believe it. Johnson OD'd. Weiss is deliriously happy. And we're both golden."

"Did you accept his offer?"

"I told him I'd have to speak to you first. So what do you think? Weiss or Fat Freddy?"

"I can't think straight. I'll call you first thing in the morning."

"Don't be the schmuck that you are, Rob. Let's do it."

"Maybe."

"Fuck the both of us," he says.

What to do?

Freddy, the good life, and at least a part-time return to live on-court action?

Or Nancy, the good life, the short-term benevolence of Weiss, and a return to the sidelines?

Should I make an appointment with one (or all) of the many psychics, Tarot readers, palmists, numerologists, or astrologers that abound in Woodstock? Consult the *Me Ching?*

Or just flip a coin?

SECOND
OVERTIME

CHAPTER TWENTY-THREE

Oh, well . . .

Back in the day, I was always eager to have my number called in the clutch.

To take the win-or-lose shot.

So, betting (my life, my soul) that even the *promise* of love will eventually conquer, I send Freddy back his money.